W9-AXQ-359

Who Ate Up All the Shinga?

Weatherhead Books on Asia

WEATHERHEAD EAST ASIA INSTITUTE, COLUMBIA UNIVERSITY

Literature DAVID DER-WEI WANG, EDITOR

Ye Zhaoyan, *Nanjing 1937: A Love Story*, translated by Michael Berry (2003)

Oda Makoto, *The Breaking Jewel*, translated by Donald Keene (2003)

Han Shaogong, *A Dictionary of Maqiao*, translated by Julia Lovell (2003)

Takahashi Takako, *Lonely Woman*, translated by Maryellen Toman Mori (2004)

Chen Ran, *A Private Life*, translated by John Howard-Gibbon (2004)

Eileen Chang, *Written on Water*, translated by Andrew F. Jones (2004)

Writing Women in Modern China: The Revolutionary Years, 1936–1976, edited by
      Amy D. Dooling (2005)

Han Bangqing, *The Sing-song Girls of Shanghai*, first translated by Eileen Chang,
      revised and edited by Eva Hung (2005)

Loud Sparrows: Contemporary Chinese Short-Shorts, translated and edited by Aili Mu,
      Julie Chiu, and Howard Goldblatt (2006)

Hiratsuka Raichō, *In the Beginning, Woman Was the Sun*, translated by Teruko Craig
      (2006)

Zhu Wen, I Love Dollars *and Other Stories of China*, translated by Julia Lovell
      (2007)

Kim Sowŏl, *Azaleas: A Book of Poems*, translated by David McCann (2007)

Wang Anyi, *The Song of Everlasting Sorrow: A Novel of Shanghai*, translated by
      Michael Berry (2008)

Ch'oe Yun, *There a Petal Silently Falls: Three Stories by Ch'oe Yun*, translated by
      Bruce and Ju-chan Fulton (2008)

Inoue Yasushi, *The Blue Wolf: A Novel of the Life of Chinggis Khan*, translated by
      Joshua A. Fogel (2009)

Anonymous, *Courtesans and Opium: Romantic Illusions of the Fool of Yangzhou*, translated
      by Patrick Hanan (2009)

History, Society, and Culture CAROL GLUCK, EDITOR

Takeuchi Yoshimi, *What Is Modernity? Writings of Takeuchi Yoshimi*, translated with
      an introduction by Richard Calichman (2005)

Contemporary Japanese Thought, translated by Richard Calichman (2005)

Overcoming Modernity, Yasuda et al., translated by Richard Calichman (2008)

Natsume Sōseki, *Theory of Literature and Other Critical Writings* (2009)

PARK WAN-SUH

Who Ate Up All the Shinga?

AN AUTOBIOGRAPHICAL NOVEL

TRANSLATED BY

YU YOUNG-NAN

STEPHEN J. EPSTEIN

COLUMBIA UNIVERSITY PRESS   NEW YORK

Columbia University Press wishes to express its appreciation for assistance given by the Daesan Foundation toward the cost of translating and publishing this book.

Columbia University Press
Publishers Since 1893
New York   Chichester, West Sussex

Library of Congress Cataloging-in-Publication Data
Pak, Wan-so, 1931–
   [Ku mant'on singa nun nuga ta mogossulkka. English]
   Who ate up all the shinga? : an autobiographical novel / Park Wan-suh ;
translated by Yu Young-nan and Stephen J. Epstein.
        p. cm. — (Weatherhead books on Asia)
   ISBN 978-0-231-14898-6 (cloth)—ISBN 978-0-231-14899-3 (pbk.)—
ISBN 978-0-231-52036-2 (ebook)
   I. Yu, Yong-nan.   II. Epstein, Stephen J., 1962–   III. Title.   IV. Series.

   PL992.62.W34K82513   2009
   895. 7'34—dc22

                                                              2009000332

Book and cover design: Chang Jae Lee
Cover image: © Bettmann/Getty Images

Contents

Introduction

PARK WAN-SUH (ALSO ROMANIZED AS PAK WAN-SŎ), although little known in the West, is by common consent the most notable female author in contemporary South Korea, where she is held in high esteem by both the literary establishment and the public for her skill as a storyteller and for the wit, compassion, and incisive social criticism evident in her writing. Her works not only have received numerous prestigious literary awards but also routinely appear at the top of best-seller lists; several have been successfully adapted for the screen. Remarkably, Park did not publish any work until she was almost forty. Her prizewinning first novel, *The Naked Tree*, created a minor sensation, however, not least because a debut by a woman her age was so rare. Since its appearance in 1970, Park has maintained a prolific output of high-quality work, with some 20 novels and more than 150 shorter pieces to her credit. Awareness of her talent is slowly reaching an international audience, as her writing is translated into a variety of languages. Works available in English include *The Naked Tree* and two collections of short fiction, *My Very Last Possession and Other Stories* and *Sketch of the Fading Sun*, as well as a number of short stories that have appeared in journals or anthologies.

Park's fiction has occasionally been described as reminiscent of stories told by a chatty neighbor. Although such a description captures the warmth and colloquial flavor of much of her writing, it belies her razor-sharp critiques of Korean society and her versatility and virtuosity as a stylist able to range with equal success from the earthy to the elegant. Her favorite themes include the tragedy of the Korean War, the hypocrisy and materialism of the middle class, and the concerns of women—topics that she embeds within lively tales about compelling, realistically drawn characters. Far from running out of ideas, Park has become even more accomplished and imaginative as she continues into the latter stages of her career, remaining productive well into her seventies.

The author's potted biography informs us that she was born in 1931 near Kaesŏng, in what is now North Korea. She entered Seoul National University, the nation's top university, in June 1950, but the Korean War, which broke out almost immediately afterward, cut her studies short. These two spare biographical details, which essentially bookend the memoir that follows, hint at the upheavals of Park's early years but not the skill with which she re-creates this turbulent period of Korean history. Simply put, *Who Ate Up All the Shinga?* is an extraordinary work about extraordinary times. Although deceptively little in the book, until its final page, suggests that the protagonist herself will eventually become the grande dame of Korean literature, her evocation of the dramatic vicissitudes experienced by her family is enthralling. The work became a best seller in its native South Korea and has remained a steady favorite since, having sold more than 1.3 million copies.

Non-Korean readers will also find that the story has ready cross-cultural appeal and that the author's insight into human nature resonates with those outside the conservative, patriarchal Confucian framework in which Park was raised. Of course, introductions to works of Korean literature in translation often do have to provide background that authors have taken for granted in their audience, and readers of *Who Ate Up All the Shinga?* should be aware of at least the broad outlines of the troubled middle decades of the twentieth century in Korea—all the more so, since South Korea's current image as an economically dynamic, culturally stylish, and technologically savvy nation is effacing memories of darker days, when extreme poverty was rife and the Korean people experienced the successive hardships of occupation by Japan and a devastating internecine war. Nonetheless, even in 1992, when Park published *Who Ate Up All the Shinga?*, she was conscious of how remote the period had become for many of her readers, who were coming of age amid rising prosperity and the optimism of a freshly democratized polity, and she fills in necessary information while avoiding didacticism.

This feature, in conjunction with the author's eye for colorful detail and her gifts of characterization, makes the text a rich and thoroughly accessible source of social history. For Park, spinning a good yarn has always been the primary concern, and the personalities who surrounded her in her early years stand out vividly, exemplifying the mores of the day without becoming reduced to types. Most particularly, the author paints a sympathetic but critical picture of her mother, highlighting her numerous contradictions. In Park's eloquent rendering, we see a resourceful, determined woman who kicks forcefully against the strictures of the time while conforming to many of them. She is desperate to shift her daughter from the countryside to Seoul so she can become a "New Woman" (*shin yŏsŏng*), equipped with a modern education, but has an incomplete understanding of what such a project entails.

Colonization by Japan, which began in earnest when Korea was annexed in 1910, brought a contradictory mix of enlightenment and oppression, which is still being disentangled in Korea's fraught relations with its close but distant neighbor. Even now, Korean popular discourse speaks too often in simplistic terms of noble, downtrodden Korean victims resisting evil Japanese oppressors and their collaborators. Although Park does not shy away from pointed criticisms of the banal everyday violence of colonial existence, her reminiscences, in their nuanced sense of how people went about their lives amid a demeaning political structure, offer a useful corrective to such black-and-white portrayals. Most notably, Park portrays the experience of assimilation into the Japanese Empire from a child's perspective. In doing so, she uncovers occasionally surprising combinations of acquiescence and resistance. The author describes with good-natured humor, for example, her own tribulations of learning Japanese in school, seemingly interminable school ceremonies in honor of the emperor, and benighted attempts to make students devoted subjects of the empire. Descriptions of fears among the Korean populace about having daughters abducted to become "comfort women" in Japanese military brothels or seeing sons forcibly conscripted to work in labor camps appear in conjunction with approving comments on the fairness of Japanese financial institutions and their role in enabling Park's family to obtain a loan toward purchasing a house in Seoul.

Of particular interest is the debate that arises within her family over whether to comply with the policy of assuming Japanese names, an issue that underpins Richard Kim's fine fictionalized account of growing up under the Japanese occupation, *Lost Names*, and the two texts can profitably be read in tandem. Park's tale, however, reveals that the policy was by no means as compulsory as often suggested and that self-interest rather than coercion often drove capitulation: while her brother insists on clinging to the family name, her uncle worries that doing so may hurt his business. The author herself longs for the family to take a Japanese name for a much more trivial reason: the resemblance between the Japanese pronunciation of her Korean name and the word for "air-raid drill" led to frequent teasing by her schoolmates that she longed to escape.

Park experienced adolescence during the heady era of post-Liberation Korea, when new political concepts excited the populace and a growing ideological divide penetrated even high schools. Park draws from personal example to show how initial euphoria over freedom from the Japanese yielded to serious concerns that society was teetering on the brink of chaos. Ominously, her laconic, thoughtful brother becomes involved with the underground leftist movement. The book's last sections are also its most harrowing in their depiction of how one not atypical family becomes trapped in the crossfire of the Korean War's destructive passions: when the Communists capture Seoul in their initial blitzkrieg attack, neighbors kowtow to her family, assuming that her brother has a high place in the leftist hierarchy. Soon after General Douglas MacArthur's landing at Inch'ŏn, however, the United Nations forces and the army of the Republic of Korea (ROK) retake Seoul, and a period of excruciating hardship descends on the family as presumed Red sympathizers; the author is regularly summoned for interrogations and made to literally crawl before her tormentors. Her brother, forcibly conscripted by the Korean People's Army (KPA), eventually straggles home from the front, suffering on his return from what we would now diagnose as post-traumatic stress disorder. The final scenes are riveting: Park must take flight with her mother, her now lame brother ("accidentally" shot in the leg by an ROK soldier), her sister-in-law, and their two infant children, one of whom was born prematurely and remains desperately malnourished.

Park readily acknowledges the extent to which *Who Ate Up All the Shinga?* draws on the often unreliable medium of memory. As she writes in a piece that became the foreword to later editions of the text, she frequently found herself forced to fill in the interstices of erased recollections with the mortar of imagination. And while she concedes that such a technique is perhaps only to be expected, a more serious problem for her involved confronting discrepancies in the memory of events between herself and other members of her family. Such comparisons, reminiscent of *Rashomon* (or, perhaps more appropriately here, the work of the acclaimed director Hong Sang-soo), instilled in her a realization that memory may ultimately be no different from imagination. In the hands of a less skillful writer, that declaration might prove alarming for those who want a reliable picture of the author's experiences, but Park has a deserved reputation for unflinching honesty. She notes the difficulty of resisting the temptation to embellish herself, but the portraits she draws of herself and her family are astonishingly frank, verging on the confessional and even self-flagellating. Throughout her career, Park has written herself into her protagonists, but clearly fictionalized elements have rendered problematic easy identification of the author with her protagonists. Those elements are entirely absent here, and to pursue the question of whether *Who Ate Up All the Shinga?* should be regarded as fiction or nonfiction is unlikely to prove profitable. Indeed, Park has been described as acting like a surgeon wielding a scalpel in the way her writing exposes hypocrisy with almost clinical precision. The metaphor is no less applicable when she turns her attention to her own life story.

* * * * * * * * * * *

A few additional remarks before we begin. Those about to embark on the work may rightly wonder just what a *shinga* is. Although the nature of this edible plant, which grew in abundance around Park's native Kaesŏng, will become clearer as the text proceeds, curious readers should rest assured that they are not alone in their perplexity. The author deliberately opted for a title that would leave the majority of Koreans scratching their heads, and the Korean name of the plant has no precise English equivalent (the Latin name seems to be *Aconogonon alpinum*, for the insatiably curious), hence our decision to romanize the term in our title.

And since the issue of romanization has come up, it is perhaps germane to note that we have, after considerable reflection, settled on the McCune-Reischauer system of transliterating Korean words for our translation, except for names that have become well known in English by more idiosyncratic spellings (for example, Syngman Rhee). Such exceptions are most obvious in the case of the author herself, whose clearly stated preference for the romanized spelling of her own name as Park Wan-suh has been honored, even though the alternative McCune-Reischauer rendering, as Pak Wan-sŏ, can also occasionally be found. When we refer to her clan name as a whole, however, we do adhere to its standard romanization as Pak.

My co-translator, Yu Young-nan, and I wish to acknowledge the generous support of the Daesan Foundation, which provided us with a grant toward the translation of the text. We also extend a note of deep thanks to Park Wan-suh, who was unstintingly generous in fielding queries about difficult points in her text. We have long been cognizant of her prodigious talent, and over the years we have experienced firsthand her graciousness and kindness as well. It is a privilege to translate one of her most important works.

Finally, those who follow the translation of Korean literature will be aware of the increasing trend toward teams that bring together native speakers of the source and target languages. Although both of us often had worked on our own in translation, collaboration proved highly productive. As we sent versions electronically back and forth a dozen times or more with extensive annotation and commentary, teasing out the finest nuances of the original text and possible renderings, we found ourselves engaged in a rejuvenating project of discovery. Both of us agree that we have put more energy into this translation than into any other text that either of us has worked on, not least as a measure of our respect for *Who Ate Up All the Shinga?* and its author. We hope that the end result justifies the effort.

Stephen J. Epstein

Who Ate Up All the Shinga?

1. Days in the Wild

I USED TO GO AROUND WITH A RUNNY NOSE. Not the occasional droplet, either, but thick yellow mucus, the kind you couldn't just snuffle back up. I was hardly alone. Back then, all kids were the same. You can see it in the nickname grown-ups gave us—"snifflers." Not too surprisingly, when I became a mom, the thing I found most remarkable about my kids was that they never had a runny nose unless they had a cold. And not just mine, but all kids. Children used to have a handkerchief pinned to their chest when they first attended school, but that custom is long gone. At this point, even I wonder why we always had mucus dangling from our nostrils, instead of finding it strange that kids these days don't.

When I was small, cloth was hard to come by. So was paper. I didn't even know such a thing as handkerchiefs existed. As the snot got down to my mouth, I'd swipe at it. By the end of winter, the edges of my sleeves would be clotted with a greasy black layer, like thick ointment. One well-padded jacket tided me over for the season. When my

mother changed its collar, she'd take advantage of the opportunity and scrub my sleeves to get rid of the gunk that
had coagulated, but it didn't make much difference.

Under the jacket, I wore a skirt held up by a bodice
rather than one with the usual opening at the back, and
beneath the skirt, drawers with wadding. The fabric was
cotton—coarse, dyed in vivid colors, and beaten smooth
with iron paddles.

I was born in a village with fewer than twenty households,
some twenty *ri* southwest of Kaesŏng. Its full name was
Pakchŏk Hamlet, Muksong Village, Ch'ŏnggyo Township,
Kaep'ung County. In the countryside, dye was precious,
and my grandfather had to go to Songdo for it. Songdo was
what the villagers called Kaesŏng, and for a small child like
myself, it was the place of dreams. In addition to dye, that's
where you had to go for hoes and sickles, rubber shoes and
kitchen knives, fine-tooth combs and ribbons stamped
with gold.

Other families' women would go to Songdo, but not
ours. Only my grandfather and uncles went. There was one
other family in Pakchŏk Hamlet that didn't let its women
go to Songdo either. They also had the surname Pak and
were related to us. Even though everyone else was from the
Hong clan, the village took its name from us Paks. According to my grandfather, we were *yangban*—aristocrats—and
they were commoners.

I'm not sure what the villagers made of my grandfather's
yangban pretensions. People from the Kaesŏng area tradi-
tionally didn't put much stock in class distinctions, so he
must have been something of a voice in the wilderness. But
even though the women in my family couldn't visit Songdo
as they pleased because of Grandfather, don't go thinking
that they accepted his authority at a fundamental level. One
day I asked my grandmother what a *yangban* was, and she

snorted, "A *yangban* is what you get if you sell a dog." Grandmother was punning on how *yangban* sounded like the name of an old-time coin. She spoke bluntly and cracked frequent jokes. But for Grandfather, she put on a show of acting like she was walking on eggshells.

It wasn't just Songdo that was off-limits. My grandfather didn't allow the women of the family out to the fields or rice paddies either. This was another difference between other families and ours. Grandfather seemed to think that restricting women's activities came part and parcel with being a *yangban*.

And so, in Pakchŏk Hamlet lived two families of aristocrats and some sixteen or seventeen commoner households. This division didn't correspond to a split between landowners and tenant farmers, however.

Our village nestled between low, gently sloping hills that were free of boulders and commanded an unobstructed view over vast fields. A small river snaked through the broad plains in the center, and brooks were everywhere—"tiny brooks babbling tales of old," as the poet Chŏng Chi-yong put it. Even a trip to the outhouse for us meant crossing a little stream. When these streams met rice paddies, they often formed pools. We called these pools "bonus wells." This was to mark them off from the ones from which we drew water. In retrospect, they were more like small reservoirs. The entire expanse of these fertile fields, which hardly ever yielded a bad crop, belonged to our villagers. No one family had a monopoly over the fields; no family had to struggle along without any. They were all diligent independent farmers and had no need to worry about food at any point in the year.

Growing up in a community like this until I was seven, I didn't have the opportunity to learn that there were separate classes of people known as "rich" and "poor" in this world. Neither did I have much opportunity, when I went off hand in hand with my friends, to visit other villages. Even when we walked and walked through the fields, we never reached one. Only by climbing over the hill behind us could we reach a neighboring village, and there was nothing especially remarkable to me about it. Houses, flanked by vegetable patches, nestled at the foot of a hill, and broad fields billowed in front of the village like a skirt. I assumed everyone lived the same way.

I thought that no matter how many hills and brooks you crossed, the whole world was Korea and everyone in it was Korean. The first name of a foreign country that I heard was "Dutchland." Only years later did I learn that Dutchland was what we now call Germany, but even before I was able to make this connection, the very idea of a foreign land filled me with wonder.

My grandfather usually went to Songdo for dye shortly before the Harvest Moon Festival or New Year's. He made a point of saying, "This dye comes from Dutchland," as he pulled out the packages he'd bought. Marks distinguished the different colors—a red mark for red dye, a blue mark for blue dye. The marks were triangular and about the size of a postage stamp folded diagonally. They were so vivid and shiny that it was as though a brilliant flower petal were embedded within them. Despite my complete ignorance, my heart raced whenever I glimpsed those German dyes. Looking back, I think they must have given me my first whiff of civilization, my first taste of culture.

The women in our house—my grandmother, my mother, and my aunts—fell helpless before those dyes. The air of dignity that Grandfather exuded would reach its peak when he brought them home, and the respect his daughters-in-law held for him became closer to servile flattery.

Not that their respect always came wholeheartedly. Sometimes they laughed at him. To be irreverent about it, Grandfather seemed almost flighty when he vented his fury and dashed into the inner quarters. At this omen that a violent outburst was in the offing, his daughters-in-law would drop whatever they were doing and exchange furtive jokes, awaiting the impending thunderbolt.

My mother was the most talented at these wisecracks. "Hey," she'd whisper in my aunt's ear, "looks like rice is burning in the kitchen." Auntie practically became apoplectic trying to stifle her laughter. My mother didn't mean that rice was really burning in the kitchen, of course. Grandfather had been nicknamed "Rice Scoop" because that's what his flat, jutting chin looked like. His whiskers sprouted in sparse clumps instead of growing long, which only heightened the impression. And so I suspect that the awe my mother and aunts expressed before him when he brought German dyes actually had little to do with his character, but simply reflected what people nowadays call a taste for imported goods.

I wasn't afraid of my grandfather, and I never acted as though I were. My father had died when I was two years old, so Grandfather treated me with special affection. Even at my age, I could tell he felt some intense spark of emotion toward me. His eyes normally had a stern, upward slant, yet they would relax a little when he gazed at me. Maybe pity softened him, but I could tell that I'd latched on to his fatal weakness. I was confident he'd take my side no matter how naughty I was. I never went out of my way to cause trouble because I could count on his support, but when he wasn't around, my spirit drooped.

Once my grandmother nagged him for being so soft with me and spoiling me rotten. She mused about whether he realized how pliant I became when he was away, and he blew up: "Oh, so it gave you a little thrill to see her feeling down when she had nowhere to turn, did it? I'll bet it did!" He screeched at her, wagging a finger right in her face.

But Grandfather did go on frequent trips. In addition to visits to Songdo, he represented the family at virtually every function that relatives or friends held. His all-white garb meant a lot of work for the women, especially those traditional socks, which must have been a horror to mend. I would awaken to see my mother and aunts patching tattered stockings beneath the dim lamplight and speaking in low tones. Those socks were big enough for me to wear on my head, which I actually did often enough.

Once Grandfather left, he could be gone for several days, but looking forward to his return was my greatest childhood pleasure. The outer quarters of our home consisted of two rooms. In front of them, facing an open yard, ran a long veranda divided by a post. As I sat with an arm wrapped around it or leaning against it, I could see the wagon path stretch beyond the village until it grew indistinct and disappeared around the hill.

That white clothing had a wonderful quality to it. In the evening, smoke billowed from every thatched roof, and as it spread slowly like ink into the heavens, it gently erased the borders between the paths, the paddies, the fields, the forest, and the hills until everything blended together under an ash-colored sky. But even then, it was easy to make out a white-clad figure rounding the hill toward us. Although all the villagers dressed in white, especially for outings to Songdo, when they decked themselves out in spotless garb, I never mistook anyone else for my grandfather.

I can't quite describe it, but there was something unique about Grandfather's gait that acted as a beacon to me. "Grandpa!" I'd think and shoot off to the entrance to the village. I was never wrong. I'd huff and puff, clinging eagerly to his coat. The edge of it was cold and like a blade, its stiffness a product of arduous paddling. The coat smelled of Songdo, a scent I adored. Immediately, Grandfather would hoist me up, saying, "All right, all right, my baby." His arms were trustworthy, and his breath was warm and redolent of alcohol. I liked my grandfather's warmth and that whiff of liquor.

After putting me down, he'd rummage through his coat pockets and press some treat into my hands—amber-colored candies in yellow paper wrappers, perhaps, or sweetened rice balls and tiny cookies he'd sneaked into his pockets from a party table, while turning a blind eye to dignity. My spirits rose as high as the sky as I let go of Grandfather's hand and skipped on ahead, savoring those goodies. Grandmother would scold me for acting like a spoiled brat. I'm sure I cut an unpleasant figure in her eyes with the special patronage I enjoyed, but I simply felt that I was getting my proper reward for waiting.

My patience was not always rewarded, though. Sometimes others appeared on the path rounding the hill, or no one showed up at all, and I would choke up with sorrow. When the weather turned cold, I'd shiver wildly. But I refused to budge, no matter how often people came out of the house to fetch me. The grown-ups said I was wallowing in self-pity, and Mother would cluck her tongue and order me to stop acting so miserable. Grandmother would even rap me on the head with her knuckles. I put up with it all, vowing to myself, "I'm going to tell on you to Grandpa. I'm going to tell on you." But I never tattled. All that was just part of the pleasure of waiting.

I had other ways to have fun while anticipating his arrival. I'd count off syllables by touching my thumb to my fingers one by one in an old children's game, saying, "*Ch'ŏk ch'ŏk*, thumb stop, middle finger, if Grandpa's at Black Kite Hill." If my thumb didn't stop where I wanted it to, I'd just change my chant: "*Ch'ŏk ch'ŏk*, thumb stop, middle finger, if Grandpa's at Wardrobe Rocks Hill." I knew the names of lots of hills and streams, even if I didn't know exactly where they were, so it was fine for my thumb and middle finger to come together at any old name I chose—just as long as they came together. Once they did, I would stealthily follow Grandfather in my imagination from that particular point as he climbed hills, passed through fields, and crossed streams.

Sometimes my grandfather traveled a pitch-dark path, sometimes a path brightly lit by the moon. Even at the new moon, with no illumination but the twinkling of stars, the fluttering sleeves of his coat gleamed so brightly that I had no worries about losing him. With his quick strides, he would arrive at the village entrance in a flash. I'd picture running after him, panting, as I anxiously waited.

But sometimes Grandfather made no progress and never appeared around the hill. After pursuing him in my imagination, I would watch for him impatiently until my concentration slackened and I began to drift off. When the adults came to gather me in their arms and bring me inside, I'd pretend that I'd fallen into a deep slumber.

This era of anticipation, which occupies the bulk of my early memories, did not last long. One day Grandfather collapsed in the outhouse. He shouted for help, unable to get up, but our outhouse lay at the edge of our vegetable patch. To get to it, you had to climb down three stone ledges, traverse the outer yard, cross under the surrounding mulberry trees, and ford a small stream. A passerby eventually heard him and rushed over to tell us. Everyone dashed out and, with difficulty, managed to carry him back to the outer quarters. People said he'd had a stroke, a condition for which there was no cure. In particular, no one doubted that a stroke that came upon someone in an outhouse lacked a remedy.

Like most scholars in those days, Grandfather had a better-than-average knowledge of Chinese medicine, so he personally prescribed medicines for his children and collected herbs to make his own pills. These he kept in a chest and dispensed to villagers when they needed urgent treatment. Nonetheless, he gave up treating his own malady early on and simply became short-tempered instead. Whenever my grandmother took Grandfather's chamber pot out from the men's quarters, she would mutter a litany of his misdeeds, from his itinerant lifestyle to his fondness for drink and even for friends, as though to suggest that he deserved what had happened. Dark clouds hung over the house, and I fell into a sorry state, like a fledgling whose wings had been clipped. I remembered nothing about my father's death because I had yet to turn two then, but witnessing Grandfather's powerlessness after his stroke was tantamount to losing a father for the second time.

To make matters worse, that year Mother left for Seoul to care for my brother. He had graduated from the four-year primary school located in the seat of our township and gone on to Songdo to finish the six-year elementary-education course of the revised school system. My uncles also had graduated from the local primary school, but since they were the only ones in the village blessed with such modern education, Grandfather regarded the two additional years of schooling my brother received in Songdo as genuine erudition. For my brother to go to Seoul to pursue his studies not only drained our finances, but clashed with the expectations placed on him as eldest grandson to carry on the family name.

Both my uncles were married and lived in my grandfather's house, but neither had children yet, which was far from usual. Grandfather often likened Brother and me to his jewels. After his stroke, he must have hoped to keep his only grandson near him and marry him off early, rather than send him out into the world. That way he'd be able to instruct him in his duties—continuing the family line with male offspring and tending the ancestral tombs.

Without consulting my grandparents, however, Mother sent my brother to a commercial school in Seoul. Given that there was a similar school in Songdo, this constituted major rebellion on her part. The event threw the whole house into turmoil. That a widowed eldest daughter-in-law would neglect her duty to care for her in-laws with the excuse of her son's studies was absolutely unheard of, and it dealt my grandparents a severe emotional blow. More importantly, it meant a loss of face for the family. Even in a tiny hamlet like ours, if Grandfather wanted to play *yangban*, he had to run his household in line with what was expected of an aristocratic family. It didn't matter if anyone else acknowledged it; Grandfather believed we had a responsibility to set an example. He was furious. And so when Mother cast aside her obligations to the family, she wound up having to cast aside far more.

Mother harbored an almost religious determination to raise Brother and me in Seoul. Changing her mind would have been impossible. She was convinced that if we'd lived in a city, my father wouldn't have died so young. When I grew older and learned more about life, I had to agree. Father was said to have been the sturdiest and healthiest among his brothers, and he never fell ill. One day, though, he began to writhe in agony with a stomachache. Grandfather consulted his medical tomes and treated Father with nothing but various herbal remedies; Grandmother arranged for a shaman ritual to ward off evil spirits. Meanwhile, Father's condition grew steadily worse.

Only when he was on the point of death was Mother able to muster enough authority to have him taken to Songdo on a wagon. What had been appendicitis led to peritonitis, and Father's abdomen became riddled with pus. Despite an operation, his infection continued to fester; since this took place before antibiotics, he died in the end. Mother refused to simply wave it away as fate. She was sure that countryside ignorance was to blame, and she wanted at the very least to rescue her children from its clutches. These beliefs came from her experiences in Seoul.

Although she grew up in the countryside among her father's extended family, her mother's side was from Seoul and quite well-to-do. Before she was married off and came to Pakchŏk Hamlet, Mother had spent time in Seoul with her cousins, who were then students at respected girls' high schools. All this provoked her admiration and envy. She called any female who received a modern education and wore a Western skirt and Western shoes a "New Woman," and she wanted to make me one. But I was still too young, and given our finances, she couldn't dream of taking me along to Seoul. So she had my brother admitted to school there and just up and left, rejecting her role as eldest daughter-in-law on the grounds that she had to care for Brother.

I was subjected to whispers critical of my mother—from not only my grandparents but also my aunts. Still, I was the only granddaughter in the house. I lorded it over my aunts like a little princess, reveling in even greater freedom, thanks to Grandfather's lack of mobility and Mother's absence.

One characteristic of houses around Kaesŏng was a contrast between the outer quarters, which were low and modest, and the taller, more extravagant inner quarters. People also gave yards special attention. Our outer yard was simple—open in front and bordered by mulberry trees and bush clovers. It held several peonies or chrysanthemums at most. But our backyard—now, that was elaborate.

Our backyard included a stand for condiment jars, a shrine dedicated to the house spirit, and a small hill, where flowers bloomed throughout the year except midwinter. All this gave me ample space to play in. Forsythias made a hedge, and beneath them lay clusters of ground cherries. You would approach the jar stand by steps that had been hewed into a gentle rise and were flanked by annuals. We had several cherry trees, a wild apricot tree, and a pear tree. The pear tree's fruit was bitter, but its flowers were magnificent. Strawberries and pungent scallions grew wild too, giving a gloomy atmosphere to the spirit shrine.

I now got to do as I wanted, so I roamed the village with my friends or invited them to the backyard, where before I'd played quietly by myself. Nobody told me that Grandfather's helplessness meant a vacuum of authority in our house, but I sensed it intuitively. I made the most of it, even turning the outhouse into part of my private playground. The outhouse did frighten me for a while, because that was where Grandfather had fallen over and become half paralyzed. I was scared about what might happen if I fell there too, but I got past my fear soon enough. Of all the spots I played in during childhood, our outhouse excited the imagination most.

In my village, every tale in which an outhouse figured involved goblins—not scary goblins, but silly and jovial ones, as in the story about a goblin with a stuffy nose who can't smell anything and spends all night in the outhouse making sticky brown millet cakes out of poo. The goblin believes that the ash there is bean flour and rolls his cakes in it over and over again, carefully molding each one. But he wants to be sure to have all his cakes at the end, so he resists the temptation to taste any while making them. When he finally finishes at dawn, he bites into one, only to spit it out, retching. Then he stirs the pieces back into the original muck, furious. It was said that if you opened the door without a warning cough and surprised the goblin at his work, he'd hastily offer you the largest cake of all in embarrassment and urge you to try it. If you didn't, there was no telling what mischief he'd play on you.

There's another outhouse tale I recall vividly. One winter solstice, a daughter-in-law makes some delicious red bean porridge for that festival. Not satisfied with one bowl, she ladles out more for herself and ducks off to the outhouse. Meanwhile, her father-in-law has absconded there to sneak some more porridge as well. When she dashes in, he is startled and tips the bowl over his head. The daughter-in-law rises to the occasion, however. Thinking quickly, she offers her own bowl and says, "Father, I brought you some more." The father-in-law replies, "Child, I don't need it. Look! My sweat is already running down just like porridge." Grown-ups used to tell these stories frequently to teach us to give some warning before we opened an outhouse door.

Children nowadays, what with their phobia about countryside outhouses, would probably gag at that tale, but in fact the outhouses where I grew up were clean enough to eat porridge in. They were very roomy, sometimes as big as three or four *kan*, with a wooden frame in one corner where adults would take care of their business. Kids just squatted on the dirt floor. This area resembled a shed, and its floor slanted to allow turds to roll downward, not into a deep pit, but into a section where ash from the kitchen furnace was dumped. In outhouses, people kept handy a long stick with a rectangular board attached, which children also used to sweep their droppings into the ash (this is why a gangly person is sometimes called a "shit stick"). You need to be aware of all this to follow the story about the goblin rolling millet cakes in flour.

Grown-ups, for their part, swept the outhouse ground morning and evening, leaving behind clear broom marks. Back then, excrement was used, together with compost, for fertilizer. The population was small relative to the amount of cultivated land, so this night soil was always in short supply. Disposing of the ash in the outhouse covered the feces and increased its value by bulking it up.

Sometimes villagers went all the way to Songdo to buy human waste for fertilizer, but they complained that the "Kaesŏng skinflints" watered it down. Of course, those who grumbled were just as miserly, for they never peed in other people's fields; even if they went to visit neighbors, they held on to their full bladders until they made it back to the edge of their own patches.

I don't think I was that calculating, being so young, but I'd go off to our outhouse with a pack of friends. If kids are playing house and one suddenly asks, "Who wants to play hide-and-seek?" the others scramble after her. In exactly the same vein, when anyone suggested a trip to the outhouse, we'd all follow. We'd squat together, our round bottoms exposed, and strain in unison, even if we didn't have to go to the bathroom. Back then, little girls wore "windbreaker knickers," with an opening underneath to make squatting easier. Even at midday, the outhouse was dark, and the girls' white bottoms looked pale and blurry, like unripe gourds on a roof beneath a hazy moon.

Although we exposed our bums, it wasn't a big deal if we didn't have to move our bowels. Crouching side by side and chatting was fantastic fun. As we squatted in our dim hide-away, excreting little corn ears of dung to mirror what we'd eaten, our trivial tales called forth flights of fancy and elicited histrionic "oohs" and "aahs." "Did you hear about Kapsun's dog? It had six puppies, but listen to this! The dog's yellow, but no puppy was yellow—just black ones, white ones, and white ones with black spots."

The most important thing was to deposit plentiful, well-formed turds in the outhouse. We knew there was nothing shameful in shit, because it went back to the earth, helping cucumbers and pumpkins grow in abundance and making watermelons and melons sweet. We got not only to savor the instinctive pleasure of excretion, but to feel pride in producing something valuable.

And while the outhouse itself was fun, after a lengthy stay within it the outside world took on an extraordinarily beautiful cast. The sunlight glittering on the greens in the kitchen garden, the grasses and trees, the tiny streams—all this was as dazzling as if we'd never seen any of it before. We squinted and sighed, feeling almost as though we'd emerged from a forbidden pleasure. Much later, when I experienced the world's brilliant strangeness after watching a movie that was off-limits to high-school students, the white collar of my uniform tucked under to conceal my identity, I felt that these outhouse adventures of my childhood were replaying themselves.

Long afterward, I read Yi Sang's essay "Ennui," about a half-dozen children in the countryside who have no toys to speak of. Not knowing how to entertain themselves, they mash grass with stones but soon grow bored. They then stretch their arms to the sky and scream. Finally, all other possibilities exhausted, they squat in a row to deposit a pile of feces each. Yi Sang describes this as a last, desperate gasp of creativity, but even without his explanation, his remarkable talent as a writer evokes a horrifyingly vivid sense of overwhelming tedium.

However, this vision depends on the sensibility of Yi Sang, who was a Seoulite to the core. People from Seoul are welcome to pity country kids and wonder how they can live somewhere so dull. But it was only after I came to the capital that consciousness of boredom sprouted within me, almost crushing me. To say that the wonders of nature were much better playthings than the toys that kids in Seoul enjoyed is not entirely accurate. We were part of nature, and because nature is alive, changing, in motion, not resting a single moment, we had no time to be bored. No matter how hard farmers work—scattering seed and tending their crops as they sprout, grow tendrils, bloom, and bear fruit—they can never gain a step. Nature has its own busy rhythms.

Children aren't any different. We had our three meals a day at home, but we were always on the lookout for snacks and coming up with ways to while away our time in the mountains and fields. There would be new sprouts galore to choose from—sweetgrass, wild rosebuds, mountain berries, arrowroot, bindweed root, chestnuts, acorns, and *shinga*. When we picked them, we were able to satisfy our creeping hunger and had the chance to please the grownups, as when we collected mountain herbs and mushrooms. Some of them, like "jar mushrooms" and "bush clover mushrooms," sprouted so fast that you could almost imagine a finger pushing them up from the ground when you turned your back.

Likewise, when we splish-splashed in the brooks that flowed throughout the village, we'd collect tiny shrimp that put on acrobatic displays as they jumped about. All we had to do to gather as many as we wanted was to bring along an old sieve. The shrimp would wind up in our bean paste soup at supper, adding a delicate flavor to it.

All our playthings were alive. We'd catch dragonflies and then cut their delicate tails and insert long stalks of straw before letting them fly off again. We'd grasp carpenter ants and tentatively lick at their sour-tasting rear ends, even though in the end our own calves wound up bitten by swarms of red ants.

Sometimes we'd make bridal dolls out of grass, wind their hair into buns, and hold mock wedding festivals. Hollowed crab shells were hung as pots, pine needles became noodles, and golden grass turned into kimchi. As a finale, we'd pull up purslane roots and rub them with our fingers. Then, eagerly chanting, "Light a lamp for the groom's chamber, light a lamp for the bride's chamber," we'd make nuptial lanterns from the reddened roots. We had an unlimited supply of playthings at our disposal and never needed to repeat a game from one day to the next.

In midsummer, under the blistering sun, we sometimes ventured on expeditions to a small river where all the tiny brooks came together. The rain showers we encountered there offered a magnificent spectacle. Seoul children may think that showers descend from the sky, but we knew the truth: they charged forward from the fields like soldiers. Where we were playing could have been bathed in relentless sunshine, but as soon as thick shadows came down over fields nearby, we'd spy a curtain of rain making its way toward us. We'd fly home at breakneck speed, shrieking, all too aware how fast that curtain moved.

Our hearts were ready to burst with a feeling we couldn't articulate. Anxiety? Ecstasy? The fields would awake from their languid sleep to fan our emotions, the grain, the vegetables, and the grasses abuzz in a communal riot. Inevitably, the curtain of rain unfurled over us before we could take shelter beneath roof eaves back in our village. The combination of the dog-day heat and our mad dash set us aflame. When the deluge lashed us, fierce as a whip but re-freshing as a cascade, we'd explode at last.

Ahh, our glee was truly explosive. We'd whoop, surren-dering ourselves to the downpour. The fields joined us in our dance of joy. At those moments, it was impossible not to feel as one with the swaying corn and the palmcrists.

Nature, though, brought not only ecstasy, but sorrow. My first memory of sorrow stands separate from any par-ticular event; it's just a mental snapshot. My mother was carrying me on her back. As the baby of the family, I often asked to be strapped on for a piggyback ride even when I was past the age for it, so I might have been as old as four. The evening afterglow had taken on an unusually crimson cast, as though the sky itself were bleeding. It wasn't that our vil-lage appeared especially dark or light, but it looked com-pletely different, the way people you know well can appear unfamiliar if seen across a bonfire.

I couldn't bear it and burst into tears. My sudden out-burst baffled my mother, and I had no explanation for it either. I just felt pure, unadulterated sorrow. Later I had a similar experience, on an evening when the wind was espe-cially dismal. It's hard for me to describe my overwhelming sadness as I returned home alone after parting from my friends. Millet stalks swayed in the vegetable patch. They were outlined in the soft persimmon tones of twilight against the contours of the ridge. This time, though, I tried to find ways to accentuate my melancholy. What could I do to make that swaying sadder, drearier? I lowered my-self, tilting my head to find the correct angle, and wound up lying on the grass on my back. And I quietly waited until the sorrow welling in my heart flowed out in tears.

In the aftermath of Grandfather's stroke, our house was a gloomy place, but the slackened discipline meant I was having the time of my life. When he was healthy, he'd been as opposed to my roaming around with my friends as he'd been to the women going to Songdo or working in the fields.

Grandfather, fortunately, hadn't become completely paralyzed, but he'd still lost the use of his left arm and leg. Immediately after the stroke, he took out his frustrations on the family, but he gradually made peace with his handicap and sought pastimes that remained within his ability.

And so he gathered the village kids and taught them to read and write. Our outer quarters became a school. The region lagged badly in accepting anything modern—our neighbors thought of my uncles' four years of primary schooling as new-fangled education. People still venerated Chinese characters, believing they represented true learning, and looked down on the Korean alphabet, which they referred to as ŏnmun, or "vulgar letters." One reason for the lack of respect was that our alphabet was easy to learn.

Grandfather's school was popular. Villagers from not just Pakchk Hamlet but the other side of the hill sent their sons to attend. The sound of recitation drifted from the outer quarters all day long. The villagers' attitude toward my family changed. Previously Grandfather had acted arrogantly without real cause, but now it seemed that even the elders nodded to me in deference.

One day Grandfather called me to the outer quarters, and from then on I was obliged to study *The Thousand Character Classic*. Thankfully, the book my grandfather gave me had the Korean alphabet written in, glossing the pronunciation of each character. Although I still didn't know that what people called ŏnmun was in fact our alphabet, I'd already got down about half of it. Mother taught me, but with Mother instruction was equivalent to coercion. She made me feel that since she'd learned it overnight, I had to do the same.

Mother was learned for a countrywoman. She wrote letters for the others, who would come late at night to ask her help. I'd wake to see her holding a brush and unfurling paper in the dim lamplight. The village women, reluctant to bother her on their own, would come in a group when she wasn't busy. As she read back the letters she'd written, some visitors dabbed at their brimming tears with their long blouse ribbons, while others sat dazed, mouths agape. Encircled by these women, Mother would undergo a transformation, her expression imposing and her voice solemn. When she experienced this metamorphosis and became so different from both the mother I knew and the other women around her, I felt afraid and proud of her at the same time, and my pulse raced. The following morning, it would seem as though it had all been a dream.

Although Mother's familiarity with the alphabet gave her license to act superior in our village, she was totally ignorant about the alphabet's history, absurdly so. She knew that King Sejong had created it, but she claimed he'd come up with it in a sudden flash while squatting in an outhouse. According to her, his inspiration came from the patterns on the door frame.

Now you can see where the story could have begun—the letters do look like they might have been modeled on the geometric patterns in a Korean door frame—but Mother stressed this point over and over, just so she could brand as fools those who took a long time to master something so simple. I believed her. Only after liberation from Japan did I learn that the alphabet was no mere set of "vulgar letters" but our proud *hangŭl*, which King Sejong and his scholars had developed with painstaking care.

I was obsessed with the fear that she'd consider me an idiot if I didn't learn the vowels and consonants right away, so I memorized the combination table. But I didn't master it. I couldn't manipulate the letters to make meaningful words or sentences, nor did I have reading material at home to test what I'd learned. In her room, Mother had several storybooks she'd copied out herself, but she'd written them in a flowing, cursive style that might as well have been a foreign script compared with the printed form she'd taught me. Master the alphabet? I didn't recognize a single word.

After Mother went to Seoul, my grandmother sometimes chanted for me, "Add *k* to *ka*, and you get *kak*; add *n* to *ka*, and you get *kan*," and so on. If she hadn't, I'd have forgotten what little I knew. Whether it was inflated confidence in me or pure arrogance, my mother wanted to believe I understood everything after learning just a smidgen.

I didn't really understand the alphabet, however. I just pretended that I did. I grasped its logic only as I repeated after my grandfather, "Heaven, *ch'ŏn*; earth, *chi*." Once I figured out that the Korean symbols written beneath the Chinese characters represented their pronunciation, I became more interested in reading the Korean than the Chinese itself.

I was killing two birds with one stone. Since I could compare the two writing systems on the sly, Grandfather praised me, saying I never forgot anything I was taught. When he caned a big boy, old enough to be married off by the standards of the time, for having failed to memorize a section of his homework, Grandfather yelled at him, citing me as an example. I felt proud of myself, but I was also anxious about being exposed as a fraud, because the book that came after *The Thousand Character Classic* didn't have Korean that I could use as a crib to cheat.

But Grandfather's academy didn't last long. He had another stroke. This second stroke lacked the drama of his collapse in the outhouse, but it was every bit as tragic. It destroyed what remained of his dignity, the very feature that made him who he was. His right arm and leg shook, and although he had managed to resume going to the outhouse, that too came to an end. Now he became clumsy even with a spoon, and he'd spill his soup when he ate. A hemp towel lay ready in his lap to wipe away the stream of spittle he produced as he spoke.

Although he slurred now, his voice remained resonant. He'd call me several times a day to run small errands or to keep him company, particularly when he got tired of sitting blankly by himself or when his temper flared. But being so young, I didn't want to see him because he looked so helpless.

Sometimes, when he wanted to write a letter, he'd have me rub down his inkstone to produce the ink he needed. His trembling hand meant it took ages to create a wobbly series of characters. They struck me as completely illegible, and I thought he was having me prepare the ink just to make my life difficult. But Grandfather was the only one in the house at that point to keep up correspondence. My mother and brother sent notes of greetings, and letters came from many others as well.

The postman came every third day. Naturally, he took his breaks from work in our outer quarters. Back then, you could give what you wanted to mail to the postman, so even when he had no letters for us, he'd stop by to see if we had anything to send. Grandfather would wait to welcome him, and then latch on to him for conversation—all the more so after his second stroke.

The postman's repertoire of stories collected as he traveled from village to village far exceeded the supply of letters in his bag. When Grandfather invited him to take a break from his rounds, I'd immediately relay this information onward, as if by tacit agreement, so refreshments could be brought out. Grandfather would be pleased and say affectionately, "Precious baby, you do just as well as my own tongue!"

But oh, how I hated his rewards—steamed chestnuts or rice cake he wrapped in the damp, sour-smelling cloth he used to wipe away his spittle and bits of food.

Sometimes I got scolded for not performing errands properly. Once he called me urgently. I rushed over, only to have him ask me to light a match for his cigarette because the fire in the brazier had died. I'd never struck a match. Now, we weren't living in those ancient times when a daughter-in-law might be banished back to her parents' house for letting the fire die, but we did keep a brazier going even during hot weather and didn't need matches often. Although I'd seen others light them, I didn't think I could do it myself and made a face. Grandfather then told me to hold the matchbox, and he tried to strike a match against it, but his hand shook so badly that every attempt failed.

It was painful to see Grandfather looking so pathetic. Smoking was hardly a necessity, I thought. Wouldn't it be better just to give it up? Then he said he'd hold the matchbox and told me to strike a match against it. I imagined the aftermath—if I struck it hard and the flame leapt at my fingertips, I'd throw the match down and fire would break out. Grandfather, unable to move, would burn to death! The mere thought of it raised goose bumps all over my body. I ran out in panic, bawling, as if I'd really made all my imaginings come to life. Back then, I cried at the drop of a hat.

My fire phobia had a basis in reason, though: people referred to me as the girl who almost burned down her house. On one of my brother's visits home from school in

Kaesŏng, he brought a small burning glass with a handle. It must have been a teaching tool in his science class.

I peered through the round, black-rimmed glass. Brother's eye looked as big as a bull's, and my finger looked as thick as my mother's. Brother saw my awe and showed me something even more amazing: he took some paper and lit it by holding the glass to it. I'm still not sure why I found this so fascinating.

The sunlight passed through the convex glass and funneled into an intense beam. It gleamed eerily, like the eyes of a cat hidden in the dark. Finally, as a weak plume of smoke rose, a hole appeared in the paper and consumed it in a thin, crimson strip. It reminded me of a shredded chili and stole my breath away. My stomach knotted up, and I felt a sudden need to pee.

That night, I really did wet my bed. As a result, I believe to this day the old wives' tale that children wet their beds after playing with fire. I still remember all this vividly, but I can't, for the life of me, remember a thing about nearly causing a fire.

Apparently, the incident occurred after the harvest. I had snuck off with the glass to play on top of a pile of straw that had been heaped up for plaiting thatch, and the straw began to smolder. In the yard opposite our main gate stood a barn of sorts—a structure that was covered but otherwise completely open, so that grain and chili peppers spread in the yard to dry could be stored right away in case of a sudden shower. Fortunately, a neighbor's wife happened to be on her way home from the well and discovered the flames. Since she had a bucket of water on her head, she put out the fire without much difficulty.

I'm not sure how this incident has been wiped clean from my mental slate, given that I could have burned down our house. I tend to be confident about my memories, especially those from my childhood, and so I can only shake my head, perplexed, wondering if the story was made up or exaggerated to stop me from playing with fire. Anyway, the phrase "the girl who almost burned down her house" weighed on me for a long time.

My match phobia lasted until I graduated from elementary school. It inconvenienced me several times, but saddest of all was when I couldn't light Grandfather's cigarette. The conflict I felt is still with me—my troubled attempt to overcome my limitations for his sake, anxiety about my inability to do so, and self-loathing for my ultimate inadequacy.

2. Seoul, So Far Away

GRANDFATHER'S SECOND STROKE USHERED IN a decline in the family's fortune. Even as a child, I recognized the thickening clouds. My younger uncle and his wife had left for Seoul. They were inspired by my mother, who was a force to reckon with. She had pioneered a life in the capital, and my grandparents' resentment toward her began to soften. Actually, let me put that more accurately: their resentment began to soften once they found themselves benefiting from her ambition.

On the previous school vacation, Mother and Brother had returned home. Brother was dressed neatly in his uniform, and Mother was the picture of confidence itself. She told everyone that Brother had been admitted to a public school, no mean feat. Not only that, she said, its graduates came up with civil service jobs easily, even at the Office of the Governor General.

I came from a rustic scholar family that was just this side of illiterate. I'm ashamed to admit it, but Grandfather had neither historical consciousness nor Korean pride despite his constant boasts about our _yangban_ status. His aristocratic noblesse consisted in looking down on families that occupied lower rungs in the pecking order, and his sense of class responsibility went no further than dictating that his sons' wives come from clans of equal status in the so-called Orthodox Faction. Whenever he sized up anyone, he'd trot out his favorite saying: "You can deck yourself out however you want, but the bones give you away."

His meager loyalty to _yangban_ ideals meant that even a civil service job with Japan's colonial administration represented high status to him, and he could dream that his grandson, the heir who would carry on our surname, was destined to bring glory to the clan. And if that's how Grandfather thought, who in the family would dare scorn my mother, whose son showed such promise of rising in the world? All the more so, since Younger Uncle, trusting in her support, had gone off to Seoul as well.

At that point, neither of my uncles had children; after Younger Uncle departed, the household became drearier. Our house was large and built with attention to detail. I'm told that Father had constructed it before I was born, in the belief that all three brothers, together with their parents and their many offspring, would live under the same roof in eternal harmony and prosperity. With fewer people around, I had even more room for wallowing in self-pity, and nowhere suited me and my wallowing better than the pillar that divided the veranda in half. I'd lean against it, preoccupied, and gaze out beyond the entrance to the village. When my family caught me at this, they immediately sensed why I was so sad and lonely, especially my grandmother. She'd scramble to snuggle me and then coo huskily over and over, "My poor baby."

They thought I was waiting for my mother as I sat like that, and because they did, I believed it too. But it was a strange type of waiting, one I hadn't experienced before, completely devoid of the sweet restlessness that had tinged my anticipation for Grandfather. "*Ch'ŏk ch'ŏk*, thumb stop, middle finger, if Mother's at Wardrobe Rocks Hill." I couldn't accept that even if I played my game a hundred times, my waiting might be in vain. Any time someone remarked that I looked so sad because I was pining for my mother, I'd burst into hysterical tears. The more I tried to deny it, the truer it became.

But a force stronger than my finger fortune-telling game was at work. One day, Mother appeared out of the blue, even though it wasn't vacation. I was relieved. Here was proof that she had longed for me so much that she couldn't bear it! But she said that she'd come not because she missed me, but to take me back with her.

"You have to go to school in Seoul too." I couldn't decide if I liked what Mother said. I thought I might have vaguely yearned for Seoul, but I'd never imagined attending school there. My grandmother practically fainted when she heard what Mother had in mind: "What? Sending a girl to Seoul for school?" Another dispute broke out in the family: "What did you do to make so much money you can talk about sending her to Seoul? Did I get that right? What if somebody hears you?"

Mother stayed silent, so she continued, "Father's only pleasure since his stroke has been watching this cute little thing come and go. And you want to take her away? How heartless can you get!"

Grandmother's shift from insult to pleading had no effect, so she switched tactics again. Confronting me, she asked, "Who do you like better, Grandma or Mommy? Tell me right away. If it's Grandma, tell Mommy you want to live with me. Right now."

I had only one way out. I exploded in tears. "I don't know, I don't know," I wailed. I couldn't cope with being torn so senselessly. Even as an adult, I hated to see children asked, "Who do you love more, Mommy or Daddy?"

Mother put an abrupt end to this pointless dispute. She didn't have time to dawdle. Without consulting anyone, me included, she took my hair, as though she were going to comb it, and then chopped it off.

Up to that point, I'd worn my hair in tiny braids, just like the other girls in the village. Until it grew long and thick enough to be gathered into a single braid, we divided it from the top in squares, like a Chinese chessboard, and tied each patch off with brightly colored thread or thin ribbons. The whole process took ages and had to be repeated daily; otherwise, you were left with a tangled mess. A single glance at a girl's hair told you how well valued she was at home.

My father's sister had tended to my hair until she got married, as though grooming it were her hobby. Afterward, my uncle's wife took over. She combed and plaited it, so it was neat and shiny, and I took secret pride in it. From a young age, I assumed that if people commented I was pretty or cute, it was because my hair impressed them. Of all my attributes, my hair gave me the most confidence.

But Mother not only chopped off this precious, precious hair of mine, but shaved the back of my head to create a high hairline. Before I could protest, she bullied me into submission with the remark that this was how all the kids in Seoul cut their hair.

"Oh my goodness! What an awful sight!" Grandmother's jaw dropped. The feeling of so much hair missing on the back of my head was even worse than having my bangs cut in a straight line. I ventured out of the house tentatively and within seconds became the butt of my friends' ridicule.

"Nyah-nyah nyah-nyah-nyah, someone's got a face on the back of her head!"

In those days, bobbed hair was cut so short that it really did look as though the back of the head could have a face. But their teasing didn't bother me too much because I now had a snappy comeback: "This is how kids in Seoul get their hair cut. But you don't know that, do you?" I was already looking down on my benighted peers. My bobbed hair not only made Grandmother surrender, but alienated me from the countryside. I wanted to leave with my mother as soon as possible.

I went to the outer quarters to say goodbye to Grandfather. He refused to look at me straight, but he seemed to know about everything that had gone on. He expressed his displeasure loudly: "Damn awful sight is right."

Then he rummaged through his pouch and tossed out a fifty-chon silver coin. I felt hurt. Why did he have to throw it toward me if it was a present? I slapped the rolling coin to a stop with my palm and then grasped it and thanked him. Grandfather seemed to need consoling for his heartbreak more than I did for being insulted. I thought I'd start bawling if he showed any cracks in his gruff exterior. He snapped at me to leave right away.

What Mother did may have deserved my grandparents' anger, but she was still the senior daughter-in-law. More to the point, they had few descendants, and she was mother to the grandson who'd carry on the family line. Besides, she was a plucky woman who had the wherewithal to set up house in Seoul, where they said your nose would get stolen right off your face if you dozed off. The packages waiting outside made it clear that, whether my grandparents approved of her or not, they could not simply spurn her. They even hired a porter to carry an A-frame piled high with all sizes of bundles, stuffed with grain and red pepper powder. Grandmother went so far as to accompany us, decked out in her finest dress.

The twenty *ri* to Kaesŏng seemed unimaginably far. We crossed fields and climbed hills. Everywhere that a field and a hill met was a village, some bigger than Pakchŏk Hamlet and others smaller, but the way they sat in their surroundings was familiar, as was the way the houses looked. I had accepted villages as part of a larger natural order. The fourth and final hill, Wardrobe Rocks Hill, was particularly steep, or so I must have thought because my legs hurt so much by that point. Mother told me to keep going. Songdo lay just beyond, she reassured me. I puffed. I huffed. Mother pushed me from behind. My mouth was parched with the exertion, but at long last I managed to scramble to the top.

And then a sight I'd never witnessed before spread beneath me: the Songdo I'd heard so much about. I let out a cry, awestruck at this beautiful city gleaming silver. Its roads and houses dazzled me. I later learned that all its large new buildings were built in granite. The sandy soil gave the city its characteristic rocks and roads of white. *So people live in places like this!* I gaped as I stared, enchanted by the artificial order and neatness.

Suddenly a blinding flash shot from a building straight into my eyes. The light was unlike any I'd seen before. There was no fire, but it was more intense than any flame. I clung to my mother in fear. She told me to stop being silly, that it was just the sun reflecting off a glass window. I could make out that a sunbeam was hitting something and giving off a ray, but I didn't understand what she meant by "glass window." She then explained to me that in big cities like Songdo and Seoul, everybody used glass for house windows.

In Pakchŏk Hamlet, too, we had something made of glass. The grown-ups called it a saké bottle. It was placed under the veranda and stored kerosene poured from a canister. *People live in houses with windows of glass!* I was amazed, but at least half my fascination when I gazed on Songdo was anxiety. I sensed that I was standing not so much on Wardrobe Rocks Hill as on the border of two totally different worlds. I felt inexorably drawn to this unknown realm, but at the same time I wanted to take a few steps back.

I could almost hear my heart pound. An instinctive fear gnawed at me—I was at a crossroads, about to turn from the easy life I had known onto a path of challenge.

The descent wasn't hard. Halfway down, we passed a cluster of huge hexagonal rocks that had given the hill its name. Sweet spring water gushed forth among them, and they really did look like a slew of wardrobes scattered about. I sat on one that resembled a long, long money chest and quenched my thirst.

Finally, we marched into Songdo. We crossed railway tracks and passed alleys flanked by trim houses with tile roofs. Eventually, we turned onto a main thoroughfare of packed earth, lined with two- and three-story homes with glass windows. Songdo was filled with things I'd never seen before, but Mother's attitude made me feel like I shouldn't cower or gawk.

Mother's confidence as she strode along struck me as slightly unnatural, even if I couldn't explain why. She seemed to be setting an example for me. All the girls had short haircuts that revealed the pale backs of their heads. I felt a newfound respect for my mother. Some older girls did have long braids tied off with a ribbon, but not a single girl wore the tiny braids I had sported in the village.

Finally, we reached Kaesŏng Station. It was magnificent, and people were bustling about inside. What would I do if

I lost sight of the grown-ups? I was terrified. I'd never imagined such a possibility before, and that made my fear all the more vivid. I clutched tightly at Mother's skirt, as she piled up our bundles near the gate and went to buy tickets. We showed them to an inspector and went out to the platform, where I saw a gigantic ladder suspended in midair. Mother called it an overpass, but even then, she made sure to boast that it was nothing in comparison with the one at Seoul Station, which was much bigger and more crowded.

We had an arduous trek, laden as we were. But when a train pulled in, Mother began to run, bundles in her hands and on her head, followed by Grandmother, who had bought a platform ticket so she could see us off. I darted after them, bundles in my hands too. Other passengers joined in the mad dash. I sprinted with all the speed I could muster and boarded amid all the confusion. The train made me think of a huge snake with glass windows. Grandmother helped us hoist our bundles on the rack above and went back out alone.

She then stood on the other side of the window by where I sat. She was saying something, but I couldn't make out her words. Of all those seeing off families and friends, Grandmother looked smallest and shabbiest, but that very shabbiness drew me to her. How amazing glass was! I could gaze clearly at her as her eyes welled with tears. I wanted her to gather me in her arms, so I could weep with her and have her caress me and murmur, "My poor baby." I pressed against the window, squishing my face against it as though against a sheet of ice, but couldn't get any closer.

The train shrieked out a piercing, melancholy whistle and then began to chug away. Those saying goodbye to loved ones walked alongside until they gradually disappeared from view. I couldn't see whether Grandmother had followed the train or just stood there. My tears poured forth in a torrent. I'd often sobbed loudly without crying, but I'd never wept silently when so many tears flowed. The heartbreak I felt was unbearable.

Finally we arrived in Seoul. Mother and I, with all our bundles, lagged at the tail of the crowd. Panting, we climbed a pedestrian overbridge that was indeed several times bigger and busier than Kaesŏng's. Other people's loads were much lighter than ours, and they could hand them to porters in navy blue uniforms and red caps. Mother, however, flailed about nightmarishly, struggling under the weight of our packages. A long, long time seemed to pass before we exited the ticket gate and reached the plaza in front of the station. Right in the center of it, Mother shed her burden, the way she might pour out buckets of water, and plopped down in a heap. I was so overwhelmed by the crowds passing around us that it didn't even register with me that we'd arrived in Seoul at last.

A-frame carriers in tattered dirty clothes rushed to us, like a band of beggars, competing noisily to carry our bundles. Some tried to lift them away unasked. When it dawned on me that we could hire a porter, as we'd done from Pakchŏk Hamlet to Kaesŏng, I felt a semblance of hope return. But Mother shook them all off, saying we'd take a streetcar.

A tram was running through the street. It was blue, shorter than a train carriage, and looked as though it had horns stretching from its back up to lines in the air. When I saw sparks leap between its horns and the lines, my curiosity turned into fear. Mother stayed sprawled on the ground, and the porters who had scattered approached again, one by one.

Mother chose a porter and began bargaining, but the criteria she used to pick one were beyond me. She pointed across the street with her chin. How much to go over there, to the other side of Sŏdaemun? The carrier quoted a price. Mother refused. She began pulling down the bundles he'd placed on his A-frame. How much did she have in mind, then? After a long bout of haggling, mother and daughter were at last liberated from their burden. We walked on ahead in front of him.

We passed a crowded street, dirty and noisy. Its dust and grime were reflected in the clothes of the people who walked along it. After crossing a big intersection through which streetcars traveled, pedestrians thinned out and the road began to look more like the one I'd seen in Kaesŏng. Farther ahead loomed a large gate that blocked the street.

"That's Independence Gate," explained Mother. The A-frame carrier, trailing behind, asked breathlessly whether we'd arrived yet.

"Just a little farther." A wheedling smile flickered on my mother's face.

"How far is 'a little farther'?"

"Over there, Hyŏnjŏ-dong."

Before she finished her sentence, he stopped in his tracks. His eyes bulged in anger. Was this some kind of joke? Who'd go all the way up that hill for the amount of money she'd offered? Mother held her ground, retorting with a question of her own: Why would she pay several times more than the tram fare, instead of riding in comfort, if her destination was in the flats of Seoul? She coaxed him onward, saying she was considering adding a tip so he could buy some rice wine. He grumbled, cursing his luck for the day, but followed anyway. Once the name Hyŏnjŏ-dong had come out of my mother's mouth, though, he became noticeably rude. It was all too clear that he looked down on us. Where on earth was Hyŏnjŏ-dong to make him behave as he did? My spirits sank at the change in his attitude.

The double streetcar tracks that had accompanied our journey came to an end. Mother entered an alley that soon turned into a series of precipitous steps lined by houses. It was a strange neighborhood. The houses clustered together on a steep hill and looked ready to tumble down its side at any moment. The houses had simple plank gates, but you could see everything that went on inside them. Drainage grooves running along the steps brimmed with a fetid mix of cabbage leaves, rice grains, and urine.

We struggled to the top of one hill without stopping, but the neighborhood continued. On we went, following an alley that twisted and turned, barely wide enough for two people to pass, until we came to steps even steeper and less regular than those we'd climbed below. Finally, about half-way up, my mother stopped in front of a thatched house, one of the few even in this poor neighborhood. But that house wasn't ours, either. Mother was merely renting a room next to its gate.

The room was cramped and gloomy and had a tiny attached veranda. The only furniture was a chest of drawers, papered in a brightly colored pattern of deer, turtles, and the so-called herb of eternal youth.

Since the women in my family didn't have to work in the fields, they must have had time to burnish our furniture, for the chests that lined one side of every room in our house gleamed. Grandmother had brought a three-tiered chest with her when she got married. Although some nickel hinges were missing from its doors and they didn't open properly, the wood of the chest had a deep, subtle sheen. In the corner of one room, an opaque blue-gray vinegar jar with a long neck and fat tummy sat beside the wardrobe. For years, vinegar had been stored in it, its acidity staining the jar naturally. I found the jar very beautiful. It struck me as mystical, just like the shrine to the household spirit in the yard. As far as I could tell, vinegar was made by pouring leftover liquor or rice wine into the jar. Sometimes small moths flew out. My grandmother considered that jar precious, saying our vinegar was the best in the village. If anyone asked for some, she refused, saying she was afraid that her recipe might be stolen. She issued this pronouncement with such solemnity that she didn't sound stingy, and I felt a mysterious power in her words.

Heartbreaking images of that long-necked jar, the wardrobe of fine-grained wood, and the harmony they created within the room came to me. It was a scene of paradise lost. My own sense of beauty had developed under the influence of aesthetics handed down for centuries. The chest that confronted me here, with its hasty paper job and tacky colors, insulted my eyes.

3. Beyond the Gates

"ARE WE IN SEOUL?" I WHINED.

To my surprise, Mother said no. "We're outside the city gates." In a soothing tone, she continued, "Later on Brother is going to get a job and make lots of money. Then we can live inside the gates and hold our heads up high."

I heard people coming and going outside our window until late at night, bellowing out gibberish: "*Manjū na hoya, hoooya!*" It sounded like they were selling something, but I didn't bother to ask. I wasn't especially curious.

Sometimes, back in the countryside, the howling of animals beyond our fence woke us.

"Don't tell me it's those damn wolves again." Grandmother would grumble and sit up, concerned that they might make off with our chickens. I heard their howling, but I never actually saw any wolves. I longed to be able to fall asleep amid their baying once more.

From the next morning, I began to adapt to life in Seoul—or, better put, to life in a rented room. I had no choice. When I woke up, I asked Mother where the outhouse was, but she told me to wait until the people inside were finished before I went. I'd already learned on the train that an outhouse was also called a "toilet," and that only one person at a time was supposed to be inside it. The night before, I'd gone to the toilet in the house. I now learned I was going to have to wait my turn even just to go squat.

Mother went a step further: "Do you know how much trouble it was to get you here? I had to be really careful. I told the landlord that I just had your brother with me. I thought they wouldn't like you being here because they have kids your age." Was this my mother, my oh-so-proud mother, talking? How could she pretend I didn't exist? I'd been spoiled rotten up to that point, and now here I was suddenly finding myself feeling unwelcome. I'd been tricked, I thought. I now saw Mother in a different light. I wanted to go tattling to Grandfather and to ask Grandmother to rescue me, but, alas, they were too far away.

Being a tenant, though, demanded a whole lot more of me than just holding it in when I needed to go squat.

"It'd be better not to play with the kids inside. If you fight, the grown-ups might get into a fight too."

"Don't watch the kids when they're eating."

"Don't touch their toys."

"Don't go acting all jealous either."

"The less you go inside the house, the better."

Better? Better if she looped a straw rope around my ankles and tethered me to a post. What in the world did she want me to do? Become invisible? That seemed to be what she was hoping for. She refused to understand how difficult all this was for me, a seven-year-old girl who'd gallivanted around our village at will. Even the village's boundaries were too confining.

Living in a rented room was hard enough. Worse yet, the school year was fast approaching. Mother said we lived outside the city gates because we were poor, but she'd already made up her mind that I had to go to a good school in Seoul itself. She didn't care what I thought. Back then, schooling wasn't compulsory, so children had to pass an entrance exam first. This didn't mean they could take the test for any school they chose, since each district had its own designated school, just like today. Mother was obviously well aware of this, as she'd already officially transferred our residence to our relatives' house in Sajik-dong.

Mother thought about how far I'd have to walk and settled on Maedong Elementary School. To get there, I had to climb over a ridge that skirted Mount Inwang. I'd go up from the center of Hyŏnjŏ-dong just beyond the ruins of a fortress. From there, a path led down to Sajik Park. The track was not steep, but not many people used it. Supposedly, lepers swarmed in the forest just off this path. Mother laughed off these horrid rumors when she took me to the school on a reconnaissance mission several days before the test.

"Don't believe everything you hear. Lepers don't kidnap kids or steal their livers to eat. They're people, just like us. They can't bring themselves to do things like that any more than anybody else could. Only idiots are scared of stories that aren't true. If you meet a leper, just act naturally. Don't be frightened. Don't run away. Just look straight ahead and keep walking, and don't stare."

My mother's tone always had an overbearing smugness that made even reasonable advice come across as a bullying harangue. But I could sense her waver when she talked about the lepers. Of all her advice, what she said about them made the most sense to me, and so I wasn't afraid of running into them. After our scouting journey, I began preparing for the entrance test in earnest. *I'm sure you'll do great.* But Mother's confidence didn't stop her from making my life miserable. She'd drill me several times a day on questions she thought might come up. She quizzed me on writing my name, telling time, counting, adding, subtracting.

I was good at all that, but I hated having to memorize two addresses. The first address my mother taught me was, of course, the one in Sajik-dong, the house where we were officially supposed to be living. Memorizing that was a cinch. It would have been enough, too, but she suddenly became apprehensive about what might happen if I got lost and gave that address, so she had me memorize our address in Hyŏnjŏ-dong as well. It was long, complete with a subdivision number, but I had no trouble with that either. At that age, I could parrot anything easily enough. But Mother turned into a complete worrywart. I assume it was fear sparked in part by a basic innocence, pangs of guilt about a mildly fraudulent application. I mastered both addresses in no time, but then she began to worry that I might get confused and give the wrong one during the test. In trying to acquire peace of mind for herself, she almost drove me crazy.

Out of the blue, she'd blurt, "Where do you live? Where's your house? What do you say if you're lost?"

Then I had to give our address in Hyŏnjŏ-dong.

If, though, she said, "Where is your house? Now you're taking the test in front of the teacher," then I had to give the fake address in Sajik-dong. Mother was petrified that I'd confuse the two. I wouldn't have, but the way she acted made me freeze and I'd get nervous about mixing them up. And then everything turned into a mess. With each passing day, I did worse and worse on Mother's blitzkrieg spot checks.

My mother sorely regretted what she'd done, saying she should never have taught a stupid girl like me two addresses, and just to forget about Hyŏnjŏ-dong until after the test.

But you can't just forget something because somebody tells you to. The more she pressured me, the more tenaciously my brain clung to the information. Although I've forgotten almost all the many addresses I've had in Seoul over the course of my life, including the one at Sajik-dong, I still remember Number 418, Lot 46, Hyŏnjŏ-dong.

And so came test day, with my head in a whirl because of my addresses—and it was hardly certain a question about them would surface. I remember wearing a long, pale green silk coat, the one Mother had brought with her when she came to fetch me from Pakchŏk Hamlet, and getting a fresh haircut at a barbershop.

As it turned out, there wasn't a question about my address on the test. Instead, they set down three *go* pieces in one spot and four in another and asked me how many there were in total. They showed me a picture of a man in a Western suit and a student, and then a picture of a fedora and a student's cap and told me to match the hats with each figure. Then they showed me smoke rising from a chimney and asked which direction the wind was blowing in. I got only two out of three questions right. I answered that the wind was blowing in the opposite direction from the smoke.

Mother's relief upon hearing they didn't ask my address turned into bitter disappointment when she heard that I'd given a wrong answer. If she had just considered that I'd failed and left it at that, things wouldn't have been so bad. But she couldn't conceal her disgust. She pointed vehemently at everything in sight—fluttering hair, billowing coat tails, the Japanese flag waving from the pole in the school playground. "What direction is the wind blowing now? What direction? Good lord! If you don't even know that much, who'd want you, anyway?"

Why did the wind have to blow so strongly that day? To make matters worse, we were in Maedong School's broad, open playground. There were almost no surrounding buildings, and we were exposed to the wind's full force. That evening, Mother relived her fury for my brother's benefit.

"You don't know what's under the lid until it's been lifted."

Although Brother was still in secondary school, he was much older than I was because he hadn't started elementary school until he was nine or so. He was taciturn and thoughtful.

The result was due to arrive by postcard. Of course, if good news came, it would go to our Sajik-dong address. After waiting long enough for the card to have arrived several times over, Mother dressed me in my silk coat and took me to visit our relatives in Sajik-dong. It was my first trip to the house whose address had practically driven me insane. On the way, Mother kept stressing that the house was located inside the city gates.

The neighborhood was indeed in much better shape than Hyŏnjŏ-dong, and cozier too. Above all, I liked it because it was on level ground, instead of clinging to a hill. Our relatives' house had a long outer portion that lay on the street. The inner quarters lay behind a gate. The outer quarters had tile roofs but were shabby, rundown, and smelled terrible—completely different from those in our country house. I learned later that, in fact, the outer section was for the servants; they were not outer quarters as I knew them. In a yard in front that looked like an alley, a maid was washing clothes. When she caught sight of my mother, she stood up, her face beaming.

"Missus, congratulations! I heard Young Miss passed the test." She bowed again and again.

It was the first time we'd ever been addressed as Missus and Young Miss. It was also the first time I saw my mother act so haughtily. With sudden arrogance, she said, "What's the fuss? All she did was get into elementary school."

Once we passed through the inner gate, a different world appeared. A veranda, enclosed by immaculately polished glass doors, rose on gleaming terrace stones of granite. The yard was neatly swept and contained a tap and a cement water basin. The housemaid had followed us in. She scooped water from the brimming basin into a pail. I marveled, filled with envy, at the tap and its infinite supply of water.

Not a single house in Hyŏnjŏ-dong had running water. Everyone either bought water from vendors or carried it home themselves. On the flat ground below all the steps was a set of communal taps. A long line of pails always stood in front of them. The vendors had pails made of zinc, with wooden handles that had been bored so they could be hooked to a carrying frame. These buckets were different from the ones used by people who carried their own water. The professionals' pails were rectangular and the size of an oil canister. Everyone else had cylindrical pails about twice as big.

The water sellers made dozens of deliveries each morning. Their goal was to exert as little effort as possible, since delivery cost one chon regardless of bucket size. Those fetching their own water, however, tried to carry as much as they could on each trip.

Mother didn't know how to fit herself with a yoke for carrying water, so she had two buckets delivered every morning. Those buckets had to last not only for cooking and drinking, but also for bathing and laundry. For over a month after my arrival in Seoul, Mother nagged me. She was intent on my becoming, first, a model tenant, and second, a frugal water consumer.

"Don't throw the water away after you wash your face. Wash your feet with it, and then use it to wash the rags. When you're done, I'll sweep the yard and wet it down with what's left."

Mother called the alley in front of our house "the yard." She swept it daily, so she could have just cause to look down on neighbors who didn't follow suit. Sometimes I'd blunder, and the water she had doled out for me wound up in the drain before reaching its final destination. She'd tut-tut in dismay as though a prized possession had accidentally been thrown in the garbage.

The area inside the front gate doubled as our kitchen, and one corner held a jar buried in the ground. The water seller came at the crack of dawn, but I never heard the crossbar being lifted. Either the landlords had already removed it for their own water delivery, or they just left the gate open all night because they didn't own anything worth stealing. I'd wake to the splash of water poured into the jar. That splish-splash of successive pails being emptied was the most depressing thing of all about life in Hyŏnjŏ-dong. It brought home to me our poverty in all its degradation. Survive all day on two buckets? In the countryside, it had never even crossed my mind to be careful about water, let alone treat it as a precious resource.

In Pakchŏk Hamlet, a brook ran down from the forsythia shrubs and through the vegetable patch in our yard. It never flooded or dried up, so for the most part it either gurgled cheerfully or whispered almost inaudibly, but our main room faced directly onto it, and during the rainy season it jabbered at us. In winter, the edges froze, but water kept flowing in the center of the brook. The ice was dappled with patterns that I found mesmerizing. I'd defy the cold and break off pieces and then crunch them up in my mouth.

The sensation was incredibly refreshing. I felt like it was cleansing me to my veins.

Mother and my aunts drew our water from the well in the center of the village, but I'd often scoop it up from the brook with my hands when I was playing in order to quench my thirst. The brook was where we washed our clothes, peeled our potatoes and yams, rinsed our greens, and, of course, washed our hands on the way back from the outhouse. That any of this might be unsanitary never even entered our heads: we had a never-ending supply of fresh water.

My one conservation lesson came in winter. We'd heat our water in a huge cauldron. If I took a whole basin for myself, I'd get a harsh scolding. The grown-ups said that if I wasted so much water just washing my face, I'd be punished in the next world by having to drink up an entire tubful.

That early dawn splash of water imbued me with silly fears as I lay in bed. I imagined that I was slowly drying out, like a fish hung up to preserve. At the Sajik-dong house, however, water spouted endlessly from the tap.

The lady of the house welcomed us. She looked the same age as Mother, but she had on a fashionable pale yellow blouse with purple breast-ties and called my mother "Great Aunt." She even spoke deferentially to me: "Congratulations on getting into school, Auntie." I learned later that we had a higher generational standing in our clan, so her rank was equivalent to that of a grandson's wife to my mother. She addressed Mother with honorifics, while Mother used less polite forms back to her.

The lady called the housemaid and told her to make lunch. Then she took out the admission notice the school had sent and set it down in front of Mother. Mother barely glanced at it, treating it instead with the pleasure she'd re-serve for rice cake that had spoiled.

"Well, it looks like she's passed," Mother said, with a mild frown. "I was hoping she wouldn't get in."

I was dumbstruck. Why was Mother saying the exact op-posite of what I knew she felt? Our relative jumped up in protest. She praised me, saying that many neighborhood children, even those who'd gone to kindergarten, hadn't managed to get in. Mother must have been waiting for just that opening. She lied blatantly once more, claiming not to have taught me a thing before the test. If I hadn't passed, she went on, she'd been prepared to accept that schooling wasn't in the cards for me and to just ship me back to the countryside. That would have made things easier on her, and she'd at least have been able to tell herself, without any regrets, that she'd done what she could. Confusion roiled within me as I stared at my mother. Here she was, acting as though she'd practically been praying that I wouldn't pass, pretending she'd never made an enormous fuss.

The housemaid brought in the lunch tray. It was respect-ably full, with white bowls and small covered dishes spread across it. But when we lifted the lids from the bowls, the helpings were minuscule. There were barely a dozen stewed black beans, and you could have gathered the fermented clams and seasoned dried pollack with a single swipe of the chopsticks. I was hungry, but the stingy city portions made me lose my appetite.

Afterward, the woman wrapped up a huge bundle of ma-terial for Mother to sew. It included items for her own family and piecework she'd collected after spreading word about Mother's skill as a seamstress.

"I'm really indebted to you." Mother expressed her thanks in simple terms, clearly struggling to retain her dignity. I wanted to get away from these adults who acted so unnaturally, but they kept going on.

"Oh, come on, don't even mention it. Have you thought about what I suggested the other day?"

"You mean about sewing for *kisaeng*? Yes, I'd appreciate it if you have any good leads. I didn't want to resort to it, but I can't be choosy any more, seeing as I've got another mouth to feed and more tuition to pay this year . . . "

"You've made the right choice. It's no picnic sewing for families. But those girls are always wearing new clothes, and they can't even tell what good tailoring is. It doesn't matter to them how the collar or tie strips look as long as the blouse is comfortable and the flaps come together. . . . Why even hesitate, when they aren't picky and pay so well?"

"I didn't want to give my in-laws anything to criticize me about at all. I hate the idea of hearing them ask how I can afford to send my daughter to school."

"It'd be one thing if you worked as a *kisaeng*. But what's the big deal if all you do is sew for them?"

"You know how those *yangban* types are."

"Don't worry. I'll stick up for you if they say anything nasty."

"It looks like I'll have to keep relying on you to find me work. I'm such a burden."

"One of the pieces I gave you today is from a concubine who lives in our neighborhood. Concubines are cut from the same stock, right? I'll just have her ask around since she knows lots of *kisaeng*. She likes your sewing, so I'm sure there won't be any problem. I can send the maid. You won't have to go anywhere near a *kisaeng* house."

I was sorry I hadn't missed one more question on the test. That way, I could have spared my mother all this trouble, but it was too late. All along, she had been sewing for a living. Besides the gaudy chest, the most significant items in our room were a small clay brazier and a sewing basket. As soon as Mother finished cooking, she'd take the firewood, which she bought one or two bundles at a time, and load it in the brazier before the fire died out. Then she'd press down on the wood with the iron. It was impossible to sew traditional clothing, with its delicate collars and the like, without smoothing it constantly, and so she used the iron all day long, heating it against the brazier.

Even before Mother took up sewing for *kisaeng*, she was often given soft, beautiful silks to work with that were incomparably finer than the dyed cotton we wore in the countryside. Mother had lots of leftover scraps of pretty fabric and kept a heap wrapped in a small blanket. When I was bored, I'd put them together, pretending to make a crazy quilt, but Mother would jump up in horror and snatch them all away. In Pakchŏk Hamlet, girls my age knew how to hemstitch and broad stitch, and quite a few could even attach bodices to their own skirts. But Mother didn't see the point in my learning any of this.

"You need to study hard and become a New Woman."

Such was Mother's mantra. I didn't understand what a New Woman was. Nor, I suppose, did she. The phrase had been coined during Korea's "enlightenment" in the early years of the twentieth century, and it remained as compelling to her as it was mysterious. It was impossible for me to understand the resentment-cum-fascination she exhibited toward women living lives so different from the traditional norm.

Despite being my mother's daughter, with her blood and her temperament, I had yet to experience enough of a woman's life to want anything but freedom from all her dos and don'ts as soon as possible. She discouraged me from playing with our landlord's child, and the thought of my going out and playing with the neighborhood kids was something else that made her jump up in horror.

"The kids in this neighborhood don't have any manners. You, though, come from a family with real pedigree. Don't go out. If you play with them you'll end up becoming one of them."

In the midst of sewing for *kisaeng*, she'd prattle on about pedigree. I wasn't sure what exactly "pedigree" meant, but it was easier for me to get a handle on than "New Woman." I could sense that she was talking about our family's pride and emphasis on dignity. Maybe its meaning was also easier for me to grasp because I missed life in Pakchŏk Hamlet, and I felt different from the other kids in the neighborhood. But all this gave me fodder for thinking of Mother as pathetic. Why was she so confident that everything she did was right? When she puffed herself up with pride over our country roots, her face had the same expression as when she bragged about her urban sophistication on visits home. This double face of my mother—arrogance because of Seoul in Pakchŏk Hamlet and vice versa—confused me, but only I saw through this weak point of hers.

Mother couldn't tether me to that sewing basket permanently, though. Her work may never have ceased, but she still had to take the finished products to our relatives' house, so their maid could relay her piecework onward to the *kisaeng*. Mother would say that our debt of gratitude to her relative was as high as a mountain.

You can't keep a seven-year-old girl cooped up when her mother is away. I developed a taste for the outside world. In our neighborhood lived a tinker, a chimneysweep, and an A-frame carrier, together with their families. The A-frame carrier's wife sold sieves and carried some twenty to thirty of them around her neck and shoulders, with different styles of meshing, from fine to broad, all hooked together by loops on their rims. She was a short woman, and her head would get buried amid these hoops and bob into and out of view as she walked. They had a daughter older than me who didn't go to school.

The sieve seller would depart her house in silence. In contrast, the chimneysweep beat a brass gong when he left his gate. He too shouldered his equipment, a long sliver of bamboo that could be rolled up and unfurled. At its end was fastened a massive brush, as big as a man's head. It had traveled so often between chimney and furnace that it resembled a huge cake of soot more than a brush. The chimneysweep's dark beard looked as though he'd attached a clump of the brush to his face. Given that you couldn't quite see his mouth, it seemed completely logical for him to announce himself with a gong.

Many other chimneysweeps passed through the neighborhood, but even those with visible mouths beat gongs. It was all very strange to me. Everything about the chimneysweeps had a dullness to it except their gleaming gongs. When they struck them, using a small club padded with cotton or the like, the gongs gave off a subtle, lingering tone. They beat them patiently, waiting for the reverberations to die away before giving another blunt stroke. Every time I heard this sound, I felt a sorrow similar to that I felt when I watched the ears of millet dance in the autumn wind.

The chimneysweep had several offspring. There were many other kids in our alley whose parents' livelihoods I knew nothing about. One day, one of the children started teasing me, "Hillbilly, hillbilly!" Soon, all the others, even the big kids, chimed in. I was already mimicking my mother's smugness, though, and found the taunt ridiculous, considering the contrast between what I'd left behind in Pakchŏk Hamlet and the circumstances they lived in. I refused to cry in front of them, and in order not to, I drew strength from that pedigree my mother harped on. I had to develop a thick skin, if for no other reason than to defend the honor of the countryside.

Although they excluded me and teased me when in a group, they'd call to me if they were alone when they saw me: "Let's plaaay." I liked the way Seoul kids said it. Our country dialect was similar to Seoul's except for the endings we put on verbs, but I found it impossible to say "Let's plaaay" in such a sweet, enticing way. Still, even when I agreed to plaaay with them, there wasn't a whole lot to do. We didn't even have enough level ground for hopscotch.

One day, a friend and I were drawing on the ground or house walls with a slate pencil we'd picked up in the street. She suggested that we pull down our knickers and sketch each other's private parts in the dirt. Why such a ludicrous game? Because we were bored stiff. When I grew older and saw odd drawings, including sketches of genitalia, in public toilets and so on, I remembered the time I'd done it. Instead of curiosity or disgust, I felt pity—I knew how bored the artists must have been.

Once we had enough practice sketching each other's privates, we showed off our skill on the wall of our house. Mother caught us and gave me a real hiding. She blamed my companion, but all we'd done was play together. It wasn't as though she'd ordered me to make the drawings or anything. The way Mother ran down not just my friend but her parents was harder to take than the beating itself.

I promised never to play with that girl again, but still did so behind Mother's back. One day, while my mother was away, the two of us escaped from our neighborhood. I followed my friend through the convoluted alleys and stairways of Hyŏnjŏ-dong until we reached the street below, where we could hear the tram.

Suddenly I was seized with anxiety. "Do you know your address?" I asked.

"What's the use of knowing that?"

"But what if we get lost?"

"Don't worry. Just make sure to stick with me. All right?"

She put her arm around my shoulder. No one had ever put an arm around my shoulder in Pakchŏk Hamlet. The girl was at least a hand's length taller than me. As we walked, with her arm draped around me, I could feel myself becoming more animated. My friend was trustworthy. Mother, who'd branded her a bad girl and grilled me about whether we still played together, was the ignorant one.

We walked along in high spirits, matching our stride, and crossed the streetcar tracks. A huge lot appeared. It was bordered on one side by a red fence that sat on ground several feet higher. The fence looked like it must have extended for at least ten *ri*—much too far for us to tell where it ended. It was also too high to peer over and see what was inside.

A broad road ran alongside the fence above the lot; a set of steps, wider and straighter than the ones leading to our house in Hyŏnjŏ-dong, connected the road and the lot. On each side of the steps were smoothly grooved drains that had been set with cement. They were a perfect fit for a child's bottom, and a number of children were sliding on them.

My friend and I joined in the fun. I became so caught up in this new game I could never have experienced back home that I didn't realize the sun was going down. For the very first time, coming to Seoul seemed worthwhile.

Across the road encircling the fence was an intimidating high iron gate that no one would dare climb over. On either side, a policeman armed with a sword stood guard. We had to keep climbing up the steps to slide back down, and every time I saw them, I cowered. My friend said they wouldn't come after me and not to be scared, but each time I slid down I felt a tingle in my spine, nervous that they might grab me by the nape of my neck. But the added anxiety just made our sliding that much more thrilling.

The road had been deserted, but on one trip up the steps, we spied a group of strange men approaching along it in ranks. They were guarded front and back by sword-clad policemen and dressed in a sinister red, the color of dried blood. As they came closer, I noticed that they had iron shackles around their ankles. I froze.

Fear registered on my friend's face as well. She stomped her feet three times and spat. "Hurry up and do what I do," she told me. "Otherwise, you'll have bad luck." Bewildered, I followed suit.

We left quickly. On our way home, my friend said we'd just seen jailbirds. Seeing them could bring bad luck, so you had to ward it off. She couldn't explain exactly what jailbirds were, except that they were bad people and that they lived behind the fence. The clanging of the shackles around their ankles made me believe that maybe we really had done something wrong in seeing them. I had spat and stomped the way my friend showed me, but I couldn't rid myself of fear and disgust.

And so I told my mother I'd seen jailbirds. I was already prepared for a whipping because I'd been so caught up in our sliding fun I hadn't realized that the seat of my webbed leggings, which Mother had bought to replace my old windbreaker knickers, had worn through. Mother seemed to consider my playing in a prison yard a much bigger deal than my ruined leggings. She blew up in anger and became teary-eyed, lamenting, with long sighs, having to live near a penitentiary. She threatened to kick me back to Pakchŏk Hamlet right away if I ever played there again. I promised her I wouldn't. I wasn't really afraid she'd send me back, but for her to cry in front of me was enough to whip me into immediate shape.

Mother wasn't daunted easily. While my aunts would sulk by the kitchen stove after a scolding from my grandmother, my mother would lighten the mood right away with a joke. I was shocked by how humiliated she was by my playing in a prison yard and meekly promised I wouldn't be friends with the girl anymore. Grandfather had simply looked down on his fellow villagers as commoners, but Mother went a step further. She called our neighbors "trash."

Fighting was a constant backdrop to life in our neighborhood. Even the arena for marital quarrels shifted to the street. After a round of curses—"Bitch!" "Bastard!"— husbands and wives tried to enlist neighbors as allies: "Argh, I'm dying. He's killing me! Ain't anybody gonna help me?"

When these skirmishes arose, my mother would press her iron firmly along the delicate curve of a *kisaeng* blouse and sigh in a low voice, "What trash! When are we going to escape from this horrible place?" Did she really forget at those moments that we got by only thanks to those who had lower status than we did?

Mother was a woman of many contradictions. Although she was very polite to our neighbors and their families—the sieve seller, the chimneysweep, the plasterer, the tinker— the underlying message she conveyed was that she didn't want to have much to do with them. Mother treated the water carrier differently, however, even though his social position was no higher.

I never saw a water carrier during daylight hours. They seemed to work through the night and sleep during the day, a schedule I assume they kept because they wanted to be efficient and avoid long lines at the taps.

Hiring a water carrier meant not only paying for his service, but becoming part of a rotation that served him dinner. Since each carrier had several customers, every family's turn came about once a month. Mother treated the water carrier as a highly honored guest when she cooked for him. She certainly never referred to him as trash even beforehand, but her incredible deference when he came for his meal struck me as out of line. Clearly, from the way our landlords treated him, there was no rule that said water carriers had to be fed well. They would simply scoop up a mound of rice that had been cut with other grains, and set it out for him along with a pot of bean paste stew and some chunks of pickled radish. They didn't bother serving him on the veranda or in a sitting room, but just spread a thatched mat in the yard or on the kitchen floor.

Mother, though, made a special trip to the market, and then boiled and seasoned all sorts of vegetables. She even saw to it that there was meat. The savory aroma of sizzling oil wafted from the pan-fried treats she prepared. She'd make a pot of rice, scoop the gleaming grains into a large bowl, and then, with thorough precision, add another bowl's worth of rice on top of it. I doubted that anyone could match Mother's skill in this. We seemed to be preparing for a feast when we served his monthly meal.

My family in Pakchŏk Hamlet loved to look down on others, but the idea of serving them inferior food was appalling. Several times, I heard Grandfather caution the women sharply that families that treated guests differently depending on who they were never prospered from generation to generation. But in fact what my mother did amounted to reverse discrimination, for she prepared a better tray for the water carrier than for my brother on his birthday.

It wouldn't have mattered so much if she'd served this fine repast in our kitchen area by the gate, but she'd call the carrier inside and offer him a cushion, embarrassing him deeply. Maybe Mother would have accepted the veranda as appropriate too, but ours was too narrow to set a tray down on. The water carrier, aging but sturdy, seemed to fill the room when he entered and took his seat. Even my young eyes found it distasteful—back then, separation of men and women remained strict.

Mother's servings were so generous that the carrier couldn't finish the side dishes, let alone his mountain of rice. When he could eat no more, Mother took the left-overs, set them in a new dish on a wooden tray, covered it all with a piece of patchwork fabric, and sent him on his way. Mother said that was what we were supposed to do with a water carrier's table. She seemed to have deliberately made so much just so he'd have some to take home. The vendor, at a loss over how to express his thanks, told Mother to let him know if she ever needed more water than usual. He meant he'd carry a load for her for free, but it was obvious that Mother would never take him up on it.

I thought my penniless but usually oh-so-arrogant mother was much too nice to the water carrier. She treated him as more than an equal, and the respect she showed him annoyed me. I misconstrued it when she tried to get me to go out and play, for he seemed to pose a challenge to my territory. My presence seemed the best strategy to repulse this grave threat. I sat and glared at him as he ate, not budging from the corner of the room.

But my ridiculous suspicions were soon dispelled. One day, Mother mentioned in passing that the water carrier deserved not merely respect but envy—he was putting his son through college by peddling.

"I can't help but look up to that old man when I think how he's managed to get a college beret on his son's head," she sighed.

To her, it was pathetic that the best she could do was a commercial high school, although she was practically killing herself sewing day and night. I was relieved not to have doubts about the water carrier, but I began to pity Mother and her dreams.

Even today, I sometimes hear the expression "water carrier's table," referring to a table from which every last morsel of food has been cleared. Small things arouse my curiosity. Did the metaphor get started because of how ravenously water carriers ate or because of how they took leftovers home? More than anything else, the question reflects my humble upbringing in Hyŏnjŏ-dong.

4. Friendless Child

THE ADMISSION CEREMONY WAS HELD IN APRIL.
Once more, I donned my silk coat and climbed hand in
hand with Mother up and over the hill to school. The other
children clearly had genteel backgrounds; most wore attractive, trim Western clothes. They looked different from
the kids in my neighborhood.

Parents were requested to accompany their children for
the first week and no more. We didn't enter the classroom
for roughly a month, but merely sang songs and played
games in the grounds as we tagged along after our teacher,
gradually becoming acquainted with the Japanese terms for
the school facilities.

The first Japanese word we learned was *hoanden*. This was
a small gray house that sat in a well-tended flower garden to
the right of the playground. We learned that we were to
show it the utmost respect. The perpendicular bows we were
supposed to make as we passed it were far deeper than the
ones we performed for our teachers. The *hoanden* had no
windows, and its doors were shut tight except on national

holidays, when we attended a ceremony instead of class. A podium would be set up. On it stood a lectern draped with a black velvet cover with golden fringes. We would form a line on both sides of the podium all the way up to the *hoanden*.

The principal appeared, decked out in black suit and white gloves. He soon passed in front, together with an entourage of several dignitaries, toward the *hoanden*. His beaming expression matched the medals that adorned his suit. We were allowed to stand upright as that solemn procession entered, but as soon as they emerged, a shout rang out as fast as lightning: "Most deferential bow!" At this, we were expected to virtually prostrate ourselves and be content with glimpses at the shoe tips of those VIPs.

I raised my head furtively and stole a glance at the principal as he walked. It gave me the same anxious thrill I'd felt when I snuck a peek into our house's spirit shrine back in the village. The principal held a black lacquered box at eye level, and during the ceremony, he unfurled a roll from it, which he read out in a quavering voice.

Stored in the *hoanden* was the emperor's message. It was long and so difficult that I couldn't understand a word even once I had learned Japanese. The principal's speech was even longer. The ceremony itself dragged on with such interminable tedium that some children fainted. Afterward, though, we were rewarded for enduring this incomprehensible ceremony with the forbearance required to survive torture—we received two Japanese rice cakes each.

The next item we learned after *hoanden* was the Japanese word for "toilet." And then, in turn, "teacher," "school," "classroom," "playground," "friend," and how to say our year and class. For a month, we followed our teacher around the playground, learning these terms. From the moment we enrolled, we were forbidden to use a word of Korean.

The teacher repeated the names of everything around us and every action she or we did in Japanese, in order to help us commit them to memory. Every object was reborn. For a child like me with no prior knowledge of Japanese, that period was extremely difficult.

Mother, however, believed that study consisted solely in reading and writing: "You mean they still didn't have you do any writing today?" She would then complain that they weren't teaching us anything—and with tuition at eighty chon a month, no less.

Most kids brought one-won bills and bankbooks and deposited the twenty-chon change in accounts provided by the school. Mother would give me exactly eighty chon. Sometimes, though, after I expressed envy for the kids who made deposits, she upped it to ninety chon. But Mother's resentment of my monthly tuition lasted only through that crucial stage when we were being trained so the teacher could guide us and communicate with us at a basic level without Korean.

In my teacher I thought I'd finally found a model of what Mother meant by a New Woman. She was beautiful and smelled nice. All the children loved her. We would scramble about in a group as we moved around the playground, each of us eager to hold her hand. She was kind too, doing her best to dispense her attention and affection fairly among the children, who followed her like chicks waddling after a mother hen. She'd call the ones farther away to come closer, so everyone could have a turn clinging to her hands and skirt.

For some reason, I always lagged on the periphery and never made it within range of the teacher's carefully distributed affection. From the fringe, it was easy to observe what was going on in the center. I could tell that a fixed group of children would hold the teacher's hand or skirt, no matter how hard she tried to be fair. Most of those kids were attractive, smart, and outgoing. They were true natives of Seoul, different from my friends in the countryside and in Hyŏnjŏ-dong.

I practically drooled with envy at the children who monopolized center stage, but I had no confidence I could become like them. We all have something we couldn't accomplish even if we were reborn. For me, becoming a core member of a group is an impossibility; it simply lies beyond me.

The first thing we learned once we made it to the classroom was a string of Japanese sentences: "Spring has come. Spring has come. Where has it come? It has come to the mountains. It has come to the fields." We also learned a tune to go with the words.

Our textbook had a picture of cherry blossoms in full bloom, and cherry blossoms were already falling from the trees in Sajik Park. But although I climbed a hill every day on the way to school, I thirsted after real mountains and a spring worthy of the name. Not a single blade of mugwort sprouted at the foot of Mount Inwang, whose arid soil resembled pulverized rock. All that grew from it were doggedly clinging acacias. I'd never seen such trees in Pakchŏk Hamlet and found it impossible to warm up to them.

Worse, nothing grew in their shade and tempted me to stray from the well-trodden path into the forest. No unique mountain fragrance, no twittering birds. And no lepers either.

I had to make my way to school alone. Mother's only concern was to send me to an elementary school inside the city gates. She didn't give any thought to how unhappy I'd be without friends my age.

What I missed even more than my friends, though, were the hills of the countryside. I found Seoul's hills odd, with their barren ground exposed between sparse, tired-looking trees, as though we were in the grip of a drought. To me, mountains, like fields, meant a constant supply of treats, and I knew well that the tasty snacks were found in the shade, rather than high up in the trees. Our hills back home had pines, but they were also thick with deciduous trees like chestnut, alder, zelkova, and various oaks. When autumn came around, piles of fallen leaves were heaped roof-high in every yard for use as winter fuel.

Even so, not all the leaves could be scraped off the hill. They decomposed over the years into soft, moist soil that made a fertile bed for grasses, herbs, mushrooms, and wild flowers of all sorts, although, of course, not all these grasses were useful to us.

Along the path from our outhouse to the backyard was a sea of what we called "dayflowers." As we trampled their dark blue petals, the clear dewdrops on them bathed our feet. Joy would course into our bodies from the earth, invigorating us like sap, filling us with an impulsive delight. We'd take the leaves of the dayflower and make flutes from them that sang a faint, quavering tune.

At the foot of the hill grew a thicket so lush that when kids passed through it, nothing could be seen of them but bobbing heads. It wasn't uncommon to find snake skins that had been sloughed off in the thicket's midst. Some of these skins weren't much to look at, but others had delicate patterns set against a white background so pure that I imagined them as the sashes of a wizard who'd descended from the mountains and ungirded himself to go to the bathroom. The hill that lay behind our house was hardly big or beautiful enough to make a worthy precinct for a mountain wizard. Even so, my eyes would dart about unconsciously, seeking traces of his visit.

Any time we spotted a snake skin, we were expected to take it home. The adults welcomed them even more than mountain herbs and mushrooms, for there was a superstition in our village that if you stored a skin inside a wardrobe, it would bring you good luck. As a rule, though, these luxuriant thickets hid nasty, sharp blades of grass. At times, our reward for retrieving a snake skin would be lacerated calves. Overall, though, the hill behind our village was like a baby—gentle and easy to approach, but bursting with a wonderful vitality.

The bare, enervated ridge in Seoul made me think instead of a dying old man. To relieve my loneliness on my daily climb, I dwelled in memories and found excuses to look down on my peers in Seoul. They could never know the translucent blue of the dayflower's petals or the beautiful music that lurked within its leaves. Or how if you carefully scratched away the thick, gleaming flesh, you'd discover veins that were thinner and more delicate than summer silk. Or the sound the veins gave off when you vibrated them against your lips. I could barely get a noise to come out, but some kids could make beautiful, plaintive melodies.

After the cherry blossoms fell in Sajik Park, acacia flowers came into bloom. They permeated the whole of Mount Inwang with a nauseating milky smell. Packs of boys would travel from ridge to ridge, hunting for branches laden with blossoms, and then harshly snap them off so they could eat the petals.

Watchmen patrolled the forest. If they spotted boys snapping large branches, they'd rush over and wring their wrists until they cried out in pain. Most of these kids came from our poor district of Hyŏnjŏ-dong. At their age, three meals a day wasn't enough to fully satisfy their hunger, but they seemed to break the branches more for the thrill of it—getting caught, fleeing, being yelled at by the watchmen. After the boys swept away, acacia branches with withered flowers would be strewn about the ground like rags.

That year was the first time I saw acacias and their blossoms. I learned that children in Seoul could also draw snacks from their surroundings. The more experienced ones would take a bunch of acacias and pluck one flower after another, savoring them like grapes. Once I surreptitiously tried a bunch, afraid I might get caught, but their milky, tepid, sweet taste made me nauseated. Only something fresh, I thought, could settle my stomach.

Suddenly *shinga* came to mind. In the countryside, they were as common as dayflowers, growing everywhere, at the foot of hills and along roadsides. They had jointed stalks and were at their plumpest and most succulent about the time wild roses came into bloom. We'd snap the reddish stalk, peel the skin, and eat the tangy inner layer. I thought their puckering tartness would be the perfect antidote for acacias.

I combed the hill frantically. I was like an animal looking for grasses to rub against a wound. But I couldn't find a single stalk. Who ate up all the *shinga*? The Seoul ridge had run together in my mind with the hill behind our village. I retched until I was dizzy.

* * * * * * * * * * *

In early summer, the teacher was supposed to visit her students' homes. Mother always demanded complete honesty from Brother and me, and from herself as well. They lavished a lot of attention on teaching us to be honest at school too. Our ethics textbook consistently emphasized that honesty came next to loyalty to the emperor as a virtue, and children who lied were subjected to severe humiliation from the teacher. We were repeatedly taught that if we found lost articles or money at school, we should take them to a teacher, and if we found them in the street, to policemen.

Mother scoffed: "If something's lying on the ground, ignore it. Why pick it up? Whoever dropped it is bound to come back, so let him find it. Only showoffs take things to police or teachers."

Mother's logic was plausible, but open to an objection. What if the item was taken before the owner returned, I countered. Her response was unequivocal: it was wrong to make off with somebody else's possessions, but it wasn't our place to worry about it. Did Mother envision an ideal society where a lost pouch of gold could be found exactly where it had been left? Or was doing a good deed for her limited to when she could prove to herself how upright she was?

The real issue, though, was that Mother's fastidiousness about honesty drove her to be fastidious in her lies. She'd gotten me into the school she chose by lying about our official residence, and she was determined to stick to her fraud even through the teacher's visit. I assume that her insistence stemmed from rural literal-mindedness and fear that I might be expelled if the truth came out. But I was sick and tired of going along with Mother's hypocrisy and wanted us to be done with it all. Mother knew nothing about my life at school and seemed to think we could just cobble an act together for the impending visit. The date the teacher would go to Sajik-dong had already been set, so Mother asked the understanding of our relatives in allowing her to play resident for a day.

That day, the kids from Sajik-dong remained after school and went home with the teacher. The visits were organized in order of distance from the school, but since I didn't say where I lived until the last moment, I was put last. No one paid any attention to me, a nobody in the classroom. Most pupils lived close to one another or crossed paths on the way to school, so they largely knew who lived where. When a girl said she'd never seen me in the neighborhood, the others chimed in and cast suspicious glances my way. Given my hick clothes, which differed so obviously from theirs, the remark was enough for them to consider me an utter heathen. I quickly smoothed over the crisis, saying we'd just moved from the countryside, but my relative's next-door neighbor, a girl who looked both smart and sweet, stayed with me to the end. She suggested that we start going to school together the following day. I added another lie on top of the one I'd already concocted: "I can't. We're moving again in just a couple of days."

Mother remained in the dark about all this. Sitting high on the veranda, she welcomed my teacher. The housemaid brought out fruit punch on a brass tray that had been polished until it gleamed. After getting through the day without mishap, Mother let out a sigh of relief. Unfortunately, the girl who lived next door to my relatives plagued me for a long time to come.

From then on, I was unable to hold my head high in front of her and wound up doing everything she told me to do. Milder indignities included tying a cord to a pole and making me hold one end of it for her so she could play rope-skipping games by herself without letting me have a turn. Worse, she'd doff her shoe at random moments, throw it, and order me to bring it back. I had no choice but to go and fetch it. A rumor began to circulate among the kids that I was her servant. I'm still not sure whether she lorded it over me because she thought my lie about our address was a fatal error or because my guilty conscience made me a cinch to push around. Which came first here, the chicken or the egg?

Hierarchies among children are hard to change once they're established. School became hell for me. At home I was bored and restless, unable to sit still. The kids in my neighborhood naturally mixed with their own school friends and looked askance at me, the arrogant hick who climbed over the hill to go to school inside the city gates.

The path through our neighborhood traveled up toward a steep hill. If you kept following in that direction, instead of branching off along the ridge toward Maedong Elementary School, you'd reach an outcrop called Fairy Rock. By this point, all the houses had petered out. A shaman shrine lay on the right as you continued onward up a valley that had no stream, and across from the shrine soared a monolith, rising at a short distance from the cliff behind it. Everyone who gazed on it believed that it was sacred. It was called Brother's Rock and looked like two people standing shoulder to shoulder.

An endless procession of people prayed before this massive stone. Prior to major ceremonies inside the shrine, shamans would go there to make preparatory offerings, complete with loud ritual cries and offerings of food tossed to the rock. Pieces of rice cake always lay strewn about the ground.

Whenever the exquisite traditional music from the shaman rites reached my ears from up the valley, I'd dash to the shrine to join in, swaying my behind in time to the rhythm. I don't remember exactly when I got into the habit of attending these rituals, but it became a hobby of sorts, a respite from my boredom.

Shamans were hardly a novelty for me, since they'd been part of my life in the countryside. Not far from Pakchŏk Hamlet lay Mount Tŏngmul, a celebrated shaman site. It had a shrine to the great fourteenth-century general Ch'oe Yŏng. Every three years, a major ritual was performed there, and shamans flocked to it from all over the country. The mountain's many shaman dwellings also meant that wealthy Kaesŏng residents were constantly hosting all types of ceremonies, large and small. The rich would fawn over General Ch'oe Yŏng at his shrine in grand rituals, praying for his help in making money, even though during his lifetime he had taught that gold should be considered the same as any old stone. Rumors of a big ceremony had a magical ability to set people buzzing, whether it had anything to do with them or not.

The shamans also did a brisk trade catering to the many families whose menfolk were traveling merchants and thus had a regular need for fortune-telling. It was taken for granted, even in the countryside, that people would have their fortunes told within a fortnight of New Year's. Although there were no fixed district divisions, typically a single shaman cared for several particular villages. There was no shaman living in Pakchŏk Hamlet, so we had to go elsewhere.

If you came across a throng of white-clad women with sacks on their heads, you knew that an expedition to the shaman was in the offing. The villagers would first pour two or three bushels of rice into a sack as payment and then travel en masse to hear their fortunes for the coming year. In our family, Grandmother took responsibility for learning what lay in store for us, and I tagged along.

Women filled the shaman's two rooms. There wasn't a lot of variation in her predictions, though, for no matter how rich an imagination she might have, the simplicity of her clients' lives imposed limits on what she could come up with. Grandmother would inquire about everyone in our family, adding my name as a seeming afterthought. The shaman then gave generic advice applicable to any child: "Don't go near the water in midsummer." "Be careful with fire in winter."

The grownups didn't take their fortunes very seriously unless dramatic events were occurring in their lives. Their pleasure came from chatting with those whom they hadn't seen for a while. The shaman's was a place to relieve stress and exchange information—sometimes, for example, they talked about prospective marriages. No woman ever left just because she'd already received her fortune.

It goes without saying that rice cake soup was served after the New Year fortune-telling was over. The shaman household didn't do any farming. Since the rice she received from her guests made up the bulk of her family's provisions for the year, this gesture of gratitude was understandable. In other words, the shaman's home was a site of exchange as well. The tiny balls of rice cake were especially delicious. I followed my grandmother just to be able to eat them.

Mother didn't discourage me from tagging along with Grandmother, but she was very cynical about shamans and their predictions and didn't seem to pay any attention to what Grandmother relayed about our fortune for the year. Her resentment had deep roots. Not a moment should have been lost in treating my father, but Grandmother put her trust in the shaman and tried to cure him with an exorcism. The common proverb "A novice shaman is a killer" means that pretending to know what you're doing can lead to disaster. You could feel a real barb when Mother used the saying.

But I was not my mother. I felt not just an affinity with shamans but awe toward them. I went to Mount Tŏngmul just once, again in Grandmother's tow. It must have been the grand festival held only every few years, because we traveled along with a horde of fellow villagers. The excitement and amusement of a major ritual usually lasted for several days, but what left an indelible impression on me was the extraordinary, baffling General's Rite, a ceremony held to appease the wronged spirit of Ch'oe Yŏng, whose life had been cut short.

A rough mat was spread and a pail brimming with water placed on it. Then a wooden lid was placed over the pail, followed by a sack of rice, and two gleaming, whetted straw cutters were set side by side. I don't remember what time of day it was, but in my mind's eye, at least, the blades glint grotesquely in dazzling torchlight.

Next, a shaman, attired in a general's uniform complete with bamboo hat, took off her padded cotton socks, revealing toes contorted from binding. The soles of her feet were dainty and white, and glided over the parallel blades of the straw cutters nimbly, like butterflies. The music beat faster. Faster and faster, faster and faster it went until it climaxed in a sudden silence. The shaman vanished into thin air, leaving only two white butterflies behind. What I witnessed was not a shaman's rite, but the sole mystical experience of my life. Just that once, I glimpsed a divine realm that can't be explained rationally.

The rituals on Mount Inwang were child's play in comparison. Some shamans may have brandished swords, but none of them walked on blades. Still, I always adored watching a rite. I especially loved the spectacle of the shaman leaping up and down, wearing those enormous, pointy-toed socks and with the tails of her long blue coat flapping. I would gaze on it all, bursting with tension.

The shaman would hold out a colorful rolled flag to her audience, and when someone took it, she'd relay a dead ancestor's words. I didn't know exactly what she was saying, but I always suspected that she was making up stories. I felt pity for grownups who rejoiced or fell into despair over her off-the-cuff remarks. In this, I took after Mother without even realizing it.

After a large rite, rice cakes and rainbow-hued candies were distributed to the spectators, adults and children alike. Actually, if I hadn't expected this payoff, I might not have felt such a thrill in watching a ceremony. At that age, I wanted to eat all the time. I never had to skip a meal because we didn't have enough food, but I can't even begin to describe the tedium of those long summer afternoons with nothing to snack on.

These little windfalls, however, were precisely what led to a ban on my going to watch the rituals. My summer uniform consisted of a short-sleeved white blouse and a blue skirt with a bodice. One day, streaks on my skirt from the brightly colored candies gave away what I'd been up to.

Mother berated me, just as she had when I'd gone sliding in front of the prison. Out she trotted her usual lament: "When will we ever escape this damn neighborhood?" I bet she wanted to up and move, head held high, just as tradition claims that Mencius's mother did for her son's education. Unfortunately, we weren't living in Mencius's day. Mother had no money, and I was cleverer than sage Mencius. I pleaded with her, saying that I'd never do it again. And then I quickly figured out another way to amuse myself.

With the weather getting warmer as summer approached, Mother's stitching orders changed to thin silk and cotton blouses. A sewing machine became essential. But because we didn't have the money to buy one, Mother chose to incur the debt of our relatives in Sajik-dong once more. After seeing Brother and me off to school, she'd go there to sew all day long, relying on their generosity for lunch as well, and then hurry home to prepare dinner. This pattern continued for a long while.

My first-grade lessons finished, alas, all too early. Before the clock struck twelve, school was over. Loneliness and bitter frustration would seize me when I returned home to find nothing but a lunch bowl the size of a fist waiting for me in the corner of our gloomy rented room. My bowl had been brought from the countryside, and its subtle gleam of deep bronze clashed with the poverty of our abode.

Mother was a real pro at sowing conflict. She had brainwashed me into believing that I came from a family with a real pedigree, and so the children of our landlord and the other neighbors weren't to my taste. I'm sure they found me just as unappealing because I went to school elsewhere and turned up my nose at theirs. Days were long, and I had no place, inside the house or out, where I felt at home.

I can't vouch for what other kids would have done in my situation, but to entertain myself I rummaged through Mother's and Brother's belongings. Stashed in that gaudy chest between layers of Mother's socks, I discovered a wallet, or, more accurately, a coin purse. Grandfather's pouch had been made of oiled paper, but Mother's purse had been fashioned out of fabric.

When Mother sent me to fetch bean sprouts or scallions, she'd take out a one-chon coin or maybe a five. In other words, it wasn't sheer boredom that made me search through her things. I had a goal in mind. Usually she let her purse lie anywhere, but when she was going to be away all day she stuffed it in the chest. After I returned from my errands, change in hand, she'd tell me just to put it in the purse without checking too carefully to see if I'd brought back the right amount. When she had to pay a large bill, like our monthly tuition fees or our rent, she counted every note, down to the smallest crumpled denomination, and sighed, "It's like a thief has been at my money." I knew she wasn't really suspicious. The expression simply reflected her frustration at being chronically short of money, despite scrimping and saving.

I took out a copper one-chon coin. Knowing how lax Mother was about small change, I didn't worry about being caught or think I was doing anything terribly wrong. Farther up from where we lived was a family that ran a small shop. Unlike the grocery store at the foot of the hill, where I often went to run errands for Mother, they targeted children's snot-streaked money and specialized in cheap snacks that cost up to five chon. I headed over to them right away, having always longed to buy something there.

A single chon bought me five toffees. Mind you, I hadn't had to forgo satisfying my sweet tooth in the countryside. We'd make taffy in the winter that would last for several months. On special occasions, we'd also take down the molasses and honey that was stored in the loft, so I actually had more rotting, blackened teeth than the kids in Seoul. Still, the cookies and candies Grandfather brought back from Songdo were always a real delicacy. They had a more refined sweetness than our homemade taffy and didn't leave your stomach feeling heavy and bloated. I was always left wanting more.

My first taste of something sweet in months sent me into rapture. The five candies turned a boring afternoon when I wouldn't know what to do with myself into luscious, thrilling hours. Mother didn't realize that one chon was going missing daily. Once every several days, I took a five-chon coin, the kind with a hole in the middle. Five chon opened the door to a much wider range of taste sensations.

Around this time, I think, we had a guest one day when Mother was at home. When the heat set in, ice-pop vendors would pass through even our steep neighborhood. The visitor apologized for not bringing anything, but when she heard the shouts of an ice-pop vendor, she handed me a five-chon coin and told me to go and get some.

"A whole five chon's worth?" Mother asked.

"We can both have one, too," the visitor said, wiping away her sweat.

Thinking I'd have a hard time handling five ice pops, Mother gave me a pot to carry them in. But by the time I rushed out, pot in hand, the vendor was nowhere to be seen. I thought I could still make out his cry, but I wasn't sure from where.

I wasn't about to let this golden opportunity slip, though. Clutching the pot, I bolted down to the streetcar terminus, where I knew there was a good-size ice-pop stand. I asked for five chon's worth, and they even gave me an extra. But the return home was not easy. I huffed and puffed my way up those damn steps under a relentless sun. When I finally arrived, panting, about all that remained in the pot were ice-pop sticks and some reddish-brown water. The visitor tut-tutted in disbelief.

"Why didn't you eat them yourself instead of letting them melt?"

Mother rebutted her guest's dismay in no uncertain terms: "My daughter is honest to a fault."

Nonetheless, this daughter in whom Mother put such adamantine trust was siphoning off one coin after another from her purse—and without the slightest pang of guilt. But as a proverb says, "The longer the tail, the easier to catch."

At the time, corner stores kept their candies and biscuits lined up in long rows of wooden containers with glass lids. One day, I tried to open a container in the back row, but as my hand pressed against a lid in front, I broke it.

The owner was a brusque man who holed up in a dark room attached to his shop and just collected payment without helping to take the candy out. He showed no emotion despite my shock and tears, but simply told me to take my candies and go home. I thought he might take the money and not let me have the candies, so I assumed he'd forgiven me. I fled.

That evening, while Mother was cooking by the gate and Brother was studying in our room, I heard a sudden ruckus outside and a sharp retort from Mother. My heart pounded with foreboding. As I dreaded, Mother called me outside. There I saw the owner of the store, his wife and children in tow, waving an accusing finger at Mother. Their expressions showed that they were fully prepared to resort to their fists. The boy, who was a little bigger than me, was holding the container lid. All that remained of it was the frame.

Mother asked quietly whether it was true that I'd broken the lid. I nodded in confession, more frightened and humiliated about being caught stealing than breaking the glass. My shame made me feel faint. I wanted to die on the spot, but Mother readily agreed to pay for the glass. The family left behind a hollow frame and demanded that it be refitted before another day passed.

And that could have been that for the incident—an unusually civil denouement for our dirt-poor neighborhood, where everyone was ready to plunge into a do-or-die showdown over half a chon. As they turned to go home a bit abashed, however, Mother spoke loudly from behind, "Now I've seen everything. Of course I'd pay for the glass if my own child broke it. What kind of a man is he, bringing along his family and making a scene like that? He's raising his kids really well, really well."

Having the husband and wife gang up on my mother for something so insignificant must have really wounded her pride. But they weren't the sort to pretend not to have heard a taunt. They spun round, as if waiting for just such an opportunity, and the quarrel blew up out of control. The man grabbed Mother by the throat. Instead of fending him off, though, she called my brother, probably wanting to show off that she too had a son. I'm sure that Brother, prudent and retiring as he was, had been hoping that everything would be settled without his having to intervene.

He ran out after Mother's plea for help, intending to tear the man away from her, but in the confusion of the moment wound up knocking him over. The man's wife helped him up and yelled that a young lout had hit an adult. Spectators gathered. Encouraged, the woman straight away got a dig back in at Mother. "You're raising your kids really well, *really* well!" she shouted. This put an immediate end to Mother's retorts. Brother bowed his head, and the battle concluded with great embarrassment for my family. The three of us withdrew without a peep.

We retreated to our room and waited, with heavy hearts, for the woman's raving to end. In the meantime, I set about concocting my alibi, since Mother was sure to ask where my pocket money had come from. I made up my mind to lie that I'd found it on the street and picked it up. Better to die, I thought, than admit my theft.

But Mother didn't ask where the money had come from. It had shocked her for Brother to be insulted as an ill-bred lout. She remained despondent for a long time. She apologized to him, and he lowered his head, repeatedly saying how sorry he was. It was clear what their mutual apologies were about, even though neither said so explicitly.

The insult left Mother so heartbroken that she apparently forgot to investigate why it had all happened in the first place, and I avoided the feared interrogation. Nor did she bring it up the next day when she went down to the shops to have the glass refitted, and, in fact, never mentioned it afterward.

Mother may have seemed meticulous, but she could actually be very lax in some ways. Although everyone, including herself, acknowledged her skill in managing money, she never realized that coins had been missing from her own meager purse. I still feel gratitude and affection toward her for these lapses.

If she'd been suspicious and pressured me, she'd have pried the truth out. Even now, it makes me reel to think of the shame I might have wound up feeling.

After that incident, I never stole Mother's money again. Ditto other people's possessions. As she wished, I never picked up money on the street. Actually, I've never spotted a sum of cash or anything else enticing enough to tempt me to be greedy, but whenever I pass money lying on the ground, without the slightest sense of conflict I find myself smiling, remembering Mother. Of course, I don't for a moment think I'm doing a good deed. It's just a habit I picked up and only I'm aware of. I cling to it with equal amounts of fondness and annoyance, the way you might hold on to a useless old item for no other reason than it has your parent's thumb stains all over it.

It's hard to say what would have happened if Mother had discovered my penchant for theft. I was very sensitive to being humiliated. If I couldn't preserve my pride, I might have been so hurt that I'd have begun acting up and become unmanageable. Personally, I don't believe that people are born good or evil, but that we keep reaching crossroads between the two throughout our lives.

A dreary, brutal atmosphere hung over Mount Inwang through the summer. Only toward the end of the monsoon did water trickle down into the valley.

The path that led up to the shaman shrine was lined on both sides with a stone wall. Off on one side, a sparse thicket remained. Toward dusk, the cries of dogs being clubbed to death drifted down from this area. Boys would rush in swarms toward the forest at these heart-rending yelps, their eyes glinting with excitement. A straw-plaited cord dangled from a tree where the hounds were hung and bludgeoned. The smell of roasted dog meat lingering about the place made the bare ugliness of the forest frightening and revolting.

As the summer heat grew more intense, even my reserved brother found it hard to remain cooped up in the room. As soon as we finished dinner, he'd lead me by the hand to Fairy Rock for some fresh air. They were my happiest moments in those days. I would swell with pride because, of all the people who came out to enjoy the breeze, Brother was the most handsome.

To show my affection, I roamed far and wide to gather nettle flowers. I'd then have him hold one side of their leaves and plait them into a curved dipper for him. As I plucked the flowers, I'd look for snacks out of habit, but only tough, inedible grasses grew on the barren earth around Fairy Rock. Sometimes my hands would fall to my side, and I would wonder idly: Who ate all the *shinga* that were so plentiful back in the countryside? Brother recognized my homesickness. He'd count off on his fingers to show me how many days were left until summer vacation.

The countdown hit five days. Mother took me to the market that went on in the evenings between Yŏngch'ŏn and the crossroads at Sŏdaemun. Daily sundries were available—kitchen knives, chamber pots, brooms, and the like—but most stalls specialized in fabric. Cloth curtains were draped along these stalls beneath makeshift awnings. The vendors kept up an energetic patter as they hawked their wares. I was captivated by their rhythmic cadences and the splendor of the gauzy fabric under the electric lights. Unsurprisingly, the fabric stalls were surrounded by the largest, noisiest crowds.

Mother intended to make me a Western-style dress. As soon as she draped a piece of fabric over me, the merchants fussed about how perfectly it suited me, and my pulse raced. Mother, however, was no pushover. She bargained at several stalls, giving up when she couldn't get the price she was looking for. Closing a deal was even harder because she was determined to buy just enough material for a short dress, and the traders sold cloth not by the bolt, but by the length of a blouse and skirt. Finally, she settled on a scrap of white fabric with navy blue polka dots.

After taking my rough measurements with a ruler, Mother cut the fabric sloppily, tossed it over me, and made some large preliminary stitches to sew it up. She then finished it the following day on our relative's sewing machine. It made for a decent dress. Mother's stitch work was renowned; in addition to clothing for *kisaeng*, she had once sewn every item for a rich family's wedding, but she had no confidence in her ability to make a Western dress. She had me model it for her several times, anxiously checking front and back. Brother offered some stingy praise. Not too awkward, he said. Mother was grateful for even that.

Going home seemed real at last. I had butterflies of excitement in my stomach and couldn't sleep, a feeling I hadn't experienced even on my first school outing, when we went to the grounds outside the Government-General building, the imposing structure that served as headquarters for the colonial administration. It inspired awe in a country girl like me. Instead of a wall, it was surrounded by high iron bars that let you see what went on within. Policemen armed with swords stood guard at each gate. When we arrived in the vast yard behind it, our teacher repeated a list of things we were forbidden to do and dismissed us. I ate lunch with Mother, who had come with me. The only real pleasure I got from the outing was amazement at seeing with my own eyes that this huge building was where she wanted Brother to work someday.

On the last day of the semester, my teacher asked the pupils who'd be going to the countryside to raise their hands. We were required to come to school twice during vacation, she said, but those who gave prior notice that they'd be going home to the countryside wouldn't be marked absent. Only then did I learn that just two or three children per class spent their vacation in the countryside. I

felt genuine pity for the native Seoul kids who'd be spending their whole summer in the city.

All day long, you're going to be stuck in alleyways, playing marbles or skipping rope. The best treat you'll have are
the snacks you get by begging one chon at a time off the
grownups. Meanwhile, I'll be jumping around in the country like a puppy. Everything there is alive and breathing and
moving around in the breeze. Tomorrow, I'm going to get
to climb up hills and walk through fields and splash in
streams. I'm going to get to breathe in air that's got the
smell of grass and wildflowers and soil.

Just imagining this brought me an elation reminiscent
of stepping at dawn in early summer onto the dewy, green
path and its carpet of dayflowers. I wasn't just homesick. I
had a ravenous hunger, and it was about to be satisfied. For
the first time, I felt a sense of superiority over my peers in
Seoul. Having a reason to pity them put me in a terrific
mood.

My joy was a little premature, though. On the last day of
school, I received my report card. It was just my first term
of first grade, but we were still marked. We were evaluated
on a scale from six to ten, and my average was eight. My
score seemed to have been rounded up, for other than two
nines and a six in singing (the lowest possible mark), the
rest of my marks were sevens. Mother never nagged me to
study or looked over my homework carefully. She might
have been aggressive enough in pursuing my education to
violate zoning rules, but that was more or less as far as her
concern went. Her indifference came, I think, from an arrogant belief that her children would excel without any special attention on her part. Brother had always been first in
his class, although she'd simply left him to his studies. He
had even skipped a grade at the country elementary school.

She took great pride in all this. And so, when she saw my report card, she almost fainted. Her grief-stricken remarks had their own unique flavor: "Dear Lord, what a disgrace! Flying geese in my own child's report card! I never dreamed I'd see the day."

Mother referred to sevens as geese for a reason. The son of the housemaid at our relatives' in Sajik-dong was in elementary school, and the maid never tired of boasting what a good student he was. But Mother once caught a glimpse of his report card and saw that he'd received a seven in every subject. The Chinese character for seven, 七, when written in a cursive series, certainly can seem like geese in flight. Mother had a knack for lightening serious moments with jokes, but her reference to geese in that boy's report card doesn't strike me as an example of her sense of humor. Instead, I think it reflects her smugness in looking down on other people's children, while considering us paragons. Mother's disappointment made her regret her previous mean-spirited remark.

Only when Mother intimated that now we wouldn't go to the countryside because she was too ashamed to face my grandparents did I burst into tears and kick and stomp. I didn't think I'd done anything wrong, and I had no confidence that I could do better. Fortunately, Brother found a fitting way to comfort Mother and her bruised pride. He pointed out that I had nines in Japanese and math, so it didn't matter if the other grades weren't too high. His interpretation thrilled Mother. She immediately took it a step further, adding that only children without academic talent did well in singing, gym, and drawing.

Late that evening, my aunt and uncle came to see us, since Brother and I had just received our report cards and we'd be leaving for home the following day. Mother was no longer dejected at all; she showed them my report card, embellishing Brother's reading of the situation. She made it sound as though she'd never come across a scholastically minded child who had received good marks in gym or singing. As the saying goes, "Whatever goes wrong is your ancestors' fault." And so, in keeping with this maxim, I still blame Mother for the fact that I am tone deaf.

My aunt and uncle agreed wholeheartedly with Mother's strained interpretation. They were our only close relatives in Seoul, and the customs of the day dictated that when a man passed away, his brothers become surrogate fathers to their orphaned nieces and nephews. We were constantly visiting and consulting each other. Since Auntie and Uncle had no children of their own, the bonds of love and affection between us all went beyond mere obligation.

Uncle lived in Pongnae-dong, on the other side of Yŏmch'ŏn Bridge. He made deliveries for a Japanese fish wholesaler, while Auntie worked as a bookkeeper at a trading company. Uncle always had the whiff of fish about him. He looked like a true laborer. Auntie, however, appeared more sophisticated by the day. I really admired her. She wore a fashionable hairdo, with the front and sides swept upward Japanese-style, and put on her makeup tastefully as well.

Once I went with Mother on a visit to Auntie at her workplace, a large warehouse stacked high with crates of goods. Several teenage boys were bustling about. They were clad in jackets that resembled Japanese *haori* robes and had the store name emblazoned on the back. My aunt wore a blue clerk's smock over her blouse and skirt, and the way she directed the boys, adding the title "mister" to their names as she addressed them, made her seem very professional.

I learned later that Auntie had started out as a live-in maid in a Japanese home. Meanwhile, Uncle had had to struggle terribly, sleeping in an attic above the ice storage of the fish merchant. Auntie spoke decent Japanese and was a quick study in everything she did. Within a few months, she had earned her employer's trust, and he gave her a job at the general trading outfit he managed. At that point, she was finally able to set up house with Uncle again.

My aunt and uncle would often pick days they weren't working to invite us over for a feast. The meat and fish they treated us to suggested that they made good money, but their living conditions were even worse than ours. A row of a dozen or so perpetually sunless rented rooms stood around a yard that seemed more like an alleyway. Sheets of galvanized iron blocked the sky, and the ground was uneven and soggy. Uncle's home lay at the end of this cul-de-sac. To reach it, you had to wend your way painstakingly (and often unsuccessfully) among puddles of filthy dishwater. The neighborhood might not have had Hyŏnjŏ-dong's water problems, but it was less sanitary.

"Inside the gates." "Inside the gates." For Mother, the neighborhoods within the four great gates of Seoul were the only desirable places to live. She hoped to move there, but there were slums like the one Uncle lived in "inside the gates" as well.

＊ ＊ ＊ ＊ ＊ ＊ ＊ ＊ ＊ ＊ ＊

Finally, we arrived at Kaesŏng Station. Mother disembarked proudly, showing off a son in a fresh summer uniform and a daughter in a Western dress. My grandmother, elder uncle, and aunt were all there, waiting for us. Grandmother embraced me and then turned around to offer me a piggyback ride. I refused.

The mountains and rivers in my hometown were green and fresh. As I climbed the hills, plucked wildflowers, and rinsed away my sweat in the streams, I again felt pity for the children stuck in Seoul. *Shinga* stalks were as abundant as ever, but by this time of year they had grown too tough to snack on.

Nevertheless, fresh produce had come into full season in the vegetable patch. Nothing can match the sweetness of that freshly picked, steamed corn. And to come upon a slender, sensuous squash, lying under lush, dew-laden leaves early in the morning, before the heat spread—ah, sheer rapture. The expression likening an ugly woman to a squash? Obviously an invention of ignorant urbanites. The phrase is unfair even if it refers to old squash: Who'd be afraid of aging if we ripened as gracefully as squash?

Grownups were at their busiest, which made the season even more delightful for kids. Little boys went around shirtless, their bellies protruding like a frog's. Some even had their little peppers exposed. If melon juice dripped onto their tummies and they were annoyed by swarming flies, all they had to do was jump into one of the many rivulets.

The tiny brook on the way to our outhouse wasn't deep enough to jump into, but its banks sported tiger lilies in full bloom. Since the blossoms from the trees in our backyard—apricots, cherries, wild pears—had already fallen, the flowering tiger lilies with their orange petals speckled with purple struck me as all the more gorgeous.

Seeing all this delighted me, but the one who delighted in seeing me was Grandfather, whose condition had declined dramatically over the previous six months. His paralyzed left cheek had become horribly sunken and twitched with occasional spasms. Now he even lacked energy for the anger he'd shown when he tossed me the fifty-chon coin. He looked so pitiful that I thought I was going to cry. As I kneeled next to Brother to offer him a bow, I pledged to myself that during vacation I'd do all I could to run the errands he wanted.

That summer, a baby girl was born into our family, providing me with a cousin for the first time. Given that Auntie was taking care of the household chores, I must have seen her swollen belly; presumably, too, my delighted grandparents would have been fervently praying for a smooth birth, since this was her first child and she was already in her thirties. For some reason, though, in my memory the baby just arrived out of the blue.

One night my eyes fluttered open, either because I'd sensed there was no one next to me or because I'd heard low murmurs. I found myself alone. I'd fallen asleep in the main room, but now I was in the room across from it. I went out to the veranda to be by Grandmother's side, but I noticed that the main room was lit up and tugged open the door. Mother waved her hand behind her, motioning for me to shut it again. Grandmother was kneading something in a basin. "Grandma, are you killing a chicken?" I asked groggily. Mother shooed me out, trying to stifle a smile. I returned to my bedding and fell back asleep.

Although we reserved beef and pork for New Year's and the Harvest Moon Festival, we served chicken for guests and on birthdays, so I'd seen them slaughtered often enough. It still baffles me that I could have thought that Grandmother was killing a chicken. Surely my baby cousin cried as she was bathed? My absurd question gave the grownups something to chuckle about for a long time to come.

With the baby's arrival, our house became livelier than it had been for ages. This tiny being brought bright smiles to a home that had been darkened by the shadows of death and disease. Grandfather was overjoyed. He chose the baby's

name, combining the character for "bright," *myŏng*, with *sŏ*,
the syllable that all the children in my generation of the
family shared. With a trembling hand, he wrote out in cal-
ligraphic Chinese "Avoid Impurity After Birth" and had it
pasted on our front gate. Where I grew up, scrolls, instead
of the more usual ritual pieces of rope, were hung to announce a birth and bar outsiders.

Some relatives and neighbors expressed regret that it had
not been a son, but Grandfather would have none of it. We
should be grateful for a smooth birth, he rebuked them;
asking for more was to invite bad luck.

I started hovering over the baby and rarely went out to
play. I no longer felt the way I used to with my friends. Part
of it was that the Seoul look Mother had foisted on me
made things awkward with my former playmates, but the
real problem was in my heart. After half a year in the capital, I felt superior to the other children in the village and
consciously tried to convey that. I'm sure I must have
seemed terribly obnoxious to them.

Our homecoming during winter vacation that year
was even more of a spectacle. We didn't have special winter
uniforms at school; instead, we were encouraged to wear
long navy blue frocks. I went home wearing mine over a
black blouse and skirt and had skates draped over one
shoulder. I'm not exactly sure when Brother started skating, but I do remember him bringing a pair home as an
award from school and watching people gliding on the
pond at Ch'anggyŏng Palace.

Although skating was the most familiar of the sports that
people in Seoul enjoyed, I never had an urge to try it myself. I'd never even worn skates before. Wherever it was that
we acquired them, I do recall that when Mother had me try
them on, she pronounced them a perfect fit, saying that I'd

be able to skate on the frozen paddies. But I couldn't even stand upright with them on in our room. Nevertheless, Mother assured me that I'd be able to glide right along in them when I was on the ice. Since I'd seen Brother skating gracefully along with several others, I accepted that it would come naturally as long as you had the right footwear.

What most appealed to me was the idea of going home with skates slung proudly over my shoulder, when the other kids had never laid eyes on such a thing. Mother and daughter understood each other perfectly in this without having to exchange so much as a word. Although we were struggling to get by in a hovel beyond the gates of Seoul, we were determined to impress those back home. The way we strove to realize our dreams of coming home in style, with a Western dress and ice skates, strikes me now as something out of a comedy movie.

I don't, in fact, remember if my friends found the skates a source of envy or amazement, but I am quite sure that they provided entertainment. Winters back then were much colder than they are nowadays. The very next day after we returned home, I took my skates out to the paddies, which had frozen as smooth as glass. With children on sleds watching me with curious eyes, I donned my skates and laced them up. So far, so good. But gliding gracefully? Ha! As soon as I made it to my feet, I tumbled right back down. I am not blessed with great natural coordination, but I felt an obsessive need to prove myself. I struggled so desperately that the other kids didn't even laugh.

Fortunately, Grandfather rescued me from the nightmarish ice follies show I was putting on. The paddies weren't ours, but they lay between the brook in our yard and the wagon path that led out of the village. Grandfather had grown fond of gazing at the outside world through a small piece of glass set into the mulberry-paper door, and when he saw my bizarre flailing about, he shouted out to alert the rest of the family and ordered them to bring me to his room at once. Without even asking what I had been doing, he rapped me on the top of the head with his long tobacco pipe.

"Don't you realize you're humiliating the entire family?" he yelled. "And a girl, at that? Don't you have any better games to play than imitating a shaman's blade dance?"

My head smarted, but it was still hard to keep from bursting out laughing. By then, I was already presumptuous enough to look down on Grandfather, who didn't even know what skating was and whose limited imagination made him think of a shaman dancing on blades. I've never wanted to learn to skate since. I've never even put skates back on. The embarrassment of that first hapless attempt has stayed with me all my life.

Except for that one incident, winter vacation was just as much fun as summer had been. My cousin was extremely cute by this point, and, following Grandfather's wishes, we celebrated New Year's Day by the solar calendar. There was delicious food everywhere. Back then, the solar New Year was called Japanese New Year, and the lunar New Year, Korean New Year. The colonial government, of course, encouraged us to celebrate the holiday Japanese style, and schools and government offices were open on Korean New Year, as on any other day. Some people in the city celebrated both, but in the countryside, people didn't even know when Japanese New Year fell. All this was before the government began to crack down on lunar New Year celebrations.

New Year's celebrations lasted an unusually long time in the countryside, almost a month and a half. During the preparations, everyone scurried about sewing new outfits, simmering glutinous candies, pounding rice for cakes, making tofu, shaping dumplings, and joining with neighbors to slaughter pigs. Then followed days of eating, drinking, and merrymaking, in which social bonds were reaffirmed. This period lasted from New Year's Day until the first full moon, and it included visits to ancestral graves, ceremonial bows from the young to elders, the offer of blessings in return, trips to shamans to have fortunes told, and all sorts of games in which young and old and men and women alike participated. For farmers, it was the longest and most leisurely festival of the year.

I suspect that what prompted Grandfather to take the trouble of celebrating Japanese New Year was his deep affection for my brother and me. A holiday without us would have been meaningless, so he made sure the festivities coincided with our vacation. That said, however, he always believed that the solar calendar made more sense. Every year, someone sent us an almanac published by the Meteorological Office. The calendar indicated both solar and lunar dates, with the traditional twenty-four seasonal divisions, names of the months, and the days designated in a cycle of sixty. Back then, calendars were hard to come by, so the other villagers visited Grandfather to learn the best days for fermenting soy sauce and bean paste, offering rites to house spirits, departing on long journeys, and so on.

Grandfather would even consult the calendar and predict whether the year promised a cold winter, flood, or drought. After his stroke, he took to rifling through the book with greater interest, as though it had become a hobby. In the end, he apparently came to believe that he couldn't just watch idly as the villagers continued in their belief that the lunar calendar was necessary for farming. He felt compelled to enlighten them at every opportunity.

"Why should you have to come ask me when spring officially begins this year? In the solar calendar, it's always the same. Stop and think. Which is better, a calendar where the seasons' dates are fixed, or one where they bounce around every year and you even have to add an extra month sometimes? What difference does it make if the solar calendar comes from the Japs? Let's call a spade a spade. Do we have to say something is black just because the Japs say it's white?"

But no matter how worked up Grandfather became, the farmers never bought his argument. They were used to the subtle charms of the lunar system, with its twenty-four seasons that rotated every year. The only enlightened notions Grandfather acquired on his own were about the calendar, but he lacked the authority to uproot the villagers' deep prejudices against the Japanese New Year. And so our family celebrated an outcast's holiday, separate from the rest of the community.

We pooled resources with the other Pak family to have a pig slaughtered, hiring some villagers to do the dirty work. One freezing night toward the last day of the year, we kindled a lamp by the corner room, flooding the breezeway between the front and back yards with light. A commotion rose among the strapping young men, followed by a blood-curdling squeal. I lay under a quilt in the main room, which had gotten all toasty because the kitchen was attached to it and taffy was being boiled down. Instead of feeling sorry for the pig, I was caught up in the thrill of festival excitement, what with lantern light flickering on the papered fittings, the hubbub of the hired workers, and a squealing hog in the midst of it all.

Brother, though, witnessed the slaughter and wouldn't touch either the slices of pork or the blood sausages. The grownups were dismayed. Brother wasn't just the eldest grandson, destined to carry on the family name—he was the only grandson. His refusal to partake in the delicacies deprived them of meaning. Grandfather was extremely annoyed. What good was it for a boy to be so squeamish? He lost his temper and said that Brother should be force-fed if necessary. Even worse, he pointed at me and said grandson and granddaughter should have come out the other way around. That harsh remark wounded both of us.

We could afford just enough beef to make soup for the offering table during the ancestral rite. All the other dishes, however—dumplings, meat and vegetable skewers, mung bean pancakes—had pork in them. And so crabs pickled in soy sauce were put on the table exclusively for Brother. Once he polished off a crab, picking it apart with his spoon and chopsticks, I'd take the empty shell, scoop rice into it, and then mix it with a dash of the soy sauce the crabs had been fermented in. I'd done this often at my grandfather's table before. Even with nothing left in the shell, the rice tasted sublime, far better than from a bowl.

Crabs from P'aju were said to be the best in all Korea, but the ones where I grew up were every bit as tasty. Since freshwater crabs have vanished from the peninsula, people these days might not appreciate why, if I were asked to name the single most unforgettable dish I've ever had, I'd say crabs pickled in soy sauce without a moment's hesitation. Around the season when rice stalks are turning golden in the paddies, female crabs become filled with a gooey, black substance. Words can't begin to do justice to how those crabs taste when they've been marinated and left to ferment. The only saying I can think of that adequately captures it is fairly crude: "So damn good, you wouldn't notice if your dinner date dropped dead."

Brother's refusal to eat the pork weighed on Grandfather. He seemed to question whether Brother had what it took to become the head of our clan. As we were leaving for Seoul at vacation's end, he lectured him passionately about what it meant to be a man.

My grandmother, meanwhile, wrapped a bundle of sesame cookies for me to give to my teacher. Light taffy biscuits—whose ingredients included popped rice, fried beans, and peanuts—were standard fare at New Year's in my village. They were big, round, and enticing, and made perfect children's snacks. Sesame cookies, however, were reserved for guests, as they were much more laborious to prepare—thin, airy, coated with black and white sesame seeds fried separately, and shaped carefully into long diamonds. As Grandmother wrapped them, she said that she'd put extra care into them for my teacher.

None of that mattered to me. I was mortified by the image of presenting my teacher with this bundle, wrapped in a crumpled yellow paper bag that had been used for cement, and then tied off with a coarse string. Back then, I couldn't even picture my teacher going to the toilet.

From the beginning, I'd felt left out from her attempts to distribute her affection fairly among the pupils as they tagged along after her. Instead of drawing her attention with such an unrefined package, I preferred to settle into the alienation and inferiority complex of a nondescript child whose name the teacher barely knew. I took the bundle to school but didn't give it to her. On my way home, I called the other children over to Sajik Park, and together we gobbled up the sesame seed cookies in the sun.

Making the bundle disappear was the simplest solution to my dilemma. First I handed out a few cookies to children who struck me as easy marks and then, teasing them, told them to stick to me if they wanted more. I ran to the park breathlessly, feeling light and free, as though I had broken out of the shell encasing me and could soar into the air. Some kids began fawning over me, but I pretended not to notice and gave more to a child who seemed to be a hick like me. I didn't make any good friends out of all this, but at least I felt as if I had put the Seoul kids in their place and gotten revenge on my teacher, who didn't seem to recognize me. Nonetheless, the incident left me with a bitter aftertaste.

In early autumn, Mother started her piecemeal sewing at home again, which was a great comfort to me. Knowing she'd be home waiting put an extra spring in my step as I walked the mountain path. Almost all the materials she worked with were elegant, colorful silks—yellow, red, pink, purple, green, and blue. They transformed our gloomy room into a brilliant, new world. After winter vacation and before the lunar New Year, sewing jobs poured in. Mother couldn't do them all, even if she stayed up all night. She'd chat with me to lighten her worries and stave off sleep. "Want to hear a story from long ago?" she'd begin.

Mother knew countless stories. There was the folktale about the tiger with the refrain "Granny, granny, give me a rice cake or I'll eat you up"; the story of the grandfather who tried to sell the wen on his chin; the tradesman who dealt in sweet-smelling farts; K'ongjwi and her evil stepsister, P'atjwi; and those two tragic sisters, Changhwa and Hongnyŏn. I'd heard Grandmother tell these stories several times, but they sounded fresh coming from Mother. And it wasn't just folk tales. There wasn't a story Mother didn't know. Her repertoire included literary works, like *The Story of Mrs. Pak*, *Mrs. Sa Goes to the South*, *A Nine Cloud Dream*, *Outlaws of the Marsh*, and the *Romance of Three Kingdoms*. She had a real talent for adapting even the more difficult stories to my age level.

My favorite was *The Story of Mrs. Pak*. I liked it so much that I begged for it again and again. When she realized how caught up I was in these stories, which she'd originally volunteered to kill time, she started to worry. "They say you'll wind up poor if you like stories too much," she'd grumble, but she'd unfurl her bundle of narratives once more, pretending she couldn't resist my pestering.

I don't think anybody in the world could retell the *Romance of Three Kingdoms* with Mother's verve. Raising her hand high, she'd intone, "Cao Cao, prepare to receive my blade!" The needle she held at her fingertip glistened, inspiring as much fear as a real sword. A thrill shot through me. I felt sorry that she was reduced to sewing for a living, when she was more than equal to wielding a weapon herself.

Mother's stories throughout our years of grinding poverty comforted me and gave me strength, but they also had a negative effect. I didn't feel deeply unhappy about not having friends at school and almost came to enjoy my loneliness. I think the stories brimming in my head helped me stay aloof.

I entertained this thought idly much later as I looked back at my childhood. For six years, I had to pass over a hill to attend school, something that was quite rare in Seoul, but I never felt scared or bored. On the few occasions when someone accompanied me, I found having to make conversation a burden. It was actually more comfortable and liberating to walk alone. The stories triggered my young and hyperactive imagination, and I took pleasure in those moments of solitude. In retrospect, though, it strikes me that the way I developed emotionally was not normal.

5. The Triangle-Yard House

BROTHER FINALLY GRADUATED. JUST AS Grandfather and Mother had wanted, he landed a job with the central government. Prior to that, my elder uncle, who'd been struggling to farm on his own, became a clerk in the township office. We just held on to our vegetable patches and gave up some productive rice paddies for sharecropping. As I mentioned earlier, there were no tenant farmers in Pakchŏk Hamlet; we offered the paddies to a villager who had more helping hands than we did.

Grandfather preened himself on his learning and mocked the villagers' ignorance all too readily. You can get an easy sense of how odious his *yangban* mind-set was when you take into account that, regardless of Korea's political situation, he felt satisfied as long as his descendants were civil servants. Central government, provincial office—it made no difference. He simply wanted their livelihood to come from pushing a pen rather than tilling the earth, and he considered a government position the prize of desk jobs. In the end, you'd have to say that my family's so-called pedigree was the servility of a petty bureaucrat that remained after you stripped a *yangban* of his scholarly leanings.

Uncle snagged his job through a distant relative who shared my grandfather's generation name and pulled some strings for him. This relative's father appears in history books as the traitorous soul whose seal stamped the Protectorate Treaty of 1905, the document that sold our country to Japan.* Because of this "service," the son also had title and rank as a Japanese noble. A job in a township office hardly deserved his mighty influence. It was hard to watch my grandfather fawn all over him in the belief that a clerk's position meant a notable rise in status.

This kinsman would come to the countryside on occasion. Despite equal generational standing, Grandfather treated him with the deference a servant shows his master. His insistence on offering hospitality far beyond our means made life difficult for the women in the house well before his arrival. Grandmother joked to my mother and aunts that two visits a year from that old bastard of a nobleman would grind us into bean powder.

In all honesty, though, for a member of a lowly *yangban* household like ours to find employment with the central government did mean great honor to the family. Needless to say, Brother's job boosted Mother's pride significantly. But within half a year, he quit to take a position with a Japanese company called Watanabe Ironworks.

Mother turned pale when she heard the word "ironworks." What, she had given him all that education just so he could become a blacksmith? Brother tried to comfort her. Yes, the company might indeed be a large smithy, but he worked in its office and his new salary was more than

---

* The Protectorate Treaty of 1905, or Ŭlsa Poho Choyak, was signed by Foreign Minister Pak Che-sun.

double what he had been receiving. But Mother couldn't relinquish an attachment to the government office. She begged Brother to tell Grandfather and the others back home that he worked for a company. God forbid he should so much as utter the word "ironworks."

The first bonus my brother brought home was more than a hundred won. Younger Uncle and Auntie came over, and we passed around the bluish banknote, admiring it with tremendous excitement. I can't vouch for the two of them, but it was certainly the first hundred-won note my mother and I ever laid eyes on. There was a drawing on it of a rich-looking old man with a bag slung over his shoulder. We genuinely wondered whether the bag was meant to contain rice or money.

Brother wanted Mother to stop sewing and take life easy, but she declared that she wouldn't quit until we bought a house. Brother's salary of roughly forty won a month and his bonuses meant that Mother had gotten closer to achieving her dream. The money more than compensated for her regret over Brother leaving the civil service. Sewing work poured in as usual, but Mother developed a new hobby. She began house hunting in her spare moments.

When she went, she'd put on affected haughtiness—and her best clothes. I have a feeling that she did so out of self-consciousness, afraid of being caught out by the real-estate agents, since she had no money in her hands on these practice runs. I doubt she went to look at houses beyond our wildest dreams, but she certainly did go to Seoul's more upscale neighborhoods. From time to time, she spoke wistfully about the huge gap between the prices of houses inside and outside the city gates. Her words made me think that we'd be escaping Hyŏnjŏ-dong the very day we bought a house.

But Mother purchased a house all too quickly, and in Hyŏnjŏ-dong, no less. Although she'd been going about her house-buying plans methodically, she wound up taking the plunge suddenly—and all because of me.

She hated to see me play with our landlord's child, but even if we'd been mortal enemies we couldn't just ignore each other while living in the same tiny compound for two years. Kids have a natural affinity for one another. More to the point, forbidden fruit has its attractions for them too. Unbeknownst to Mother, the landlord's daughter and I became close.

One day, a spat broke out between us while we were doodling in the alley with a slate pencil. Brother happened to be on his way home from work and attempted to break up the fight. But now I realized I had strong support to rely on and clawed at my playmate's face, trying to deal her a crushing blow. Our squabble then escalated into a battle between the adults.

It wasn't the first time I'd scratched or pinched another child. I never planned to, but I think insecurity about my skinny frame drove me to fingernails whenever a fight turned physical. Mother kept trying to reason with me. For heaven's sake, she implored, don't scratch. Nails leave telltale marks. If another kid smacks you, just hit back. But I wound up using my nails once more.

Our landlady was furious about the scratch on her daughter's face. More seriously, given that I generally didn't get along well with others and retaliated with my nails in a flash, I must have struck her as a real "problem child," as we say today. What was Mother teaching me? What could she expect of me when I grew up? Her abuse was tinged with sympathy. She dragged Brother into her attacks too for acting as a bystander and not stopping me.

If Mother believed she was right, she would plow on ahead, consequences be damned. Besides, snobbish as she was, she harbored contempt for the landlord, whose family life was complicated by a concubine and a child from a former wife. Mother took every opportunity to express her disdain for the way they lived beyond their means. The landlady came to borrow money from time to time, and although Mother readily lent it, she grumbled afterward.

"This takes the cake. It'd be one thing if they couldn't afford rice or firewood. But borrowing money because she's got a craving for beef in their soup? It's not like I have a choice either. If I weren't her tenant, you can be sure she'd get a real earful as I showed her the door. I wouldn't give her a single chon."

It must have hurt Mother terribly to have a woman she looked down on insult her precious children and tell her how to raise them. But Mother didn't chide Brother and me or badmouth the landlady. Seeing her like this scared me even more, because I thought she might go and do something really extreme. I once wrote about how we bought our house after this incident in the magazine *Economic Justice*, so let me just quote passages from it:

> The following day, my mother went out to buy a house and actually ended up signing a contract within a few days. The house was small—a mere six *kan*, and farther up the hill in the same impoverished neighborhood, but it was unthinkable that we could afford a house unless we robbed someone. Even at my age, for the longest time I believed Mother had gone crazy. The honest truth, though, is that she actually did rob someone.
>
> Acquaintances from the countryside visited us frequently because we'd been the first to settle in Seoul.

One of them arrived with a large sum of money from a land transaction in the hope of starting a business in the capital. He was staying with us for several days, relying on our hospitality, but had to return home for some urgent matter and left the money with Mother.

Well, Mother appropriated his cash on the sly. She signed a contract for the house, deliberately finishing the deal before she informed my grandparents and my younger uncle about the details and pleaded for their help. They joined forces and raised the necessary money, hastily selling off some land and borrowing emergency funds, in order to avoid humiliation from their acquaintance's loss.

In the aftermath, Mother had to cower before my grandparents for a long time to come. Even to my eyes she seemed very odd. How could she have done what she did? . . .

. . . Until then, I had considered my mother absolutely upright, so for her to behave like a criminal bewildered me. I was still too young to understand that she was driven by the same touching, blind maternal love that would drive a mother to steal cold rice for her starving child.

Given Mother's personality, the first dwelling we purchased in Seoul forced her to muster an almost manic courage, and she went through enormous trouble for it. At the very least, the house had a tile roof. Its six *kan* held three rooms, a kitchen, a veranda, and a gateway, each unit about one *kan* in size. The house was built on a tiny, awkward lot. The portion that nominally passed for a yard was triangular and came flush against a steep embankment.

You can hardly expect a day laborer who lives from hand to mouth to keep his home in fine shape. That house, however, was in even worse condition than usual, for its former owner was a tinker with several mouths to feed.

Back then, every house in Seoul was infested with bedbugs. People simply took it for granted. They even said that if a house didn't have bedbugs, well, it wasn't Seoul. It was anyone's guess when the previous owners had last papered the rooms—traces of blood from squashed insects coated every inch of the torn wallpaper. But never mind that Brother and I were disgusted; the solution to our money problems left Mother elated. Removing all the doors of the house, she scrubbed them with lye, and then used it to wipe the pillars and eaves as high as her hands could reach.

Mother claimed it didn't matter that the house hadn't been well looked after because it had "good bones." What she meant was that the pillars and eaves were sturdy. She was right. After several days of wiping, polishing, and papering, the house took on a new look. But only much later did I understand why Mother had bought such a spooky house, with a particular eye to its "bones." She intended to use the house as collateral to get a bank loan and pay Uncle back.

In those days, the only financial institutions low-income families had ready access to were the banking cooperatives. When a loan application was made, the cooperative sent out an appraiser to consider whether to grant it. My mother waited on the appointed day, having cleaned the house inside and out, just like for a teacher's visit.

The appraiser paid closer attention to the overall structure than to the floors and wallpaper, as my mother had expected, and asked what size mortgage she had in mind. Mother had the nerve to muse about whether the house might not be worth eight hundred won in collateral. The appraiser left without saying anything or committing himself one way or the other. Mother, however, didn't seem worried; she didn't bow deeply or fawn over him. She didn't even treat him to a glass of water or a cigarette.

Nonetheless, an eight hundred–won mortgage came through soon after, and although Mother was able to settle everything neatly, she didn't act particularly grateful or appear to consider herself lucky. At the time, low-income family loans came easily enough to anyone who followed due procedure.

My mother bought that six-*kan* tile-roofed house at the top of Hyŏnjŏ-dong for fifteen hundred won. The mortgage she took out totaled a little over half its price. She neither knew anyone at the banking cooperative nor was she endowed with unusual social skills. She was just an ordinary countrywoman, and her face would blanch when she found herself in front of a government office or a police station. Nevertheless, she wasn't afraid to knock on the bank door for the loan she desired.

I stress these bare facts because I'm concerned that people won't believe me. I'm all too conscious of the universal belief that since Liberation, corruption in our banking system has meant that loans only come via special privileges of dubious origin or a real gift for networking.

A dreary litany of minor horrors clouded my childhood and adolescence under colonial rule: petty functionaries—lowly clerks at township and neighborhood offices—who spoke to us condescendingly; policemen, whose glinting swords seen even at a distance made us cower and want to flee, innocent though we were; prison guards, who treated shackled prisoners like animals; Japanese soldiers filled with arrogance and murderous spirits; Japanese teachers, whose eyes revealed pitiful disdain for my mother, a barbarian unable to speak a word of their language.

But amid all that tiresome bureaucracy, the era's financial institutions stand out. I have no hostility to speak of toward them. Mother was able to acquire loans when we moved to bigger houses as well. I have to point out, of course, that easy credit also encouraged reckless borrowing. Ready loans played a major role in causing more than a few to unwittingly forfeit their assets.

We called our new abode "The Triangle-Yard House." We were all satisfied with it. In fact, we loved it. Brother had a room of his own on the other side of the main hallway from Mother's and mine, and next to the gate was a room that we rented out. The house had an L-shape, with my brother's room and the gate at opposite points. The line linking the two formed the base of the yard's triangle and stood along a high embankment.

Beneath lay the rear of another house. Mother asked the family who lived there for permission to expand our yard outward, so it could become like an eave for the back of their house. She made a flowerbed in the extension. The family below was happy because they had additional roofing, and I was happy because we now had somewhere to plant flowers.

The flowerbed was just soil poured onto boards shored up by wooden props, but four-o'clocks and marigolds flourished on it. In the fall, we prepared abundant rice cakes topped with red beans to ward off bad spirits and shared them with our neighbors. Although the house was higher up the hill than the one we used to rent, Mother liked the new community better. She stopped telling me not to go out. Her earlier loathing must have been particularly directed at our previous landlord and his family rather than at all the residents of Hyŏnjŏ-dong.

The house in front of ours belonged to the head of the neighborhood. It sat tidily on a lot with numerous flowering plants. Back then, alleys were narrow, and everyone kept their gates open, so the fragrance of the many plantain lilies in their lot wafted over to our house at dusk when they blossomed. Their dwelling became known to us not as the house of the neighborhood head but as "The Plantain Lily House." The family had a girl two years older than me, and although she gave us lily roots several times, the plants never thrived at our house. We nicknamed the home next door "The Single-Gate House," and Mother became friendly with that family too.

Now that we had rent coming in and Brother had a good salary, Mother didn't sew to earn money as much as she used to, but when people expressly sought out her craftsmanship, she worked behind Brother's back. Brother was extremely filial. Whenever he caught her sewing for others, his face fell and his temper rose. Even at my age, I could sense how wonderful it was to have our own house, to plan a month ahead on Brother's salary, and to live in familial harmony. Although we did not escape Hyŏnjŏ-dong, mentally and materially we began to adapt to urban life.

But as soon as vacation started, we were off to the countryside. Nothing had changed as far as that went. I continued to have butterflies of excitement for several days before going home, and I still pitied the children who were stuck in Seoul all vacation long. Yet I now thought that I couldn't live in the countryside forever. What I found especially frustrating was the dim lamplight. When we returned to

Seoul with the opening of school, the electric lights, bright as day, brought me a joy just as thrilling as the scent of fresh village grass.

Brother had to keep working during my vacation. He remained in Seoul with my uncle, who, after years of hardship, had earned enough to open his own store near Namdaemun. That's why he'd been able to lend us money when we bought the house. His first foray into commerce was an ice store, a result of the connections he'd developed at the fish wholesaler, I imagine. The shop was located in a neighborhood lined with tidy grocery shops and did a thriving business.

One of the joys of life in Seoul was visiting Uncle and Auntie. They had no children of their own and doted on Brother and me. Before heading home for vacation, I'd show Uncle my report card, and even though I was a mediocre student until third or fourth grade, he showered me with both praise and snacks for the train. He followed Mother's interpretation of my marks unquestioningly. As long as I was doing well in Japanese and math, my poor grades in singing and gym didn't matter.

Being spoiled by Uncle and Auntie was wonderful, but I was also drawn to the atmosphere of their commercial district, so different from Hyŏnjŏ-dong. There, Japanese and Koreans resided in equal numbers. Uncle's establishment had a large space for ice storage and even a telephone, a rarity in those days. Although he also sold charcoal in winter, in the district his business was known as the "ice shop."

Exaggerated rumors about Uncle's success evidently circulated back home, as a stream of country folk came to Seoul, hoping that he could arrange for them either to work in a shop or even to start up their own businesses. In return, they had to listen to Uncle's soliloquy about pulling himself up by his bootstraps. He would go on and on about arriving in Seoul empty-handed, and spending a winter living in the attic above the fish merchant's ice storage. The aid he extended did not go much beyond offering visitors his braggadocio, nor was he in any real position to help. Nonetheless, his shop, a mere stone's throw from the train station, remained a magnet for country folk.

Uncle's ties meant that he was eventually pressured into hiring a boy from our village. He tried to reproduce his own success story with the lad, first building a loft in the crawl space above his ice storage and having the boy sleep there. But my aunt was meticulous and sweet, and in my eyes, the space, as she had decorated it, was wonderful. I longed to live in a two-story house, and climbing the ladder to this makeshift loft with its tatami mat made me feel as though I were in one. I suppose at some level I thirsted for a Japanese lifestyle.

In this loft, I came across a comic book for the first time, a tale about a sword fight between Japanese samurai. Uncle caught me reading it and gave me a harsh scolding. He also called the boy and slapped him about his closely cropped head with the book—how dare he run up the electricity bill on this, when Uncle was allowing him to keep the light on late to study? I felt bad about getting the boy into trouble, but I couldn't forget the excitement of the comic book, especially because Uncle treated it as an illicit pleasure.

For a long time, the drawings remained vivid in my head. I was dying to know what happened next. I'd have stolen the comic book somewhere, if I could have, just to finish the story. It seems incredible now, but that was the first time in my life I stumbled on reading material other than my textbooks. That was partly because of our poverty, but I never saw classmates with storybooks or the like either.

Mother's storytelling talent instilled in me a love of narrative, but she of course was oblivious to the desires she had kindled. I quenched my thirst by reading all the tales in my Japanese and ethics textbooks when I got them at the beginning of a semester. When I was bored, I'd read the good ones aloud over and over. My reading pleased Mother, who assumed I was studying. Then I'd stick out my tongue behind her back and feel a strange thrill in deceiving her.

Brother had a handful of books in his room, but they were mostly novels in Korean and didn't interest me at all. Since Korean wasn't taught at school, I was one of the few children who could read and write it, but I wasn't yet mature enough to take pride in this.

I could have easily lost my literacy in Korean, as I'd acquired it in the countryside at a very young age. The reason I managed to hold on to it was that I needed to use it sometimes, much as I loathed when these occasions—letters to my grandparents—rolled around. I cherished Grandfather and Grandmother, but to me, hometown and grandparents were inseparable, almost a single entity. If they hadn't been there, I'm sure I wouldn't have felt such joy in going home. But I also thought that if they lived somewhere else, I might not miss them so much.

As far as I was concerned, Grandfather's palsy was tied to being as firmly rooted in Pakchŏk Hamlet as its guardian spirits. When vacation approached, my heart even ached for the dried persimmons and chestnuts wrapped in the hemp cloth that reeked of Grandfather's saliva. This yearning was hardly the same as wanting to eat them. It was bittersweet, filled with melancholy. Like wanting to see ears of corn waving against the crimson glow of twilight.

Who helps light your pipe when the brazier goes out, Grandfather? Cousin is still too small. When I visit during vacation, I'll do a good job running errands for you. Just like you say, I'll do the work of your own tongue. That's the sort of letter that would have expressed how I felt.

But Mother wouldn't let me write the way I wanted to. She believed that letters had to follow a prescribed format. A letter that violated it, especially to my grandparents, was out of the question. She would sit me down and dictate to me as though I were taking a spelling test.

The letters always began with similar phrases: "I offer this humble letter to Grandfather. Grandfather, I trust that your health remains in steadfast good condition . . ." Something along those lines. Then after inquiring after everyone's well-being, in hierarchical order, I was supposed to let them know that everyone on our side, again naming all of us in strict order, remained in good health thanks to the benevolent concern Grandfather bestowed on those below him. Then I would have to finish the letter by saying that I was inquiring after his health because the weather was so unpredictable that I felt concern for his well-being, varying this section slightly, depending on which season was upon us.

I'd squirm with the tedium of having to write it all down. The thought occurred to me that if I didn't know the Korean alphabet, I could avoid this torture. Not too surprising then, since this was my only use for Korean, that I had no interest in reading anything written in it. I took it for granted that Korean books would be boring.

"The Triangle-Yard House" was where we ushered in World War II, or, as the Japanese called it, the Greater East Asia War. We didn't know what it was all about, but it was an exciting time nonetheless. We were being trained to be belligerent. Japan was in the middle of its war with China, which was dubbed "the China incident" in Japanese. We held the Chinese in utter contempt and called them "chinks." This became the worst epithet to tease friends with when we bickered. The Japanese pronunciation of Chiang Kai-shek, "Shō Kaiseki," also was readily tossed about when referring to the general, because it sounded so much like *kaesekki* in Korean—son of a bitch. Every morning, we assembled in the schoolyard and pledged ourselves as citizens of the emperor's realm. As we trooped to our classrooms in time to a military march, our blood roiled for no particular reason. Our hawkish passion, our sense of elation, made us want to attack something, anything.

We constantly heard that we were defeating the chinks, so they didn't seem worthy opponents. Subtly, without even realizing it, our expectations swelled in anticipation of a greater foe. In addition to Shō Kaiseki, Rūzuberuto and Chāchiru—Roosevelt and Churchill—were added to the list of leaders of evil we had to smash. News of victories arrived every day. A famous Korean soprano sang, "Say so long to Singapore. Back off, Britain." It became a hit overnight. Torchlit processions threaded their way through downtown Seoul to gloat in celebration over the fall of each South Sea island. Every schoolchild in the country got a free rubber ball to welcome these isles, with their limitless rubber, into the fold of Japanese territories.

"A braggart's barn burns first," says a proverb: not long after, rice began to be rationed, as were sneakers and even rubber shoes. Each family received a ration card for rice, depending on its size. Rubber shoes, however, were issued to local divisions of the Patriot Association and distributed by lot. My mother would come up empty-handed at every neighborhood meeting and sigh at her lack of talent at lotteries. Necessities grew more expensive with each passing day.

The order to adopt Japanese names had come before rationing was introduced, but as the economy deteriorated, this policy grew more coercive and made life more difficult. My family didn't change its name. Grandfather was adamant that it would happen only over his dead body: "Not until my eye sockets are filled with dirt." Household heads had absolute authority in such matters. Uncle resented Grandfather for the decision, and implied that his business was going downhill as a result. My mother was also afraid that it could affect Brother's career and the way I was treated at school. She hoped Grandfather would have a change of heart.

My homeroom teacher in fourth and fifth grade was Japanese. Mother often asked me if he said anything about my name. When I answered that he didn't care, she said that I was just oblivious. She couldn't believe that he didn't discriminate against me. She tossed me leading questions, and then answered them herself to get the response she was looking for. Maybe I was lucky, but I have no memory of my teacher mistreating or putting any silent pressure on those of us who kept a Korean name, even when it had dwindled to just three or four.

Had our families been branded as troublemakers, things might have been different, but I think the situation of ordinary households like mine was similar. I may be relying too much on my own experience, but I still find it hard to fathom how the name changes took root so rapidly. In my village, only the two Pak families remained steadfast, while all the Hongs took the name Tokuyama very early on. My uncle, as a township clerk, really should have been the one to worry about the disadvantages of a Korean name, but Grandfather, even with his belief that Uncle's lowly government position meant a rise in status, remained oddly principled on this point.

The other villagers were just as inconsistent. They changed their name with little prompting, but clung to the lunar New Year, despite all the difficulties it presented, on the grounds that it was Korean. My mother was another good example of how people could succumb without much pressure.

I myself longed desperately for the change, albeit for a very different reason. My name, pronounced in Japanese, was Poku Ensho. This sounded a lot like *bōkūenshū*, or "air-defense drill." We practiced drills daily as the wartime emergency progressed, and I was teased each time. After the name changes, Chinese characters were read with their meanings rather than their sound in mind, and I envied girls with Japanese names like Hanako and Harue.

Some kids bragged about using Japanese at home. In most cases, their mothers were young and fashionable. I couldn't dream of such a thing. These tales made Mother furious. "Spineless good-for-nothings," she'd say.

Mother attended parents' meetings without fail. If the homeroom teacher was Japanese and the parents couldn't speak the language, the class monitor translated. My mother carried herself proudly, a black horn hairpin securing her bun. I found it torture to watch her in her starched, coarse cotton garb, sitting before the teacher and speaking her mind solemnly, completely ignoring the young translator.

Mother acted the way she did out of her own self-respect. I doubt nationalist pride had a thing to do with it. She was petrified that clinging to Korean names might disadvantage my brother and me, but she was thoroughly unprepared to help us cope with any inconvenience or persecution that might have resulted. Her hopes for us to rise in the world were, of course, confined to the possibilities available under Japanese imperial rule. Mother was an ordinary woman. Envisioning a sovereign destiny for Korea lay far beyond her.

6. Grandmother and Grandfather

As if it weren't embarrassing enough to put up with Mother attending every single parents' meeting, one day she burst in during the middle of class, rattling the door open. She hadn't even taken off her rubber shoes. Oblivious to the fact that my teacher wouldn't understand a word, she began explaining in difficult, ornate Korean why she'd come: she'd received a telegram that my grandfather was in critical condition and was taking me back to our village.

The teacher at least understood that something serious was up. He called me forward to interpret instead of the class monitor, but I bungled the job. My inability to convey Mother's elaborate and solemn way of speaking left me flustered. Somehow, though, I managed to get the basic meaning across, and the teacher gave me permission to leave immediately.

Even so, Mother had me double-check that I wouldn't be marked absent if I missed school for my grandfather's funeral. Only after her understanding of the rules had been confirmed did she take me by the hand and lead me out of the classroom. Mother had already made all the preparations for our departure before she stopped into school to fetch me. Strapping my schoolbag to my back, I headed with her straight to the train station, where Brother, Uncle, and Auntie were waiting for us.

On trips home during school vacations, we'd take the local train to T'osŏng, but that day, for the first time, we took the express bound for Shinŭiju. The train ran straight on until its brief stop in Kaesŏng. Although it was already pitch dark, our party of five hurried along the twenty-*ri* trek home without a break.

The outer quarters of our house were ablaze with lanterns. Folk milled about, speaking in hushed tones. Grandfather, we learned, was in a coma but still alive. This was his third stroke, and everyone was bracing for the inevitable. Those gathered in the outer quarters didn't let me in, saying that I was too young. I was just as afraid of seeing him on his deathbed and hurried away.

The inner quarters were also brightly lit, and everyone was keeping vigil. I fell into a deep slumber, only to awake at dawn to the sound of wailing. Grandfather had passed away, but tears refused to well in my eyes. In keeping with the custom of the time, not a moment of the five-day wake passed without wails of lamentation. Still, the atmosphere wasn't gloomy, as was fitting when the deceased had lived to a ripe old age.

Not only residents of Pakchŏk Hamlet, but people from surrounding villages arrived as well, accompanied by their children, and slept and ate in the bereaved household. Everyone envied the deceased's good fortune, because we were able to carry out the funeral rites generously despite being in the throes of a national crisis. This was all thanks to Elder Uncle, who cared for Grandfather until his death and at the time was the township's director of general affairs. Although Younger Uncle and Brother were known to have been successful in Seoul, when it came to hosting a funeral, it was the authority of a local civil servant that shone through.

The one who took Grandfather's death hardest was Brother. When Father died, his grief had been so extreme that it threatened his health, which caused Mother a lot of anxiety. Once again, Brother acted as chief mourner and dressed in the hat and coat the role called for. By this point, he'd grown into a dashing young man. It was heartbreaking to think of him as a boy of nine, in mourner's garb, weeping with abandon, but all this seemed to me to be his fate and to have nothing to do with me. I pitied Brother. He was a fragile youth. I fretted recalling the elders' concern when he could not bring himself to eat the slaughtered pig.

On the day of burial, a long line of people with mourning flags snaked after the bier from our house to the hill where Grandfather would be laid to rest. The large turnout was in part because our ancestral tombs were not far away. Both the bier itself and the entire scene struck me as an exquisite spectacle, the likes of which you almost never got to see in Seoul.

Although the women of the family wailed as they held the bars of the funeral carriage, they slipped away almost imperceptibly before the procession left for the burial ground. I don't know if that was the general custom back then or unique to my family.

Grandfather's death summoned even more people to pay their respects. For five days, every hour was dominated by complex procedural formalities involving the disposition of his body. They seemed to go on forever. Once Grandfather was finally taken away, a sense of emptiness and loss came over the women of the house, although much continued to demand their attention. This void pressed on my young self as terror. I was already on the point of bursting into tears, but Mother lashed out at me nonetheless.

"You usually bawl over the tiniest little thing. Why haven't you cried a single tear for your own grandfather?" She then muttered, "And he adored her so much, the useless creature. Even a dog that was loved as much would starve itself for days out of respect. Daughters, granddaughters—what's the point in raising them?"

It wasn't just the cruelty of what she said but the disdain in her cold, scornful gaze that pried open the floodgates of my tears at that moment. I wept and wept, flailing about until I almost fainted from exhaustion. Grandmother and my aunts, thinking my grief was now erupting, comforted me and rebuked my mother for speaking so thoughtlessly.

It remains clear to me, however, that I wept out of humiliation, not grief. That's not to say that Mother understood my feelings exactly. I may not have cried during Grandfather's funeral rites, but I felt his loss keenly and held on to trifling memories about him longer than anyone else. Even after I grew up and got married, I could recall in detail how he looked (he didn't leave any photographs behind), his foibles, and anecdotes about him that everyone else had forgotten. My relatives said I had a good memory, but I think it was rather my great affection for him that spurred my recall.

A tightly woven hemp cord, about as thick as a straw rope, hung from the rafters in the outer quarters for people to grab as they climbed up to and down from the veranda platform. Eventually, Grandfather recovered enough from his first stroke to go to the outhouse or the yard by himself, but he no longer swung on the cord as nimbly as he once did. On several occasions, I saw him clinging to it, his legs shaking violently.

The rope continued to hang there after his death; every time I returned home and caught sight of that cord from a distance, I was overcome by pangs of grief and would run toward it, as though running to someone who had kept a lengthy vigil for me, and stroke it. The cord had become sticky with the sweat from Grandfather's palms, but I wouldn't have had it any other way. I clasped the rope at every opportunity, feeling the same emotions I had when Grandfather embraced me. I did all of this in secret, though, embarrassed that someone might sense my thoughts.

❋ ❋ ❋ ❋ ❋ ❋ ❋ ❋ ❋ ❋ ❋

As Japan's situation deteriorated, air-raid drills became increasingly frequent. We were now told to wear roomy pants that were comfortable to work in, instead of our school uniforms. To Mother, violating school instructions spelled calamity. She bought a length of coarse black-dyed cotton and made me a pair with her own hands, but couldn't restrain a sigh after I tried them on.

"The Japs' loincloths are disgusting enough, but to let a girl's crotch be that exposed? Heaven only knows what I'll live to see."

Mother looked down on Japanese customs generally, but her greatest contempt was reserved for their clothing. She told me, as if recounting historical fact, that in ancient times the Japanese had lived barefoot, wearing nothing but a diaper of sorts to cover their midsection, so they came to Korea and begged to be taught how to make suitable garments and shoes. Koreans, she said, showed them how to turn our mourning robes into their national costume and our kitchen cutting boards into clogs. And thus were born the *haori* and *geta* of today's Japan.

Mother was absolutely convinced of this, just as she was convinced that King Sejong had created the Korean alphabet overnight after being inspired by the shapes on a door frame. No one could persuade her otherwise. She would point to the Japanese men who ambled about Namdaemun or on Seoul's central avenue in loincloths late at night in midsummer. To her, they offered concrete evidence of the remnants of their customs before we taught them how to make clothes, even if it was nothing more elaborate than our simple mourning garb.

You could never be sure what form Mother's anti-Japanese sentiments would take. As soon as we got back to Seoul after Grandfather's funeral, she urged Brother and Uncle to take a Japanese surname for the family. I'd secretly expected this and assumed it would happen as a matter of course. This time, however, it was Brother who opposed the idea. He said that since we'd endured everything up to that point, we could hold the fort a little longer. His words unnerved me a bit because it sounded as though he expected an end to the wartime emergency.

On the issue of our name, Brother's usual lack of resolution gave way to a quasi-heroic determination. Being young, I accepted at face value that Japan's end would mean our own demise. Mother held fast to the same belief, despite her contempt for Japan and her own considerable smarts. She'd apparently never dreamed that Japan's end could open a new path for us.

Brother's firmness astonished Younger Uncle even more than Mother. He complained that it would grow increasingly difficult to do business in a heavily Japanese district without a name change and that he'd become more and more conspicuous, like a husk among grains of rice. Brother said that if that were the case, Uncle was welcome to break off from the rest of the clan and change his name. Brother had succeeded Grandfather as head of the household and inherited the immense authority the role brought with it. Brother's unexpected suggestion angered and saddened Uncle: "I never felt bad about not having kids because I thought of you two as my own. And now you're humiliating me by telling me to take our name off the family register?" Mother was at an utter loss, caught in the middle. She tried to apologize to Uncle and reconcile the two.

Our family name must have created even bigger problems for Elder Uncle because of his job, but Brother thwarted him as well. Mother was very concerned. Why was Brother, who'd never given his elders any problem at all, suddenly so obstinate? The three branches of the family had never disagreed before, but they now squabbled. Given that tacit agreement was reached to follow Brother's decision, my uncles must have considered his insistence more than pigheaded rashness.

For the first time in my life, I had a sense of Brother as different from the common herd. Although my understanding was imprecise, it gave me an odd sense of pride. I had the illusion that I was unexpectedly glimpsing a soul that towered over a world awash with philistines. This impudence of mine was probably related to my reading, which was becoming ever more voracious.

In the fifth grade, I came to have a close friend for the first time. She had transferred to our school, and our teacher had her sit next to me. Teachers would usually seat transfer students with good-natured kids until they could adapt to their new environment. I was a nobody in class and never chosen for anything else, yet this was a duty that regularly fell to me. I felt insulted but couldn't openly show my annoyance. I knew that I was neither good-natured nor kind, but had no choice but to pretend to be otherwise. I didn't have the heart to betray the one expectation the teacher had of me. My new classmate now had a Japanese surname, but she kept her unsophisticated first name, Pok-sun. Her features also gave the impression of a country girl, and her clothes were on the shabby side.

In our first Japanese class after we began to sit together, the lesson was about libraries. The teacher described in detail how to borrow books and return them, and then told us where the library was, saying it would be a good experience if we went and used it. The teacher gave us advice frequently. He'd tell the story of a diligent person who became successful and urge us to follow his example. If a tale about honesty came up, he'd emphasize it as the most precious virtue. We were free to just let it all in one ear and straight out the other.

Rustic little Pok-sun, however, began to talk me into going to the library the following Sunday. She'd paid attention to the teacher's directions and thought she could find her way there. How fun it would be to go and borrow all the books we could read, she said, just like in our textbook. She knew more about books and their pleasures than I did. In contrast, for me this was all virgin territory. The library the teacher told us about stood where the Lotte Department Store is now. At the time, it was known as either the Public Library or the Government-General Library—the very building that became the National Library after Liberation. We agreed to go together on Sunday and that I'd stop in at her house first.

Pok-sun lived in Nusang-dong. I was stunned to see a house like hers within the city gates. The eaves of the thatched roof almost touched the ground. They were so low that you practically had to crawl in and out. Except for a water tap made possible because the house sat on level ground, it was much worse than ours. The six members of her family—parents, grandmother, and three children—lived in two teensy rooms the size of mouse holes. It was genuinely pathetic. On top of that, Pok-sun's younger brother, the only son, was retarded. He drooled and barked out incomprehensible syllables. Their mother, her face vacant, chain-smoked in front of her mother-in-law. I wonder if deep resentment drove her to become that rude.

I took pity on my friend and respected her for staying positive and cheerful. She went to the kitchen, took a spoon with a short stem, and began vigorously peeling potatoes with it. Then she steamed them and fed me. I was touched by her artlessness and felt I'd finally found a friend. I don't mean that I hadn't had any playmates until then, but Pok-sun was the first to satisfy my longing for real friendship.

I told Mother that going to the library was part of my homework, so she gave her permission straight away. The unfamiliar road from Pok-sun's house to the library on that holiday morning seemed long. Pok-sun herself had never visited the library. But we weren't shy about asking people for directions and eventually arrived at a red brick building enveloped in authoritarian silence. It didn't look like it would welcome children cheerfully, and we could not bring ourselves to enter.

Afraid to peer into the building's hushed, cold darkness, we nervously moved from one open door to the next, stealing glimpses in, until a uniformed guard ran toward us. I froze, as though caught red-handed doing something I shouldn't, but Pok-sun simply declared that we'd come to practice using a library, as our textbook taught us to. The guard had rushed over, his eyes bulging, to shoo us away, but her composure impressed him: "Ho, you young ones are something . . . " He told us to go to another library because the one we stood before didn't have a reading room for children.

The library the guard sent us to lay close by, right across from what is now the main entrance of the Chosun Hotel.

This building underwent several incarnations after Liberation—at one point, it housed the Seoul National University Dental School—but at the time it was the Seoul City Library, the second largest after the Library of the Government-General. Its imposing solemnity hardly inspired confidence that hick kids like us would be allowed in either, but beside it sat a detached one-story building, the size of a schoolroom, that served as the children's reading room.

There was no special procedure to enter. A man sat at a desk in front, as teachers did at school, and bookcases stood in rows behind him. The stacks were open, and anyone could enter and pick out books. We could take them off the shelves as we pleased, just like at home, and if they didn't interest us, we returned them to their place and chose others. Some kids simply browsed without reading. The man sat facing the children, but didn't order us around. He also spent the whole day reading. It was a world whose existence I'd never dreamed of.

The book I chose that day was *Ah, Cruelty*, a simplified version of *Les Misérables* for young readers. Of course, it was in Japanese, and its beautiful illustrations made reading that much more delightful. It was abridged but nonetheless quite thick, and I couldn't finish it before closing time despite trying to read as fast as I could. We weren't allowed to take books out, and in leaving the book unfinished, I had the sense that I was leaving half of myself behind. The feeling was similar to when Uncle had snatched the comic book from me, but my heart was incomparably emptier this time around. Pok-sun had read and finished *Little Princess*. Bubbling with excitement, we chattered about what we read and agreed to go straight back the next Sunday.

Mother highly approved of my going to the library every holiday and asked no further questions. Although Brother knew that I wasn't studying but reading storybooks, he didn't discourage me, for he trusted the books available there. Reading stories on days off from school brightened my childhood, and Pok-sun and I became inseparable.

I read the tale of the happy beggar who in his dreams became king every night and the unhappy king who likewise turned into a beggar. I also followed Pok-sun in reading *Little Princess*, of course. In this story, Little Princess Sara becomes a servant, but she suddenly finds hot, delicious food and a warm stove waiting for her when she returns to her room at night, like a dream. To me, entering the children's reading room was just like entering this world of dreams.

Outside the windows of this dream world grew poplar trees taller than the one-story building. In summer their leaves gleamed, as though silver coins dangled from them, and in winter their sturdy branches stretched straight up to the cold sky, suggesting a great will worthy of our emulation. In some ways, the joy in reading lay not within the books, but outside them. If I tilted my head from the book I was reading and looked up at the sky or the greenery outside the window, ordinary items I'd seen over and over again took on a completely different cast. The strangeness of things enchanted me.

The teacher put in charge of our class in sixth grade was quite strict. Preparation for middle-school entrance exams wasn't as rigorous as it is today, but after the day's classes were over, we'd stay late to study and take practice tests. Nonetheless, Pok-sun and I kept going to the library on Sundays, hurrying through our piles of homework together on Saturdays. Since we were inseparable, the teacher and our classmates treated us as a pair. Pok-sun was an excellent student, and after she and I became close, my grades improved. Fear of losing my best friend motivated me to keep up with her, I think.

Back then, from fourth grade on, school picnics were turned into study tours. The destinations were the same for every school: Inch'ŏn in fourth grade, Suwon in fifth, and Kaesŏng in sixth. Despite the name "study tour," we didn't stay overnight; we'd just take a train in the morning and return home that evening. I hated the idea of a trip to my hometown. It gnawed at me. It certainly wasn't that I knew everything about Kaesŏng and thought the trip would be dull. In fact, Kaesŏng was just a place we passed through on the way home, and I'd never really had the time to go sightseeing there. What worried me was the possibility that Grandmother or Auntie might come to meet me, since Mother had already written to them about the trip.

Our family regarded sending off and welcoming our own at train stations as a quasi-moral duty. When I went to the countryside during vacations, Mother always accompanied me, leaving my brother with my uncle, but my aunts and uncles saw us off and met us in Seoul and Kaesŏng, shouting at the top of their lungs. The older I grew, the more I hated it. I didn't like that our lives were so intertwined with theirs, and I detested having Mother and Grandmother treat me like a baby.

To buy a ticket to Kaesŏng, we had to stand in the line for Mukden, modern-day Shenyang, which lay on the continuation of the Seoul–Shinŭiju line. Ditto for when the tickets were punched. I don't think the departure times for both destinations were similar, but we took it for granted that we had to arrive hours early at the station and wait and wait, regardless of when our train left, as though such were our sad destiny. A close look at the passengers for Mukden revealed that they were very different from domestic travelers. They had lots of luggage, such as rolls of bedding. The elderly among them dozed off, leaning on bundles that had

large gourds dangling from them, while the children de-
voured roughly shaped mugwort cakes and cooked millet
that had been spread out for them on the floor. Many
groups of passengers consisted of entire families and so
were noisy. They gave off an air of poverty.

Mukden wasn't on maps of our country. I heard that it
was in Manchuria and took more than a full day and night
to reach—of all the foreign names I knew, it was the only
one that I could have reached easily. A sidestep into the
next line is all it would have taken. My heart raced when the
boarding call for Mukden was made. "*Hōten, hōten yuki,*"
came the announcement in Japanese. Murmurs rose from
the queue. The temptation to slip into the disorderly line
and out of the clutches of my family wasn't a longing for the
unknown, but a dream of escape. I was fed up with my family's meddlesomeness, and this drove my friendship with
Pok-sun to become all the more exclusive.

On the day of our trip to Kaesŏng, Mother accompanied me all the way to the station and said to have fun and
not to be too disappointed if no one came to meet me.
What wouldn't I have given for just that? But my heart remained heavy with foreboding that someone was sure to be
waiting for me when the train pulled into Kaesŏng.

My sixth grade had five classes, and we'd been instructed
to line up on arrival in the station plaza for a roll call. At
that point, I heard a loud voice calling my name, "Wan-
suh, Wan-suh!"

Grandmother. Screeching at the top of her lungs. Weav-
ing recklessly among the kids, oblivious to any rules we
might have had. Grandmother, not even Auntie! I wanted
to vanish.

She was dressed in a coarse cotton blouse and skirt,
heavily starched and paddled smooth. On her head she

carried a large bundle wrapped in hemp cloth. I made up my mind to ignore her. I turned my face away, burning with fury and shame, and held fast to Pok-sun's hand. I figured no one else but her would know my name pronounced in Korean. I felt slightly sorry for Grandmother, but I intended to wait out the crisis by shutting my eyes and acting deaf.

But no. When it proved futile to shout my name and ask one kid after another where I was, Grandmother began to call out my name in Japanese, wherever she had learned it. She mangled it so terribly that no one would have recognized it, but I could stand it no longer. I hated myself for driving her to call out something she'd find such a tongue twister. Bursting into tears was the only trick up my sleeve. "Grandma!" I buried myself in her stiff dress and began to wail mournfully. She kept patting me on the back, saying in a weepy voice, "*Aigo*, my baby. *Aigo*, my baby."

We staged an emotional reunion as though we lived thousands of miles apart and hadn't seen each other in years. The kids surrounded us to watch this spectacle. Grandmother unwrapped the hemp cloth, revealing three small bundles of crescent-shaped rice cakes. The cakes were soft to the touch and gave off a whiff of pine needles and sesame oil. I was sure she'd nagged my aunt to spend all night molding them and to steam them at dawn.

My primary sensation in having this scene play out in front of other kids was of humiliation. I wanted to escape this torture. When the teacher's whistle to straighten the lines rang out, Grandmother explained that she'd brought three bundles of cakes—one for my teacher, a second to take to Seoul for my uncle's family, and a third to share with my friends. Only then did she express her regret about saying goodbye to me.

Fortunately, my own teacher had sprained her ankle and couldn't come, so a teacher in charge of another class was guiding us. I blurted out this information to Grandmother in a whisper and pushed her away, saying she should go now, afraid that she might want to greet my teacher. I was gripped by misery, conscious of Grandmother watching us from a distance as we filed out of the plaza, one orderly line after another. Thankfully, Pok-sun, without a word, helped me carry the bundles I'd been laden with.

I was dejected during our sightseeing tour as we moved about from Manwŏl Palace to Sŏnjuk Bridge. I didn't share the rice cakes with anyone at lunch. That I didn't give the teacher her bundle goes without saying. I was old enough to feel a touch of shame at my own shame over Grandmother, but it wouldn't be accurate to say that this was the only reason for my dejection. Half of it was indeed self-reproach, wondering why I was the way I was, but the other half was resentment about why my family had to be the way they were. My family's suffocating clinginess made me crabby and impatient.

Brother was waiting for me at Seoul Station when we arrived that night. I hadn't offered Pok-sun a single bite of rice cake, but she fathomed my warped thoughts and faithfully toted the bundles along with me until we handed them over to him. Brother and I stopped in at my uncle's house near Namdaemun. As my aunt and uncle unwrapped the bundles and carefully divided up the cakes, I was subjected to gushing praise over how hard Auntie must have worked and what a wonderful cook she was. On this depressing note ended my final elementary-school excursion.

7. Mother and Brother

JAPAN'S WOES DEEPENED. OUR LIVES GREW harder. At first, Korean youth were simply encouraged to volunteer, but now they were conscripted. Brother was by then too old to be considered a youth, but a separate labor mobilization system was in place, and the possibility remained that he could be called up at any time. Mother fretted. She lamented that if he'd kept working with the Government-General, he could have had his name taken off the mobilization list. Brother reassured her that she had no need to worry. After all, the Watanabe Ironworks had become a munitions factory. But he didn't seem especially relieved himself.

At the time, a corporal named Yi In-sŏk, the first Korean volunteer for the Japanese army to die in battle, was being celebrated as a hero, and his story became the subject of a *naniwabushi*, or a traditional Japanese ballad. As Japan desperately stepped up efforts to send Korean youth to battle, the song aired on the radio daily. Brother would bark in nervous disgust to turn it off when it came on.

From the second semester, I had to concentrate on middle-school entrance exams. Our teacher had sprained her ankle badly, but as she rested at home, she kept in close contact with our class monitor, sending us tests, marking them, and instructing the monitor how to punish us. Mother was delighted by our teacher, a married Korean woman with a baby. Some Korean teachers used interpreters when they met with parents who didn't speak Japanese. For my teacher to dispense with this formality and sit face to face with Mother was enough to win her over.

The punishment our teacher subjected us to, however, was cruel, unusual, and thoroughly repugnant. Two of the five sixth-grade classes were composed of girls. My teacher encouraged competition between us to raise our marks. If our overall test scores were even slightly lower than those of the other class, we were all punished, no matter what our individual grades were. Our teacher knew how to punish us viciously without so much as lifting a finger: she had pairs of students face each other and smack the other's cheek until she told them to stop.

You might think we slapped our partners lightly. Not at all. If the teacher sensed we were only pretending to hit each other hard, she'd threaten to keep us at it as long as we tricked her, a mocking smile on her lips.

But the real reason our blows grew fierce was that it was difficult not to feel that your partner was getting the better of you. This made us lash out even harder, determined to give as good as we got. It's a hellish picture. Imagine prepubescent girls forced to slap each other until their rosy cheeks swell crimson, their mutual hatred accelerating all the while.

Pok-sun and I were roughly the same height and got similar grades, so we often wound up together, regardless of whether we were seated by height or marks. We'd end up slapping each other more and more violently, gripped by barbaric hate. After a certain point, it didn't matter who was hitting harder; we just felt a merciless whip on our backs, preventing us from stopping. When the teacher yelled "Stop!" our malice instantly turned to mortification, and we were unable to look each other in the eye. The cruelty of it all is a painful memory. Mother commented that she liked our teacher the best of any she'd met because she was sweet. I still find it incomprehensible that such a person could have tortured us so at our tender age.

Mother wanted to send me to Kyunggi Girls' High School. The trouble started when my teacher remarked that I might as well apply if I was interested. I'd never been on the honor roll in those six long years of elementary school, and even I knew that my grades didn't come close to those of the kids whom the teacher had pointed to as Kyunggi material from the start. I'm sure Mother realized this. Ambitious though she was, she wasn't foolhardy enough to take major risks. And so she needed a pretext to lower her sights. She began to express silly resentments, telling Brother that she had a hunch that keeping our Korean name would come back to bite us, and that, if we'd only changed our name, she could send me to Kyunggi. The issue of our name, which had been relegated to the back burner, came up once more.

Mother went to the teacher to confirm her suspicion, but the teacher sidestepped a definitive answer. She simply said that since Kyunggi was a public school, it was conceivable that I could be at a disadvantage if other children had the same score I did, but that there was no written rule giving preference to those with Japanese names. This remark became excuse enough for Mother. I didn't like her giving Brother a hard time, knowing full well that she was being unreasonable. I respected him for putting up with her nagging so stoically and felt it was my duty to help him, even if no one else came to his support. He had principles that Mother and I couldn't fathom.

I talked Mother into letting me try for Sookmyung Girls' High School. At the time, there was essentially free choice in application. Student preference and family situation were taken into account, and teachers used grades as a reference point in their recommendations. One reason I wanted to avoid Kyunggi was that Pok-sun was shooting for it. Maybe being so inseparable wore me out, or maybe I wanted to say goodbye because I loved her, as people put it these days. She felt the same. We were infected by the sentimentality of novels for girls and had the brashness to plot a farewell, promising we'd share more about ourselves in letters.

Mother kept agonizing about our Korean name after I sent in my application forms to Sookmyung. Then she started worrying that I'd fail the physical exam. I could tell she was preparing her excuses in case I didn't make it. Never in a million years would she have been able to say I'd failed because I wasn't smart enough. I have no idea where she heard the rumor that students were rejected if their weight fell below a certain limit, but she started doing everything in her power to fatten me up, and fast.

I had a hardy constitution, but was a twig. Pok-sun, though, was round-faced and chubby. She'd been nicknamed Ōtafuku, or Many Fortunes, after a popular figurine of the time, since *fuku* is the Japanese pronunciation of *bok*, or "fortune." Because we shared everything, the teacher joked to Pok-sun that she should give me some of her flesh. But I couldn't suddenly gain weight just because Mother was anxious. My metabolism wasn't cut out for it. On the day of the physical exam, Mother slipped dense little items like silver rings into my underwear so I'd weigh more.

Thankfully, she didn't bother with the popular customs that were supposed to bring luck in the entrance exam itself, like making me eat taffy or sticky rice. Just picturing what might have happened if Mother had followed those superstitions with the same determination makes me laugh.

We took our entrance exams before graduation. Both Pok-sun and I passed with ease, and continued attending school. Our teacher went through the motions in class, talking about modern-style plays she'd seen and what I suppose could be construed as sex education. She urged those of us who had passed to pay our respects at the Shinto shrine where we'd gone as a group before the exams to pray for success.

One day, Pok-sun suggested that we follow up on the teacher's advice. We were hardly goody-goody students who thought we had to do whatever the teacher told us, and I doubt we had any curiosity about the shrine, unlike the library, but I thought Pok-sun's idea was terrific and readily agreed.

Only a handful of days were left until graduation. We never talked about how we felt, but we both knew that each of us regretted applying to different schools. No ordinary goodbye would suffice. We needed a farewell ritual, but didn't know where to go or what to do. Neither of us had rooms of our own, where we could mimic adults and wallow in sentimentality. The shrine was the only place we managed to come up with.

But the March day we chose wound up being cold and windy, almost like a typical winter day nowadays. Sleet escorted our journey. Not a soul was visible on the high steps leading to the main shrine. We tackled them huffing and puffing, as though in anger, paying no heed to the way our sneakers sank into the slush, soaking our socks and freezing our toes. Untrodden snow made the gravel path upward look almost level. We gave a quick glance at the main shrine and instead made the gentle descent toward Keijo Shinto Shrine. This area was well known as a place for young couples to stroll in good weather, which may have been why it came to mind as having the right atmosphere for our farewell.

The weather was so foul that we didn't meet anyone all day. We couldn't resolve the unspoken tension between us even after we reached Namsanjŏng, an exclusively Japanese district, and gazed off in the distance at the lights that came on one after another in the houses on the other side of Seoul's central avenue.

Our miserable trek of penance brought me to the verge of tears. Pok-sun and I would prattle on endlessly whenever we got together. Even after hours of talking, we still felt we had more to say, but on that day words barely passed between us. We were conscious that we were drifting from each other and tried to recover our original closeness, but in vain. Our goodbyes were awkward, distant. I caught a cold that day and missed school until graduation. Pok-sun never visited me.

Brother offered me an extravagant treat to celebrate getting into middle school. He took me to Hwashin Department Store to dine at a Western restaurant, for the first time in my life. We had to stand in line all day long to get in. The queue began on the ground floor and slowly climbed to the restaurant, four or five stories up.

Those days were the hardest of all for civilians, whom the Japanese had coined "The Rear Artillery." When Brother took me out, Mother commented that I was rolling in luxury. But that's not at all how I felt. I don't even remember the main dish. What comes to me is minimal: even at a restaurant like that, people were cutting in line to get in. There were clean tablecloths. Our soup was served in a shallow dish, rather than a Korean-style bowl. And it was accompanied by two fist-size rolls.

Not only Mother and Brother, but Auntie and Uncle also came to my graduation. Pok-sun received awards for her grades and perfect attendance. I didn't receive any, but no one in the family had regrets. Mother's unshakable theories explained it all easily. Of course I didn't receive an award because I wasn't any good at singing and gymnastics. But I was also obviously a good student, since I'd been accepted into "that fine school," even though we didn't change our name. Mother had given up reluctantly on Kyunggi, which she'd branded "that fine school." But once we settled on Sookmyung and I made it in, Sookmyung became "that fine school." I felt depressed, embarrassed, and angry that so much of my family attended my graduation. I envied Pok-sun for having just her father there.

After the ceremony, we were told that we'd go pay homage at the shrine en masse before parting. Pok-sun and I exchanged a look of dismay. I could tell that she also felt as though this were a desecration of our own rite. Only a handful of days had passed since our excursion, but beautiful spring weather was now upon us. Nary a trace of the sleet we'd struggled through.

Pok-sun and I were expected to stand next to each other until graduation, and so we had no choice but to walk up to the shrine, hand in hand. We'd become even more awkward and distant by that point. My misery deepened because I realized that I was jealous and felt inferior.

And thus Pok-sun and I parted. Only after Liberation did we see each other again, by which time she'd dropped out of Kyunggi to become an elementary-school teacher in the countryside. We'd never even exchanged a single letter. This episode puts me to shame, for it highlights my insecurities all too clearly.

I no longer had to skirt Mount Inwang once I began middle school; now I could take the streetcar. Initially I'd felt no affection for Seoul's bare hills, but I'd taken that mountain path regularly for six years, and I began to miss the cherry blossoms of April, the acacias of May, and the snowy landscape of winter. It dawned on me that I'd enjoyed a rare privilege for a Seoul child. Walking to school alone for six long years had a significant effect on my character. For one thing, I learned how to entertain myself. Even now I prefer to go about by myself unless I'm with those so close to me that I don't have to be conscious of their presence.

The other girls invariably traveled back and forth from school in pairs. Most considered walking on their own a hardship and would wait if their partner had to stay longer at school—for example, when it was her friend's turn to clean the classroom. But I avoided a companion, not because I always preferred to be alone, but because I savored those moments of solitude. In elementary school, I'd come to enjoy the comfort of not having to worry about making conversation. I'd turn my attention to unimportant things, letting my ideas run free, and sink into idle fancies or just observe my surroundings.

I entered middle school during the waning hours of Japanese imperialism. Regular classes lasted for only a few days; almost immediately, we were mobilized to help with the war effort. After two hours of study in the morning, our classroom became a workshop. We sewed buttons on soldiers' uniforms, but our major project involved taking mica and scaling its surface with sharp knives. Pieces came to us by the boxful. They were translucent and in shapes like hexagons, pentagons, or rectangles that made them easier to peel.

No one told us how the mica was used, but we weren't curious. According to one rumor, the mica was intended for airplane windows. Maybe if such a thing as glass air-planes had existed, our work might have had a purpose, but I doubt there was enough material around to manufacture the bodies of aircraft. Nonetheless, the pile of mica in front of us never seemed to dwindle.

Hardship reached a zenith. Brass bowls were collected from every house, supposedly to make cannonballs. One bitterly cold day, we were sent out to gather pinecones. I remember wandering a hill in Shinch'on, eating frozen rice and shivering with cold. We couldn't find any cones. Everywhere stood dead pines stripped of their bark. The denuded land was more impoverished than its inhabitants.

Air-raid drills were frequent. Our school's shelter lay in the dormitory basement, which also housed a furnace and a coal heap. As we filed out, we'd find that our nostrils had turned black. When real air-raid warnings sounded, we were sent home. I would run back to Hyŏnjŏ-dong, terri-fied of being killed on the way. Even on days when we were allowed to go to school without our book bags, we still had to bring a first-aid kit with our name, address, and blood type written on it. We'd keep some very rudimentary emer-gency medicine in it and triangular bandages to stanch blood. We often practiced tying them, but none of us thought they would make any difference with a real wound.

Although newspapers carried stories of the devastation that Tokyo and Okinawa suffered in air raids, more color-ful rumors flew about. The Japanese authorities attempted to control them by prosecuting people who spread false in-formation. Mother, relying on who knows what source, confidently declared that America wouldn't bomb Korea.

One day I returned home to find Mother blanched with fear. Brother's draft warrant had arrived at long last. His assurances that he wouldn't be targeted because Wata-nabe Ironworks was manufacturing munitions had come to naught. Mother was beside herself. She talked of having Brother run away, and then stealing off with me in the dead of night. She had put her confidence in Brother's job and not made a contingency plan. But things had become so harsh that without a ration book even a meal was impossible. The first hiding place to occur to her was Pakchŏk Hamlet, but given that all our papers recorded it as our permanent residence, it was hardly an ideal refuge. In later years, we could have phoned Brother and discussed what to do, but we had no choice but to wait for his return. Each minute dragged on.

Brother did not return until nearly midnight. The factory kept him working late almost every evening. Mother did an admirable job of concealing her anxiety, presenting him with the draft notice only after he had finished supper. He simply said there was nothing to worry about and went off to bed as though everything were normal. We couldn't tell whether he was really confident or just, as usual, being careful not to worry his elders. Mother surely must have been frightened, but she didn't breathe a word all night about Brother going into hiding.

The next day, Brother announced that everything was taken care of: his company had issued a draft exemption certificate for him. Apparently the matter had been officially settled. He'd been ordered to respond to the draft notice within three days, but he continued to go to work as usual without incident. Mother repeatedly expressed her amazement at Watanabe Ironworks and its clout. She found it hard to believe. Just what did the Japanese boss see in my brother, who stubbornly refused to change his name?

Mother's thoughts jumped all around. The violence of her remarks as we sat idly in the dark during blackouts made me nervous; I was afraid that someone might overhear her say, for example, how she wished she could see the Jap bastards collapse even if it meant we all had to die in an air raid. At the same time, she could hardly have been prouder of the esteem Brother was held in by his Japanese employer. I'm sure she wanted to brag, but the situation meant that she had to keep it all to herself.

I first heard the names Syngman Rhee and Kim Il Sung from Mother. On nights when we went to bed early amid air-raid drills or actual alerts, she'd relate tall tales about them as though she were telling me tales of old. She spoke of Kim Il Sung as a general leading the resistance in the vast fields of Manchuria. He was endowed with superhuman strength and had the magical ability to make space shrink, enabling him to travel a thousand *ri* over rough mountain paths in a single night. And Syngman Rhee was a most learned scholar struggling for our independence in America. She explained that he had come on the radio and told us not to worry, because Korea would not be bombed, and that flyers with the same message were being dropped from American planes. She said that the Japs hurried us into shelters whenever a plane appeared, not because they were concerned about our safety, but to keep us from seeing the flyers. She would then laugh mischievously. She seemed less like my parent than a younger, unsophisticated play-mate, as she gleefully contemplated just how hopping mad those flyers must have made the Japs. Despite the gravity of it all, her tone was far from serious. Having Mother speak so jokingly comforted me in the darkness of that single room of ours, but ultimately, her power was limited. She could not offer me the light of courage.

Brother, however, was different. He was very troubled. But we dismissed his concern; it impressed us no end that his company had protected him from the draft.

Brother had used his influence to help a lathe operator find a job at the ironworks. He was older than Brother and married with children, but the company refused to issue him a similar exemption certificate. Brother quarreled with his boss over it, pressing him and demanding to know why, when the company needed a technician like him more than Brother.

We learned all this later when the lathe operator visited us to express his thanks for Brother's efforts, even though they had been unsuccessful. Naturally, Mother was flabbergasted, as was I, that Brother had put another's welfare ahead of his own, oblivious to the potential consequences of sticking his neck out. Brother struck me as pathetically naïve. One anxious day followed another. Every morning that he left for work, we felt we were letting a child go play unsupervised by the edge of a river.

The food ration decreased further. The grain we now received was mixed with soy bean dregs that tasted awful. Mother began going back home more frequently to get rice. As a township clerk, Uncle could elude unreasonable exploitation, as long as he donated a fixed portion of his crop. Clerks like him were generally leading the grain confiscations, and evidently Uncle himself was the target of resentment. That Brother tormented himself over the small show of favoritism he'd received at work was laughable, all the more so since he escaped hunger through riding on the coattails of Uncle's far more shameful privileges.

A disturbing atmosphere had settled over Pakchŏk Hamlet by the time we went home during winter vacation in 1944. Police and clerks had joined forces to search for food, turning the entire village upside down in the process. They carried horrible contraptions that were more terrifying than outright weapons. One was an iron spike strapped to a long pole. They shoved it anywhere—into ceilings, furnaces, bundles of rice husk, and piles of leaves. A rumor circulated that a girl in a neighboring village had been stabbed with such a pick while hiding among leaves. The story was nightmarish. A few days earlier, her parents had heard of a girl being seized for the comfort women corps by a Japanese policeman as she was drawing water. And so when the girl's parents caught sight of strangers in Western suits near the village entrance, they grew frightened and hid their daughter amid the leaves. To have loved ones abducted was far more horrific than having food confiscated. A world in which both could be stolen was undoubtedly spiraling to its end.

Apocalyptic signs were cropping up all over. A childhood friend was married off to a faraway family. Her mother held my hands and wept. Getting married at my age! I was only thirteen. It was common enough in the countryside to marry daughters off young in order to have one less mouth to feed, but the comfort women issue made matters worse. Families with sons wanted grandchildren before the boys were taken into the army.

Uncle had avoided extremes of exploitation thanks to his position, paltry though it may have been, but when all is said and done, it still was disgraceful. As director of general affairs, he didn't personally search for grain, but the grain collectors consisted of low-level clerks and local police, who turned a blind eye at his house. Not that they skipped it. In fact, they drove their instruments into every nook and cranny, poking and prodding more vigorously than they did in other households, but ignoring the rice jars. They were simply putting on a show. The villagers weren't unaware of our privilege. Before these bandits burst upon them, some neighbors handed rice bags over our fence. They would then make excuses when they took them back, saying the rice had been specially set aside for a coming ancestral rite.

Uncle and his family didn't exactly have rice to spare. Nonetheless, supporting us was his top priority, and we grew up thinking that everything in the country home was ours as well. Yes, Brother was heir to the family paddies, moderate as those holdings may have been, but more importantly, Uncle felt a deep responsibility to act as a father to us. What I received from Younger Uncle, who never had children of his own, was fatherly affection. What I got from Elder Uncle, who eventually had four children, was paternal authority and obligation.

"The salt on the stove is useless if you don't put it in the food," goes an old saying. Even if rice had been available for us, it had to be delivered before it could go into our mouths, and that was no mean feat. Police searches on trains were even more thoroughgoing than in farmhouses. Patrols to pry out black market traders often descended on the carriages, jabbing and searching suspicious bundles. Exposure meant humiliation and, of course, confiscation of the contraband. But the inspectors were only human, and since they were nominally looking for smugglers, they didn't make trouble over a handful of rice if those carrying it pleaded that it was for their families. Mother brought a little at a time. Although her travel costs were mounting, we never had enough. She grew bolder. In addition to stashing rice in bundles of clothes, she took to strapping it around her stomach. Every time she went to Pakchŏk Hamlet, I'd be nervous until she returned home safe and sound. Black-market trading was taken as an assault on the economy of the home front and strictly curbed. Control over underground rice transactions was especially tight. But the stricter the controls, the more cunning smugglers became. Tales began to circulate of smugglers who carried several bags of rice in the padding of their clothes.

Our countryside relatives urged us to just apply to transport rice legally instead of going to such trouble, but Brother would have none of it. He jumped in horror at the thought. Landholders were given a card for the right to bring a certain amount of rice to Seoul, but were then ineligible for rations. Brother insisted that we weren't real landowners and that there was no reason for us to refuse government grain and use up rice from Pakchŏk Hamlet. Brother was right, but then again, thanks to Mother, he'd never eaten rice mixed with bean dregs.

I was never treated unfairly when it came to food just because I was a girl, but Mother did cook rice separately for Brother during the emergency period. The smell of bean dregs was so disgusting that she didn't want to scoop his rice from the same pot in which they'd been cooked. Mother and I ate the rice in which they'd been mixed, but of course a distinction existed here as well. At the top of our bowls, we seemed to have a similar proportion of dregs, but the deeper we went, the more dregs Mother's bowl held. I knew, but pretended not to notice because I despised them so much.

In fact, my aunts considered Mother's general refusal to discriminate in feeding Brother and me rather extreme. Boys and girls were treated differently, and so my aunts were snide. Did she think she could marry me off when the time came, raising me as she did?

Mother, as though nothing were amiss, would reply, "Don't worry, her taste buds will be the best gift she has to offer to her in-laws." She never really gave up this belief until I married. Mother thought a daughter should be pampered with good food so she could learn how to cook well. After all, you can't make something you've never tasted. Her ideas were exceptional in an era when appalling sayings were regarded as common sense: "A daughter-in-law with an eye infection is useless, but mouth sores are no problem." Not surprisingly, then, I was the object of my aunties' jibes until I got married: "Those taste buds of hers will make a great dowry gift."

8. Spring in My Hometown

BROTHER QUIT WATANABE IRONWORKS. THE LATHE operator he'd helped land a job wound up being called up for forced labor, while Brother himself escaped. Brother's failure to extricate the technician triggered his own resignation. He was fed up, he said, and would go back to the countryside and farm. No one understood why he was agonizing about it. Why should a white-collar worker risk his own meal ticket to protest? Given the times, there was no guarantee of survival even if you were just looking out for yourself.

At first glance, you might think that Brother put aside his own interests out of a sense of justice. In actual fact, he just wanted a way out. He couldn't tolerate working in a military factory, clad in uniform, gaiters, and boots complete with plated heel and toe.

Elder Uncle had become the township's director of labor affairs. His office supervised the recruitment of young men for conscription as workers or into the Student Na-

tional Defense Corps. If he hadn't had such a plum position, Brother wouldn't have been able to give up his job so
easily. And if Brother relied on Uncle in making his decision, then he was being a baby, not a hero.

Coincidentally, Brother's resignation occurred soon after the order came for the evacuation of Keijo, as Seoul was
called back then by the Japanese. Air raids and food shortages became an excuse to shoo Seoul's population to the
countryside. The order also gave the colonial authorities
a pretext to demolish houses in the city center and replace
them with avenues. Everyone was living in terror, worried
that the food supply would be cut and starvation would follow, or that Seoul would be reduced to a sea of fire like Tokyo. These concerns eclipsed Mother's shock over Brother's quitting his job.

Uncle sent messages urging us to evacuate and come
home. It was important to Mother not to look like we were
returning because we couldn't make a go of it in Seoul. Her
attitude was perfectly understandable given the difficulties
she'd gone through to establish herself. She must have
wanted an appropriate excuse if we couldn't manage a glo-
rious, silk-clad homecoming.

Younger Uncle kept his shop open, but business had
practically come to a halt. Ice was a luxury item, and the
store was empty, save for a few bundles of the charcoal and
firewood that he also sold. But Uncle had an excellent nose
for opportunity. He was doing well as a "black market rat,"
reaping huge profits in the face of danger. The combination of a controlled economy and shortages had—inevitably—led to smuggling. Uncle was another father figure to
us, and his latent financial savvy may have played a further
role in giving Brother the strength to quit. He and Auntie
wanted to flee Seoul with us, saying they'd long been after a

reason to close up shop. As far as I could tell, a smuggler had no need to live in Seoul per se, as long as he could travel around the country on the train and get to whisper in clandestine meetings.

All this took place roughly six months before Liberation. I was about to enter my second year of middle school. The transfer process had been streamlined for the students who were evacuating to the countryside: all you had to do was visit the Student Affairs Bureau, report your destination, and state your preferred school. I applied for Holston Girls' High School in Kaesŏng, and our house with the triangle yard was put on the market. Commuting from Pakchŏk Hamlet to Kaesŏng would have been impossible, so we agreed to find a house in Kaesŏng together with Uncle. None of us was in a position to be holed up in Pakchŏk Hamlet—even a black market rat needed a nest in the city to conduct business from.

Brother had another shock in store for Mother. He revealed his information in dribs and drabs, letting on just enough each time to avoid making her faint. He had found a girl to marry.

"So, got yourself tangled up in a romance, did you?"

It bothered me for her to talk that way. Brother clearly wasn't any happier about it and frowned. "Why do you have to put it like that?"

These days, someone without a love life is considered inept, but Mother had other views. A son might have a lapse and get involved in a relationship, but what kind of girl would be suckered in by sweet talk? Considering what Mother had taught us and that she treated a romantic bond as a full-blown sexual affair, her remark conveyed obvious contempt for the young woman.

Everyone thought of Brother as filial, and being a dutiful son was an important part of his own self-image. His challenge must have come across to Mother as though he were siding with the woman against her. Mother shed tears, feeling betrayed. Brother apologized again and again for his disrespect, but pressed Mother to meet her just once.

She drew a firm line, though: "Okay, you win. I'll have a look. But that's it. I can do that much without losing face, and it won't be any skin off her nose either."

The inspection occurred at, of all places, the Red Cross Hospital. We'd sold our house and were in the middle of packing. The new semester had started, but I wasn't attending school since I'd already finished the transfer procedures. I decided to go along with Mother. Even though the hospital was only a stone's throw from our home, I felt as excited as if we were opening a door to an unknown world. The wave of events that had broken upon Mother all at once left her exhausted.

The woman was in a tidy, spacious, private room. She looked fine, which made me wonder why she'd been hospitalized. Brother had obviously given her advance warning about our visit, for she addressed us as Mother and Little Sister. Mother asked why she was in the hospital. A bout of flu, she replied, but she'd recovered. It all sounded a bit dubious.

Brother had urged us to visit her in the hospital so we could see her before we moved, but had been evasive about what was wrong. We assumed that she'd had an operation and that was why she couldn't be discharged quickly. A girl who had let herself get romantically involved didn't suit Mother's taste to begin with, and on our way to the hospital, she vowed that we couldn't welcome a woman with a knife scar into our home. But nothing suggested she'd been operated on, and she was quite a beauty. It was hard to pin down exactly what made her beautiful, but as people say nowadays, she had class. She exuded charm, in a way different from any women we'd known until then.

I could tell that Mother was drawn to her in spite of herself. Similar pangs of jealousy were gnawing at me, but they didn't prevent a growing admiration for the girl. "Too bad for Mother," I thought. "She'll lose again." Mother already seemed half resigned to the marriage.

On our way home, Mother asked me what the date was. She counted out the days since Brother had resigned, working out events, and heaved a deep sigh. I could tell what she was dwelling on—the pride and expectations she'd invested in Brother as her only son, her desperate but ultimately futile attempts to carve out lives for us in Seoul. That night, Mother curtly asked Brother why the girl was in the hospital, but Brother wanted to hear her opinion about her before he'd answer.

"Oh, I can see how she'd bewitch you, all right!" Mother spat out.

Brother said she'd had pleurisy but had fully recovered and would go home soon.

"Ah, what are you going to tell me next?" Mother moaned but kept her composure. She then grilled Brother with one probing question after another about the woman's background. Everything disappointed her except that she'd graduated from a well-known girls' high school. She was the youngest of four daughters, and although both parents were alive, the family wasn't well off. In the end, Mother's interrogation uncovered that her luxurious private hospital room had largely been Brother's doing. Mother's disappointment and anger welled up, but she seemed to have lost confidence that she could split the pair apart. When she and I were alone, she sought a thread of comfort from me; "Pleurisy doesn't always turn into TB, does it?" Back then, pleurisy generally developed into tuberculosis, a terrifying disease that could spell financial ruin for the whole family.

Several days later, my transfer went through without any further effort. Notification arrived that I should report to Holston Girls' High School. With all the turmoil, I never got to pay a farewell visit to my school before we moved. Brother remained in Seoul. We heard that his sweetheart had been discharged and was recuperating in her hometown.

The house we found in Kaesŏng sat in Namsan-dong below Wardrobe Rocks Hill. Mother and Uncle chose that neighborhood because we'd be making frequent trips to Pakchŏk Hamlet. The house wasn't far from my school either. On my first visit there with Mother, we saw impressive and beautiful buildings of granite set on a hill and a large playing field surrounded by luxuriant greenery. Cherry trees in full blossom made it all seem like another planet. For some reason, I couldn't come to grips with the idea that this was where I'd be attending high school. It was too alien. I was extremely shy and clamped my mouth shut. I didn't even glance at the girl sitting next to me. Often I was on the verge of tears, feeling helpless and infuriated over all the changes that had occurred in the span of just one month.

I went to school for about ten days, but then skipped the next several, feigning a cold. At least I meant to feign a cold. But I actually did develop a slight fever that didn't subside. I went to a clinic nearby and was told to go to the provincial hospital for a chest X-ray, my first. Mother panicked when the X-ray showed a lung infiltration. The very words threw her into near hysteria, and she asked the doctor if my condition could develop into tuberculosis. Possibly, if I wasn't well cared for, came the reply.

I was packed off to Pakchŏk Hamlet together with a bundle of Chinese medicine. I couldn't help suspecting that Mother was unreasonably projecting her fears about Brother's beloved onto me. Until then, Mother would scarcely allow me to miss a day of school even when I was suffering from relatively serious ailments like diarrhea, malaria, or stomach parasites, much less a common cold. I'd taken it for granted that if you weren't on your deathbed, missing school spelled catastrophe. Still, whatever the case, I was delighted to be off to Pakchŏk Hamlet.

For the first time, I realized how beautiful spring in Pakchŏk Hamlet was; I hadn't been there in that season since leaving for Seoul. I'd been an unbridled child, but now I had reached the sensitive age of fourteen. I wandered the hills and fields as if in a trance, friendless. Once I went out with little cousins in tow and gathered a heap of mountain herbs. Nothing made me feel more at peace than going out with a small basket at my side, like the village women. I thought that the basket suited me better than a book bag and that no matter how hard Mother pushed me, I simply wasn't cut out for study. Wasting the care and hope Mother had lavished on me would be a shame, but I had no intention of returning to school.

In my solitary mountain wanderings, I stumbled upon a damp vale where a small colony of lilies of the valley grew in profusion. They filled my heart with yearning. Without realizing it, I'd been attracted by their surreal perfume—so cool, sweet, strong, and elegant that I thought I was hallucinating. Until that point, I'd seen lilies of the valley only in pictures, but here they were, their lush, well-formed leaves carpeting a shady patch. They had white flowers that hung in clusters, like tiny bells the size of rice grains. Their gorgeous scent belied the way their heads bowed shyly.

The lily of the valley was Sookmyung's school flower, and I'd proudly worn a design of one on my chest. Our school song extolled its bashfulness and fragrance. But since I'd entered school at such a difficult time, I'd never actually seen one that was alive. Finally coming upon a real specimen of this flower I'd known only as a vague ideal depressed me. My heart ached all day. What was going to happen to the world? What was going to happen to me? The perfect joy I felt was bound up with awareness that my situation couldn't last forever. I sensed that I could trust neither myself nor the blissful oneness with nature I felt. I had also left an important part of myself behind in Seoul.

Younger Uncle evacuated to Kaesŏng at almost the same time as the rest of us. At first, he and my aunt stayed in the house we'd bought in Namsan-dong, but they soon moved to a rented room of their own. Uncle was a seasoned smuggler by this point and hardly wanted to spend his money on a house, but marriage negotiations with the woman's family had progressed rapidly, and Brother's wedding date had been set. Uncle's move had been partly motivated by concern that their presence might make Brother's bride uncomfortable.

Uncle's trips to Pakchŏk Hamlet came after he'd finished off some major deal, and he'd show up in a terrific mood. I was the most excited on days Uncle arrived. He and I had a much closer relationship than children did with their fathers back then. We'd act more like a loving father-and-daughter pair do nowadays. I played the baby, and he showered me with affection. I was even jealous of unborn cousins, thinking I'd have to behave differently when Uncle had a child of his own.

Uncle fished as a hobby, using a net rather than a rod. When he opened the storehouse door and slung a net over his shoulder, I'd follow him out in high spirits, clutching a basket. It was more than a mile to the reservoir, but there were lots of wading pools and brooks on the way for him to toss his net into. How manly he looked as he made his powerful cast toward the water!

In the local dialect, the net he used was called a "shrinky." It spread into a wide circle in the air and sank heavily as soon as it hit the water. Plumb weights hung at intervals along its edges, and the net would contract as Uncle pulled the string, sweeping fish up within it. Collecting the writhing, shiny-scaled fish filled me with delight. Sometimes, if Uncle was unlucky, the net would catch on submerged branches, and he'd have to swim in and pull the torn net out.

Every once in a great while, we'd manage to trap jumping eels. I found it impossible to keep them in my basket as they thrashed around. Once, we caught an enormous eel. It hurled itself about with such force that we wound up in a frightening do-or-die battle with it; Uncle actually had to throw it on a boulder and bash its head with a rock.

Uncle stopped fishing whenever we caught an eel. He'd say it was for me, and we'd hurry home while it was still alive to debone and roast it. The weather was getting warmer by the day, but the brazier was always going in the kitchen. We'd set a grill over it and then put the eel on it. Grilled with a sprinkling of rock salt, the eel was indescribably delicious. The fat sizzling off it sent up fierce tongues of flame. My cousins would rush over, but Uncle wanted to feed only me, because I was supposed to be recuperating. Ever since I was young, people said I had a strong constitution, but I lacked energy. I've never considered myself especially hardy.

But during that spring and summer at Pakchŏk Hamlet, I was savoring the joy of life and good health. It was as if vital fluids were coursing through my body. Being treated as sickly felt strange, but I was hardly inclined to insist that I was fine. I didn't want to go back to Holston.

One reason I may have been considered infirm was because Mother couldn't pay any attention to me at the time. After sending me off to Pakchŏk Hamlet, she was frantic with preparations for Brother's wedding, preoccupied with welcoming her only daughter-in-law and doing her very best for that most auspicious of events. Nonetheless, doubts about the young woman's health left her more flustered.

"What's wrong with me these days? When I go out to buy something, I forget what I've gone for. I'm so full of worries that I don't know what I'm doing. I'm not even sure we should go ahead with the wedding."

Foreboding swept over me when Mother sighed out complaints like that. My aunts seemed to share her feelings.

"If that's how you really feel, why not just break it off? People say sons are better for a reason. It's no big deal for a man to have a fling. You gave your approval easily enough, didn't you?"

"If I just wanted to ruin someone else's daughter, I could have opposed the marriage in the first place. I've got eyes, you know. I could see that the boy would have fallen apart if I didn't say yes. It's our fate to get a sick daughter-in-law. But who knows? A newcomer just might draw any evil eye destined for my children."

I was stunned that Mother's love for us could be so cruelly selfish. I'd had positive feelings toward my prospective sister-in-law and admired her ever since we first met at the hospital. Mother actually might have felt the same way I did, despite what she said, for she regularly embraced whatever Brother and I liked. The frailty of Brother's fiancée probably troubled her so much because she was quite fond of her.

The wedding day approached. I was almost forgotten amid Mother's worries. Everything happened so quickly that the bride's family sent a message to say it wasn't clear whether the carpenter could finish the wardrobe in time and to beg our understanding in case it arrived after the wedding.

A Western-style wedding had been planned for Seoul, to be followed by a traditional ceremony in Pakchŏk Hamlet. Love had blinded Brother. He wanted to welcome his bride in real style, adhering to all the niceties of social protocol. He wasn't his usual self. I declined from going to Seoul on the ground that I hadn't fully recovered. Instead, I watched how a grand feast was prepared in the countryside.

Early summer, 1945. Liberation still lay a few months ahead, and shortages were at their peak. Nonetheless, a woman renowned as a bridal make-up artist was brought in from Kaesŏng to adorn my sister-in-law in our regional style. She looked so beautiful under her wedding crown that I held my breath. The way her rosy cheeks and lips were set off against her pale skin put the splendor of the crown to shame. Brother wore a triumphant smile that simultaneously expressed pride in his new wife to his guests and pride in Kaesŏng's traditions to the bridal entourage.

The scene of my sister-in-law with her crown made an indelible impression on me, and I recycled my memories for the protagonist's wedding in my novel *The Unforgettable*.

After the wedding, the newlyweds went to stay with the bride's family for a few days in accordance with custom. They then settled down in Namsan-dong. My sister-in-law was unable to bring the wardrobe with her and instead just brought bundles of her clothes, as the difficulties of the era affected transport as well. But Brother and his bride, submerged in honeymoon bliss, were oblivious to the turmoil. Mother was still concerned about her new daughter-in-law's health and spent more time in Pakchŏk Hamlet than in Namsan-dong to make life easier for her.

An unusually long, peaceful summer day from that period has lodged itself in my mind. Grandmother had gone off somewhere, and my two aunts and Mother were all alone together in Pakchŏk Hamlet, a rare event. We'd just eaten buckwheat noodles for lunch, and the three of them were chatting and making papier-mâché containers, some the size of brass soup bowls, others as big as one's outstretched arms.

Making containers from paper had become all the rage in our village. Any traditional paper, from books to the taut mulberry pasted on door frames, would do. Women would first soak it (in water or caustic soda solution, I'm not sure which) until it turned white, then squeeze out the liquid, add glue, and crush it in a mortar. The resulting material was as sticky as clay. They'd then apply it to containers of all sizes, working out just the right thickness, or shape the papier-mâché as they wished and dry it. After a good polish with gardenia dye or oil from cooked beans wrapped in cloth, they became sturdy, handsome vessels. They could turn out surprisingly creative in the right hands. The containers, showing off the craftsman's talent, were used to store grain, seeds, and biscuits.

Elder Auntie got a bright idea from something she'd seen other women do; she pulled out Grandfather's books

from the outer quarters and soaked them in water to prepare material. Thanks to the stockpile of texts Grandfather
had left behind, we had the best supply of papier-mâché in
the village. The three sisters-in-law shared this windfall
with some envious villagers, oozing satisfaction and delight
as they went about their creations. Younger Auntie, quick
study that she was, was applying the material to a large
wooden receptacle on which the traces of a chisel were still
vivid. She was hoping to highlight the grooves through the
paper. Elder Auntie was pasting papier-mâché on a small
wicker jar. Mother was trying to make something from
scratch with no pattern to guide her, but since she kept
failing, her main contribution to the gathering was amusing talk.

The chatter was primarily about Grandfather, since it
was his books that they had reduced to this state. They were
making fun of him for the most part, but the comments
were affectionate enough that I wasn't upset overhearing
them. The containers were hardly the object of their full
attention. I didn't see why they found these reminiscences
so amusing, but they roared with laughter after each one—
how as new brides, they almost fainted when he entered the
inner yard at the crack of dawn, loudly clearing his throat
and clomping about in his wooden shoes; the time he'd
saved a little bit of his beef soup, a rare delicacy, as a gesture
of affection for the daughter-in-law assisting him at the
table. He'd urged her to finish it, but she was at a loss about
what to do because his beard had trailed in it as he ate.

I wonder why they laughed so much. Was it relief mixed
with a sense of hollowness now that their jitters about Brother's wedding had passed—an elusive sense of peace amid the
instability of the times, when it was impossible to predict
what lay even a moment ahead? Or was it a heady sense of

freedom from the authoritarianism that had weighed upon them for half their lives? I was a mere spectator, but the scene remains vivid with me and warms my heart.

Much later, whenever newspapers reported that old books or documents that merited the status of national treasures had been found in the houses of rural scholars, Mother would say with an abashed smile, "What we did was pretty ignorant." She regretted her actions, probably thinking that similar items could have been among Grandfather's books, but I don't particularly agree with how she felt. Not that I take Grandfather's books lightly. Their value as documents was important, but I think it was just as important for my mother and aunts to enjoy that sense of liberty.

Even now, I smile when I think of that occasion. They struck me as free. Cute. Like children. And it's not easy for adults to leave behind such an innocent image. So the old books haven't survived, and neither have the containers. But I believe that the healthy joy that Mother and my aunts felt after blowing off some stress—as people say these days— remained with them until they died. But those were the last moments of peace in Pakchŏk Hamlet. After Mother's visits to Kaesŏng to check on Brother and his bride, she'd say in distress, "Why is her family sending so much medicine, when they haven't even sent anything for the house? It breaks my heart that newlyweds can't get through a single day without the smell of Chinese medicine . . ."

"Sister, you're very odd. Just relax and enjoy the attention and respect you get when you visit. Why do you have to go sniffing around the house?" My aunts accused Mother of being oversensitive, but I had a feeling that something was wrong with my sister-in-law, which couldn't get past Mother's sharp eyes.

Summer was sweltering. I was anxious because I knew I could never bring myself to say I didn't want to go back to school after vacation, considering that I was healthy. I steeled myself for an important decision, but it wasn't easy.

Before school reopened, through, Japan fell and with its fall came Liberation. In Pakchŏk Hamlet, we learned only some three or four days after August 15 that Japan had surrendered. Uncle had reported to work at the township office on August 16, as usual, and didn't come home for two days in a row, although that was common enough behavior on his part. There were rumors that he had a concubine near the township office, but he strenuously denied it: it was work that was keeping him busy. No one gave it a second thought, because that certainly sounded plausible. Back then, low-level government officials were pushed around mercilessly, and Auntie, who should have been most keen to the issue, didn't care in the least.

9. The Hurled Nameplate

ONLY AFTER A GROUP OF YOUTHS BARGED INTO
our house, brandishing sticks, did we learn that Japan had
fallen. Strutting and chortling, the young men set about
smashing our door frames and furniture. Most of them
were strangers to me, but one or two were fellow villagers.

Elder Auntie had lived in the area her entire life and
recognized almost all of them. Although she trembled like
an aspen leaf, she maintained her dignity. "Have you all
gone crazy?" She berated. "What do you think you're doing? Tell me why you're doing all this!"

A young man from Pakchŏk Hamlet lagged behind, unable to bring himself to join in the fray. He told us that
we'd better hide for the time being. Korea had been liberated, and we were a target of their fury because we'd been
branded collaborators.

They'd already visited several other villages, he said. The
youths went from settlement to settlement in a growing
mob; when they wreaked havoc on a house, those from the
same village would hang back and merely watch. Loyalty to

families with which they'd shared well water and festivals and funerals for decades meant that much at least.

As it happened, Brother arrived from Kaesŏng just as our house was being ravaged. He'd hurried back because there'd been no news from Pakchŏk Hamlet since the world had gone topsy-turvy. He was concerned but also eager to share in the collective joy. One of the young men gave Brother a hearty welcome, even in the midst of it all. But just because one familiar face felt sheepish didn't mean the spree of destruction was to be checked. The youths were possessed. One of them smashed our front gate into smithereens, solid though it was, and hurled Grandfather's nameplate to the ground. The nameplate had been part of my life since childhood, having remained even after his death. Neither Uncle nor Brother had ever put up nameplates of their own.

I charged, screaming. I'm not entirely sure why I found it so hard to put up with what he'd done, given how blithely I'd stood by when Grandfather's books were reduced to containers. This was the first violence I'd ever witnessed, but I wasn't frightened one bit. I felt I wouldn't mind battling to the death. If Brother hadn't shown up, I can picture myself having bitten someone and then fainting. When I was younger, my uncontrollable temper had led me to faint on more than one occasion.

Brother dragged me to the back of the house and up the hill behind it, while Auntie and Grandmother pounded the ground, wailing. Several of the young men, flustered, were trying to calm them down. They did not look as though they were genuinely intent on hurting anyone. Still, Brother's behavior stunned me. With breathtaking naïveté, he politely asked them to mind the safety of their elders and led me off. Once we were up on the hill, I screamed at him, "What makes us collaborators? We didn't even take a Japanese name! It's like pigs wallowing in shit complaining about muddy dogs. Who do they think they are? Tokuyamas, Arais, Kimuras . . . and they dare to smash a house of the Pannam branch of the Pak clan?"

Brother looked down helplessly as our house was ruined. Eventually, the angry mob had enough and withdrew. He stroked my shoulders, trying to make me understand, but I was determined to argue. I don't remember in detail what he said, but basically he explained that the Tokuyamas and Arais had experienced persecution, suffering, and humiliation, while we'd been privileged. He'd been too ashamed to hold his head high before the young men of the village, but would feel less shame now that we'd been the target of their anger.

Finally, I fell silent, stricken with grief. Brother hadn't persuaded me, but as my futile rage subsided, a sense of emptiness swept over me. I was devastated to see our home ravaged. How we'd loved that house! Brother encouraged me to let it all out in tears before we went back down.

The destruction that day came from the sudden release of pent-up energy that accompanied the lifting of repression. In other words, the spirit of carnival rather than the organized violence of revenge was at work. After the young men made the rounds of several villages, they calmed down. Our fellow villagers were very sympathetic and cooperative. They helped to make our house livable once more, helping us fix broken doors and furnishings. All this was before partisan politics—the Democratic Youth League, the self-defense corps, leftists, rightists—distorted people's inherent good-heartedness.

Uncle returned. As gossip had it, he'd been keeping an eye on events from his concubine's. He took a look at our house and commented that things wouldn't have come to this pass if he hadn't become the director of labor affairs, although he'd had no alternative but to accept that notorious position. Uncle's lone contribution was to lament water that had passed under the bridge. When someone who earns a living by pushing papers around has that taken away from him, he's useless. Far more helpful were the villagers who hammered even a single nail into our door frames.

Discontent was brewing in our household. And misfortune never arrives unaccompanied: my sister-in-law started vomiting blood. Brother took her to Seoul, and Mother and I hurried to Kaesŏng. We couldn't just leave the Namsan-dong house vacant, and, in any case, we had to get ready to move back to Seoul too. Younger Uncle and Auntie had been renting a room, so nothing prevented them from returning to the capital quickly. They soon followed Brother. Uncle was full of high hopes, saying the times held all sorts of promising business opportunities.

As Mother cleaned the house that Brother and his wife had abandoned so hastily, she muttered to herself, sighing and shedding tears. The bride's furniture hadn't arrived yet. Nothing, in fact, suggested that the home belonged to newlyweds. Maybe I imagined it, but I thought I could sense in the clutter the duress that Brother and his wife were under, as though the house had been a hideout for fugitives. We kept finding Chinese medicine and natural herbal remedies, one bundle after another. And as if it wasn't disgusting enough to contend with the dried remains of enormous centipedes, longer than my outstretched hand, maggots were feasting on them.

Mother disposed of it all, hands shaking, face drained of blood; "Did I bring up my son just to witness this?"

I had trouble understanding Brother. He must have known his wife's condition better than anyone. Even though the strain of newly married life was said to be catastrophic for the tubercular, he'd rushed into the wedding as though driven, instead of helping her recover first. Neither Mother nor I ever learned why, but who can confidently claim to understand the overwhelming passions of youth? It was possible that Brother hadn't told us not because he wanted to hide his motives, but simply because he couldn't explain them himself.

The first foreign troops to occupy Kaesŏng were American. I went out to watch as they entered the city. Their relaxed marching style astonished me—chomping gum loudly, winking at women, hoisting children in the air. What kind of military discipline was this?

Around this time, we began to notice posters on the street walls. They contained words I'd never heard before, marvelous words like "liberty," "democracy," and "citizenry." Slogans ran rampant. Some advocated punishing pro-Japanese elements and national traitors, while others expressed political sentiments such as "We absolutely support so-and-so" and "We'll oppose so-and-so to the death."

Brother's wife had been admitted to Severance Hospital. He sent a message telling us to move to Seoul as soon as we sold the house. Mother went first to take in the situation. Upon her return, she acted with even more urgency, saying that the scene had been painful to watch. My sister-in-law was being nursed by her own mother, but she was old and in bad health herself. Mother said we should take care of Brother's wife because she was a member of our family now. Mother, of course, must have been distressed about Brother and the way he clung to his bride, anguishing over her health.

While we were preoccupied with her illness, Younger Uncle was busy making the most of his talents. He'd taken over the house of a Japanese acquaintance and said he could help us out if we wanted to buy a property like it. He pressed us to sell the house in Namsan-dong, even if we had to practically give it away, and to hurry to Seoul.

Around the time we sold the house, the American forces suddenly pulled out of Kaesŏng. The explanation was that they'd initially entered the city because there had been an error in drawing the thirty-eighth parallel. Soviet troops arrived. Before the Americans came, I'd often heard arguments about whether it would be better to have American or Soviet soldiers around, for the thirty-eighth parallel passed so close to Kaesŏng that it was hard to predict which side would occupy it. No one remotely imagined the binding power that abstract line would come to have.

The American soldiers, in contrast to their boisterous entrance, slipped away unnoticed. But when the Soviets arrived, the world suddenly turned menacing.

Rumor had it that they commandeered any watch they spotted, with some sporting more than ten on their wrists. A word derived from Russian, *dawai*, came into vogue. People turned it into a verb and started bandying the term about, saying that a marketplace had been *dawaied*, that vegetable patches had been *dawaied*, even that women had been *dawaied*. Supposedly foreigners couldn't tell the age of Korean women, so the Soviets went so far as to violate the elderly.

Mother was generally indifferent to this atmosphere of fear, perhaps because she had so many worries of her own. She made it sound as though everyone were overreacting. The railway was near our house, and day by day the number of people who trudged south along it grew. At that point, people could still move back and forth across the thirty-eighth parallel as they wished, so it was before anyone from the North headed across specifically for freedom. Most of the travelers were Koreans, whom dire poverty had driven to scatter to Manchuria and beyond, returning home. They had no choice but to walk, because after the Soviets' arrival, southbound trains from Kaesŏng had been discontinued. No one knew why. All the wayfarers looked tired and hungry. The lucky ones had at least managed to catch a train as far as Kaesŏng; others had made the entire journey on foot.

The rail system was in utter chaos. We were told we'd have to walk the entire way to Pongdong Station in order to get a Seoul-bound train. Frequently, I saw women whose husbands or sons had been conscripted standing around and watching the human procession all day long. Sometimes they stopped travelers to ask where they had come from and when they'd left.

Quite a few Japanese moved among the crowds. When their identity was exposed, some spectators would curse them or spit on them, saying they deserved their misery. The hardships experienced by Koreans coming home to a liberated country were every bit as arduous. Scenes of anarchy were part of the daily fabric of life.

I began to read novels in Korean. For the first time, I became curious about the Korean novels that lay among Brother's books. Most students my age didn't know how to read Korean and were frantically hurrying to master our alphabet. I felt pride and an odd delight in my ability to read without difficulty the posters and flyers pouring forth. My pride in what should be taken for granted—knowing one's native script—sparked my first interest in Korean literature.

The first book I read was Yi Kwang-su's *Love*. I had been attracted by the title. Then I read his novel *The Tragic Story of King Tanjong* and, after that, *White Flowers* by Pak Hwa-sŏng and *Tale of Escape* by Ch'oe Sŏ-hae. I also read one of Kang Kyŏng-ae's short stories, although I've forgotten the title. The works that made the strongest impression were Yi's *The Tragic Story of King Tanjong* and the tale by Kang. I couldn't fall asleep after finishing the tale of King Tanjong, while Kang's story was so disgusting that it turned my stomach. I actually lost my appetite for several days. The story describes how a baby, whose head is covered in boils, is treated by having a rat skin placed on him, like a hat. In the end, maggots wind up swarming all over his head. I'd grown up in an environment in which soybean paste was applied to burns, but the image was so gross that I felt like vomiting.

Until then, reading had allowed me to transcend my daily reality and immerse myself in joyful fantasies. This new experience of reading, however, was totally different. Korean literature pushed me to look at the world and its ugliness in a harsh, glaring light.

The Tragic Story of King Tanjong may have been fiction, but I accepted it as fact and was spurred to learn about our history systematically and in greater depth. Afterward, we studied Korean history at school, and as an adult I read several history books by different authors and from various perspectives, following my whims. I acquired the knowledge purely for its own sake. As a result, it's a mixed bag, essentially useless, like a desk drawer into which things have haphazardly been thrown. The one era I feel I have some accurate knowledge of is that between King Sejong and King Sejo, but this is probably an illusion entirely rooted in *The Tragic Story of King Tanjong*.

Given the critical nature of the input kids get when they're able to absorb everything like a sponge, I am slightly resentful about how barren my intellectual life was back then, within both my family and the larger society. Yet only after reading Kang Kyŏng-ae's stories did I begin to feel grateful to Mother for her ability to raise us lovingly and rationally in the midst of poverty.

Summer retreated. Light blankets became necessary early in the morning and late at night. Mother and I were at last able to leave Kaesŏng. But with the city still occupied by the Soviets, no trains were departing for Seoul. Some said we should head to Pongdong Station; others, to Changdan—all of it speculation. The only thing that was clear was that no southbound train left from Kaesŏng. Pongdong lay twenty *ri* distant; Changdan, fifty. There was no way we could take everything we needed, even by carrying bundles in each hand and on our heads. We were determined to walk dozens of *ri* if necessary and couldn't afford to be concerned with possessions. Fortunately, the person who bought our house didn't have a large family and agreed to hold our furniture for the time being.

To reach Pongdong, we had to cross Yadari, Kaesŏng's best-known bridge. The name derived from the ancient word for "camels," *yakdae*, which were tied there by Arab merchants who came to trade at the height of the Koryŏ Kingdom. I imagine that few Kaesŏng children, when they were scolded, avoided the taunt that they'd been picked up as newborns under that bridge. I was something of a crybaby since early childhood, and so adults often teased me: "Looks like they got you over at Yadari!"

We were far from the only wayfarers with bundles heaped on heads and backs. A large crowd filed toward Yadari, similarly laden. The scene was not unexpected now that it was the only way to get to Seoul because the trains were no longer running. The spot had always been busy with traffic to the capital, as it was. Soviet soldiers guarded one side of the bridge; Americans manned the other.

But the soldiers did not control passage or inspect travelers. Some young women, mindful of frightening rumors going around, covered their heads with dirty towels. They stooped deeply as they passed, but in fact both the Soviet and the American soldiers, with their brown hair and light brown eyes, merely looked amused. No line drawn in the middle of Yadari indicated the thirty-eighth parallel. Not so much as a straw rope was draped in the center of the bridge to mark a border.

At that point, we still had no concept of how formidable the thirty-eighth parallel would come to be, but soldiers automatically provoked fear in us, a lingering remnant of Japanese rule. We passed both sets of troops with frozen expressions and racing hearts.

Despite the absence of any official notice, a crowd had gathered at Pongdong Station. We also decided to wait there instead of traveling on to Changdan. There was no ticket booth, so we just went out to the tracks. Patiently, we waited.

At long last, a train arrived from the south. The crowd surged toward it, boarding more through the windows than the doors. Any windows that were shut were shattered. Many had already been smashed. Mother hoisted me up and pushed me through a window as someone pulled me in. I then struggled desperately to help Mother clamber in. We certainly didn't anticipate getting a seat, but the wreckage that greeted us was a shock: windows without glass, torn seats with twisted frames. Given the anarchy of the era, the mayhem might not have been so unexpected, but I couldn't understand why even plush seat covers had been slit open, exposing not just dirty stuffing but frail frames. Some passengers took it upon themselves to vent self-righteous fury, demanding to know if this was the meaning of Liberation.

The train kept stopping and arrived in Seoul only after a very long journey. Once we reached Shinch'on, people began to disembark. We followed their example. I think everyone was worried what might happen if we turned up at Seoul Station without tickets.

We settled in with Uncle at his Japanese-style residence for the time being. Thankfully, my sister-in-law was doing much better. Her doctor said that all she needed to do now was take good care of herself. She had gone to stay with her parents in Ch'ŏnan. We had to find a place of our own in a hurry, if only for her sake.

I couldn't warm to Uncle's house, although it was the sort of two-story dwelling I'd dreamed of. My shame in living there made me so uncomfortable that I might as well have been sitting on a pin-filled cushion. I had the sense that we were breaking the law, for I knew all too well from newspaper editorials and warnings issued by the American military government that there was to be no trafficking in goods or houses used by the Japanese. Enemy property belonged to the state. We were told not to cooperate with Japanese attempts to sell or to assert any form of preemptive right over property. Brother felt even more uneasy than I did. In this lay a point of difference between Uncle and my immediate family.

Most of these Japanese houses were occupied by shrewd wheeler-dealers, and so real estate in Seoul had become extremely cheap. Adding the money from the sale of our home in Kaesŏng to the sum Uncle lent us, we were able to buy a house along Shinmunno, near downtown. Even at the time, it was the most expensive neighborhood in the city. And so, just as Mother had long wished, we now lived within the gates of Seoul itself.

The house stood on good, flat land and was quite swanky—new and well ordered, with a gleaming tile roof. The house even came with a bath, a rarity in those days. We bought beyond our means, perhaps in part because Brother, with a new husband's vanity, refused to give up on the dream of a happy life with his bride.

Mother set about decorating the newlyweds' bedroom in earnest and waited for her daughter-in-law's arrival. Meanwhile, I returned to Sookmyung Girls' High School. I was accepted without a problem, as though I'd just been temporarily absent; the roster for roll call still had my name on it. Since Liberation came during summer vacation, many students from the North had yet to return. Their seats were kept vacant in expectation of their arrival. I could scarcely believe that my leave of absence had lasted just a semester—so much had happened in the meantime.

School hadn't changed much. The Japanese principal and teachers had vanished, of course, but astonishingly the teacher who had taught Japanese stayed on to teach Korean. In the terminology of the time, what is now middle school was actually called high school. Second-year students were busily learning the syllabic combinations of the Korean alphabet. Although the teachers scolded us, any time we had something complex to express, it was Japanese that rolled off our tongues. Other than school textbooks, our reading material was almost entirely texts written in or translated into Japanese.

I was able to own a set of literary works for the first time. I'd long dreamed of possessing all thirty-eight volumes of *The Complete Collection of World Literature* put out by the Japanese publisher Shinjo. One day, Brother had the set delivered for me. The books had, of course, been discarded by Japanese who'd fled in haste. Market vendors were awash with daily necessities and books that had been likewise sold off dirt-cheap or left behind. Common as these books may have been, owning the complete collection seemed like a fantasy come true. But I also felt burdened. I don't know where it came from, but a sense of mission weighed on me. I felt compelled to read them all, from beginning to end. And although *Quo Vadis* and *The Count of Monte Cristo* were so much fun that I could barely put them down, *The Divine Comedy* and *Faust* were so difficult that I'd never have made it through them if it weren't for this blind zeal of mine. I don't think that it did me much good to force myself to plod through, however. Even though I didn't understand those books, at least I felt I'd read them, and so I never bothered with them again. When people say they like such books, I always wonder whether they really understood them. I'm left torn between doubting others and doubting myself.

Next I received *The Complete Works of Tolstoy*, which Brother bought at a used-book store. My first impression on seeing the solemn brown jackets was that I couldn't possibly read them all. But over a long period, I did read Tolstoy's major novels—*Anna Karenina*, *War and Peace*, *Resurrection*. And read them again and again. They became very important to me. I rarely reread books, even if I really enjoyed them or found them too difficult to fully comprehend the first time through, but Tolstoy's works were an exception. Although they were initially hard to understand, there was something compelling about them and they piqued a growing interest within me. I think it's because, above all, for the first time I was enthralled by the power of excellent characterization. Besides, the atmosphere at home had turned somber once again and pushed me to lose myself in books.

Despite Mother's and Brother's concerted preparations to welcome my sister-in-law into the house, she was unable to go through the motions of being a young bride with us for even a month. Her parents hadn't sent her furniture and belongings. Although I know this left Mother feeling self-conscious before her acquaintans, she never let on. Later, she would profess that she'd done well to be patient and say nothing, as she'd been plagued by ominous premonitions. Brother's in-laws knew that his wife's condition was far worse than we assumed. They must have decided that it would create problems to leave so many personal items behind in the event of tragedy. Once more, my sister-in-law was admitted to Severance Hospital. This time she never returned.

One morning, I woke early to the sound of wailing. Both my mother and the mother of my sister-in-law burst into sobs as soon as they entered the front gate, for they had been unable to cry freely at the hospital. Her mother had come to our house to weep without restraint. To describe how heartbreaking her wailing was would be pointless. I had known that my sister-in-law's death was imminent, but the pain was overwhelming nonetheless. How could someone die so young? I was filled with dread, as though the loving world I inhabited was plunging into an abyss.

My sister-in-law's death occurred in the spring following Liberation, less than a year after her marriage. Brother and Mother had done all they could for her, and more. Their efforts were enough to bring tears to anyone's eyes. Our relatives were concerned but also criticized Mother. Why did she devote herself so to caring for the bride, instead of separating the couple out of consideration for Brother's health? Mother's answer was that she had failed to separate them before they got married; once the young woman became a member of our family, she wanted to do as much for her as if she were her own child. I'm told that before closing her eyes forever, my sister-in-law expressed moving, heartfelt thanks to Mother.

This side of Mother was new to me and thoroughly unexpected, and it became an important watershed in my developing pride in and respect for her. At the same time, because my sister-in-law received such devoted care, I longed for and romanticized tuberculosis even after I was old enough to know better. As an adolescent, I harbored the dream of falling passionately in love with a consumptive.

10. Groping in the Dark

AS A TEENAGER, I'D SEEN HOW PASSIONATELY devoted Brother was to his bride, but love between a man and a woman remained a mystery to me. Normal, natural sexuality was even more puzzling. I'd grown up with a mother who'd been widowed young, so I'd never witnessed parents acting affectionately or the birth of siblings. What's more, Mother's extreme views on propriety meant that any time a remark with the tiniest sexual connotation was made in my presence, she'd leap to her feet in horror: "How can you say that in front of a child?"

Both my uncles may as well have been immediate family. They shared all their possessions with us and every experience, good or bad. Yet when we were together, they treated their wives with complete indifference. Only after I grew up did I understand that, in keeping with the manners of the day, consideration for my widowed mother affected the way they acted.

But I must have been quite young when I realized that making a baby required intercourse. No particular incident stands out in my mind; I assume I just picked up this information naturally. I saw animals at it often enough when I was little, and my countryside playmates were quite precocious. Still, I was loath to admit that that was how I'd been conceived, and I refused to imagine my uncles having such a side.

Even now, at times I blame Mother for my tone deafness and my unusually poor motor coordination. Her pride in my being a poor singer and gymnast obviously played a formative role. Likewise, I'd bet that my great shame in my teen years of erotic thoughts and even the rudimentary knowledge I had about the birds and the bees stemmed from Mother's wish that I remain a child in terms of my sexuality.

My uncle's concubine was said to be a widow as much as ten years his elder. Rumors of their relationship surfaced only after Liberation. It was easy enough to understand how they'd become close, as she lived with a daughter in an isolated village between the township seat and Pakchŏk Hamlet. Everyone thought she'd seduced him, for a position like his—the local director of labor affairs—would have offered her a substantial safety net. Auntie even tried to be magnanimous and show pity for the woman. The issue, however, proved more complicated than that.

After Liberation, Uncle lost his job as a matter of course. But our home had been handed down from generation to generation, and to have it ravaged left him feeling wronged and resentful of the other villagers. He was unable to accept coming back home and farming. Auntie had quickly patched up relations with our neighbors and could even ask for their help in repairing our home despite the pro-Japanese stigma it was tainted with. Uncle, however, became aloof and kept his distance from our village. He didn't stay with the widow, since in the countryside, nobody's business

was secret. What limited power he'd wielded as a civil servant evaporated when he was dismissed, and he'd never
amassed a substantial sum. I think Auntie was secretly
pleased with Uncle's misfortune—a pity he'd lost his job, to
be sure, but she assumed the concubine would now turn
her back on him.

However, the widow had some land and was taking in
some interest through small loans she made. She left the
countryside and its gossip and bought a small house in
Kaesŏng, openly becoming Uncle's concubine once she
settled in the city. This stirring of the hornet's nest turned
our household upside down. We were shocked. Furious. We
bad-mouthed her for wantonly taking in a man, although
we'd been as charitable as could be when we thought she'd
become Uncle's concubine to support herself. My own
dirty imaginings, gathering steam amid the family's barrage of crude abuse and lewd conjectures, jolted me.

The woman refused to live in hiding. She boldly allowed
her identity to be known and over time started to assert her
position even more brazenly. Uncle was now living with her
in Kaesŏng, and anyone who wanted to see him had to go
to her home. But she soon began to win over his visitors
with her warm hospitality. Eventually, she was appearing in
Pakchŏk Hamlet on important occasions like Grandmother's birthday. And when it came to chipping in materially
and with her own labor, she was twice as filial as Grandmother's formal daughters-in-law. She stole Grandmother's heart. An old proverb says it's the concubine daughter-in-law who gets offered the embroidered cushion. And
such proved to be the case in our family. Tension between
Auntie and Grandmother hung in the air.

But this bleak development didn't prevent me from going back to Pakchŏk Hamlet during vacations. Once con-
firmation came that Kaesŏng indeed lay south of the thirty-

eighth parallel, travel to Seoul was allowed, even though the Soviets had replaced the Americans as the occupying force. I went home partly to see Grandmother, but partly because I hated to even imagine spending my entire holiday in Seoul. I no longer had to have Mother accompany me, but just like when I was a young girl, my heart soared with the approach of vacation. Pakchŏk Hamlet offered me a physical and spiritual lifeline. Going to the countryside governed the rhythms of my body and soul.

But now I faced uncomfortable obligations. When I disembarked in Kaesŏng, I had to stop in at the house of Uncle's concubine. So Grandmother wished, and although Mother's pride took a beating simply in acknowledging the presence of a concubine in the family, she said I had no other choice. It was the only way I could see Uncle. Even Auntie sharply distinguished between jealousy and a sense of duty and sent her children to visit their father.

Uncle's concubine was extremely kind to our family. She won over Grandmother, stickler for propriety though she was. When I went to visit, she'd rush out in stocking feet to welcome me, as though she'd spotted a flower in midwinter. She fawned over me, showing off her tremendous skill as a cook. But the more she fussed, the more I swore to myself that I owed it to Auntie to snub her, if for no other reason than to maintain loyalty to Auntie, who did not have a smidgen of guile in her soul.

But I couldn't suppress a strange curiosity about her. When they were together, Uncle was completely different from the stern man I had known. His eyes sparkled, and he was talkative and full of jokes. Instead of being embarrassed about the relaxed picture he presented, he appeared to revel in it. What wiles had she used to tame him? The affectionate way they acted stoked lewd, disturbing thoughts in someone like me, who'd grown up without seeing husband and wife in harmony. Even after I left their house, I'd be caught up in self-loathing, as if I'd been contaminated.

During my third or fourth year of high school, there was a long delay on one train trip home. Disruptions had begun to occur immediately after Liberation, and several years later problems still remained. Trains now habitually ran late. In winter, passengers had to tremble in unheated cars whose windows, more often than not, were broken and sit on the skeletons of seats whose covering had been stripped. On that particular day, the delay was extreme, and I didn't arrive until dusk. Traveling the twenty *ri* home by myself was out of the question. Having a potential refuge in Kaesŏng was reassuring, but I dropped in at the woman's house, taking it for granted that Uncle would accompany me to Pakchŏk Hamlet. However, Uncle showed no intention of setting off after our hearty dinner, and his concubine took it equally for granted that I'd stay the night. I had little choice but to keep my mouth shut.

Although her daughter slept by herself in a room in the back, the woman insisted that I stay in the main room, clearly considering it the best hospitality she could provide. While I didn't like the idea of sharing with her daughter, the prospect of sleeping in the same room with Uncle and his concubine terrified me. This terror likely reflected my burning curiosity, but since I felt ashamed of my curiosity, I acted as nonchalant as I could.

They spread bedding out for me on the warmest part of the floor and lay down nearby. After the light was turned off, I pulled the covers over my head and pretended to be sound asleep. Nonetheless, every single fiber of my nerves was on alert. I had no doubt that, for the first time in my life, I'd witness something physical occur between a man and a woman. I wanted that knowledge, although I feared being sullied by it. But all the two did was chat, tittering over nothing, with Uncle doing most of the listening.

Their talk was of a prosperous country household that had come to ruin. I was bored at first, as I was waiting for something else, but gradually I was drawn into the story. The family had a daughter-in-law, a young widow of outstanding beauty, known for her haughtiness. The gist of the tale was that she had an affair with a servant and became pregnant, blackening the family name. The concubine related the complex story with strokes of detail that kept me riveted. At the end she mused, "Now, just what would make an icy lady like that cuddle up with such a lowlife brute?" Then she giggled and giggled. Her lewdly suggestive tone made me shudder.

Nothing happened between Uncle and his concubine that night. An adolescent girl's imagination can be a lot dirtier than a middle-aged couple's sex life. Long after they fell asleep, I had trouble drifting off. Tingles ran down my spine as I pondered the inexplicable power that had drawn together a haughty beauty and a lowlife brute. I suspect this was my first whiff of lust, from a world still dark to me. The story I overheard that night stayed with me for a long time. Several decades later, it became a key subplot in my longest novel, *The Unforgettable*.

Those days were difficult for me, not only because of my family, but because of the political situation. Words like "freedom" and "democracy" were surging everywhere, but only recently had our eyes opened to take an unflinching look at such dazzling objects, objects we'd never expected to encounter.

Confrontations between the right and the left were intensifying all around us. Rallies and sloganeering were constant. "We Unconditionally Support So-and-So. "We

Absolutely Oppose So-and-So." A student council was established at school, and we'd hold meetings for the slightest reason. In keeping with the overall environment, we decided that some teachers should be kicked out as collaborators, while resignations from others should not be accepted.

I think we had the illusion that freedom and democracy meant unlimited rights for students. We frequently boycotted classes, and the entire student body would gather in the auditorium for heated discussions. The foundations that supported schools were located mainly in the North, and so now many institutions were struggling financially, but we didn't care in the least. In our immaturity, we just added to the confusion. But that period was important for us.

We engaged in passionate debates and then put issues to a vote. There was one senior whose logical way of expressing herself stood out, and I remember a girl in my class whose opinions carried a lot of weight. We held a meeting when our new principal was due to arrive. For no special reason, the sentiment was that we should reject him and support the former principal. But the matter was hardly ours to decide, and the newcomer took office as planned. We rebelled to the end, staying in our classrooms instead of going to the auditorium for his inauguration. In retrospect, our actions strike me as similar to the university demonstrations of recent years.

But the new principal more than proved us wrong to have opposed him. He curbed the chaos by revamping the school in expert fashion. He brought in excellent teachers and gave us the chance to take fascinating classes, completely different from the ones we'd had under the Japanese.

This tumultuous period at school ended relatively quickly. I never spoke out during the meetings; all I would do was clap or raise my hand to side with the majority. Nonetheless, I think of those days as the end of my childhood, the time when I began to look with some awareness at what was happening in the world around me. In reality, our strident opinions were about school administration matters we likely had no business to meddle in. You might say that we were simply suffering an inevitable stomach upset as we tried to digest the freedom and democracy that the U.S. Military Government regaled us with as bountifully as their flour and candy.

But I was trying to use ideology to understand it all and looking at the turmoil through the lens of confrontation between progressives and reactionaries. I had a firm conviction that my personal allegiance lay with the left and that it was the left I should applaud. As you might guess from the way absolutes were inserted into every slogan back then, people felt uneasy if they didn't have an ideology to cling to. Brother's influence was decisive in aligning my sympathy with the left.

This is not to say that Brother actively worked to raise my consciousness. He'd had a reputation for being smart since he was young. He was also handsome, careful in his words, and loving, and, as eldest grandson, would carry on the family name. Naturally we thought the world of him. He was a tremendous source of support to me, an idol. My desire to imitate him was unquestioning. That I hoped to fall in love with a consumptive because of Brother's own tragedy tells you everything you need to know.

After Brother's wife died, he became more reserved. Even in this, he seemed admirable to me, however. He came across as the only high-minded member of my otherwise vulgar family, and I included my uncles in that. My heart pushed me to believe that only I could fathom the loftiness of Brother's thoughts. I longed to comprehend

him fully and to emulate him. And so my eagerness made it
easy to ferret out his political leanings—or, to be more precise, easy to see that every book he bought had a leftist tinge.
I chose only the simpler ones to read, but those thin pamphlets were enough to influence me, since they were easy to
follow and stirring.

I still remember one story about a longshoreman in
France who became a Communist activist. One day, he was
told to dump sacks of flour into the sea rather than offload
it. Despite receiving the same pay, he was torn: How could
this happen when so many of the poor went hungry? He
learned that it was a plot to keep prices high by reducing the
grain supply, because capitalists feared that wheat prices
would fall as a result of that year's bumper crop. Realizing
that those driven by the profit motive did not care if the
masses starved, he began to hate capitalists and became a
top revolutionary. The story dazzled me, as though opening my eyes to the world afresh. I wanted to use my enlightenment from these clear, straightforward truths as a yard-
stick to measure everything against. And it was reasonable
to think that Brother would not be satisfied with just reading those agitating pamphlets.

Our family left him alone, afraid to aggravate his pain
over his loss, but he became harder and harder to understand. He would invite a roomful of strangers over and
sit whispering with them. Sometimes they trooped out en
masse to head who knows where. At other times, they wrote
crude, fierce slogans denouncing the mayor of Seoul, the
chief of police, and Syngman Rhee. Then, under the cover
of darkness, they would paste them on fences and telegraph
poles. Once I'd discovered Brother's handwriting on se-
ditious flyers on my way to school, I knew for certain that
his political beliefs mirrored my own. But that gave me
little pleasure. Brother deserved to be a bigwig; it hurt my

pride to imagine him skulking around at night to paste up slander.

But not long after, Brother wound up on the run when a genuine bigwig was arrested. Mother sobbed and begged for Younger Uncle's help. Uncle, in turn, requested a favor from a connection. The reply came that it was safe for Brother to return home, but from this point on persistent conflict broke out between Mother and Brother.

Mother tended to adopt our tastes and beliefs without questioning them. If I spoke favorably about teachers or school friends, she would take an immediate liking to them and remember their names. Conversely, instead of scolding me when I bad-mouthed or showed dislike toward others, she hated them more passionately than I did. I'm sure that she would have preferred to agree with Brother in all that he did.

But she was unwavering in her belief that a Red's actions would ruin himself and his family. As she understood it, a Red's primary goal was to oppose Syngman Rhee, and she always emphasized that she had that much sympathy with the cause: "I don't like the man either. But shouldn't we give him a chance to be president? After all, he's an elder who's fought for independence all his life. It's no wonder Reds are so disloyal. They don't even respect their own parents properly. I hear they call them Comrade Mother and Comrade Father."

Mother's cajoling just provoked a bitter smile from Brother, who didn't respond either way. She sighed: "Fine. Go ahead and call me Comrade. Just tell me what you're thinking."

It was taken for granted that those arrested for leftist activity would be tortured until they were broken. Mother had never even spanked Brother. She was plagued by the nightmare that he'd be tossed in jail and beaten half dead.

She detested having suspicious characters murmuring conspiratorially at our house. She blamed everything on them and seemed to think that Brother would come to his senses if she could just shield him from them.

A police investigator came to our house on Shinmunno looking for one of Brother's friends. That was it. Mother suddenly made up her mind to sell it.

We moved to a smaller house in Tonam-dong. Brother no longer had an income, and we were relying on Uncle to make ends meet. By then, Uncle had brokered all sorts of deals, and, as the situation stabilized, he'd begun to think about starting a business that would be a safe bet. A building with a large storefront and living space came up for sale along an avenue with tram tracks, and Uncle wanted to buy it. Mother's idea, then, had been to move to that smaller home, volunteer the remainder from our house sale to Uncle, and in return receive money to live on from him with a clear conscience.

As the saying goes, "You don't stretch your legs unless there's room for them." Only when it looked certain that money would be available did Brother apply to enter the night program at Kukhak College—the college of "National Learning." But Mother and Uncle regretted not giving him a college education, and they urged him to attend a better school during the day instead. Uncle tried to talk Brother into attending a prestigious private university. I'm not sure whether to believe it, but Uncle implied he'd paid to finagle a spot for Brother. Maybe he had. It was all the rage to go to university at that point, and quite a few students from my high school attended, long before their official graduation. Mother and Uncle eagerly welcomed Brother's entry into college. But they were more interested in the opportunity for him to get himself out of the leftist movement than in academic credentials.

Brother's motives were not at all what Mother and Uncle wished, however. He had no intention of pulling away from the leftists; he wanted a general education, buoyed by the wave of enthusiasm to learn more about Korea, which was cresting in the wake of Liberation. In fact, leftist organizations in colleges were much stronger than their counterparts in society at large. Mother pinned a strand of hope on sending Brother to college only because she was clueless about what actually went on.

In the end, we never had a chance to settle in comfortably in Tonam-dong and wound up moving almost yearly until the Korean War broke out in 1950. As soon as Mother judged that our home had become a den for subversives, she would pull up stakes in near hysterics. Once we absconded in the middle of the night, leaving behind our furniture and kitchenware, and went to stay with Uncle. If Brother ever wrote an account of his revolutionary struggle, the way those types like to, and been honest about it, he'd have had to admit that its most heroic feature was his struggle with Mother. I was caught in the middle and unavoidably torn: I supported and cheered Brother, but pitied Mother.

When the academic system changed, secondary education was lengthened from four to six years. Because attending secondary school for up to six years could get boring, some students dropped out and married, while others, as I just mentioned, went to university. It was considered acceptable to pull strings to get in, either because we were in a transitional period or because we'd been admitted under the older four-year system.

In my third year, I learned that our school had a Democratic Youth League. I don't know how I came to its attention, but when a student I wasn't friendly with invited me to join a reading group, I immediately understood what she meant. I accepted without hesitation, even though I was slightly nervous. Being given instructions on how to find our secret meeting place certainly satisfied my desire for intrigue, but the texts and discussions we shared weren't up to the insight I obtained from the pamphlets I'd already read. I was very disappointed but content: I had become Brother's comrade-in-arms.

May Day arrived. Leftists held an event at Namsan, and right-wingers gathered at Seoul Stadium. The members of our group were ordered to skip school and go to Namsan. I had trouble making up my mind whether to participate. Thoughts of Mother held me back, but rallies, demonstrations, and chanted slogans held no appeal for me, regardless of political views. My individualist streak regularly came in for harsh criticism at our reading-group meetings. I recognized it as a weak point that I'd eventually have to overcome.

Finally I made up my mind. I skipped school and went to Namsan. The grand rally aimed at mobilizing as many workers and students as possible. We shouted out violent slogans in response to the leaders' cries, and endlessly sang along with songs of the masses. I returned home that evening, thoroughly drained. Unable to hold out against Mother's probing questions, I confessed what I'd been up to. Mother was mortified. She dredged up all sorts of frightening scenarios, gleaned from who knows what source: Did I have any idea what happens to girls who are sent to prison? She persisted. She discouraged me from going to school the next day—she'd phone to say that I'd been sick and would have to miss the next few days as well. I was being a coward and I knew it, but I succumbed to her pleading.

I asked around while I was absent and found out that the students who'd missed school on May Day were called to the teachers' lounge and interrogated. If it came out that they'd gone to Namsan, they were harshly reprimanded. Their parents were summoned and had to appeal to the school for forgiveness. Other schools handed over students who'd attended the rally to the police, but thankfully ours was more moderate and treated it as an internal issue. No one tipped off my attendance, so nothing happened when I finally returned to school several days later. I escaped both questioning and punishment.

For a long time to come, I was ashamed of myself. I'm sure I must have looked completely spineless to my friends. The thought drove me into deep self-loathing. Not only did the teacher not suspect me, but no one in my class imagined that I'd participated in a leftist rally. Did their obliviousness come from seeing me as some straight-arrow, model student? I felt like a hypocrite. No more contact came my way, although to this day I'm not sure why. Did the Democratic Youth League collapse, or was I ostracized?

Whether all the upheavals for my family affected me or not, I became half-hearted about school. I wasn't interested in friends, the major concern of adolescent girls, their primary cause of joy and sorrow. I don't even remember who my friends were at that point, for that matter, or what I did with them. My only comfort came in reading. I weaned myself off political works and gravitated toward Korean literature. I never bought any of these stories, but simply picked them out from Brother's bookcase. I was still under his influence. The one literary journal he read was entitled, plainly enough, *Literature* and published by the leftist Literary Writers' Union, since Brother's standard for deciding what books to buy was ideology.

Of the books I read from Brother's collection, a piece by Kim Tong-sŏk stands out for me, although I'm not sure if it was a work of criticism or an essay. His prose was clear and easy to understand. At that point, I still struggled with Korean texts, because my sensibilities had been cultivated with Japanese novels. One particular passage of Kim's that spurred my interest and agreement was about the *Tale of Ch'unhyang*. He refutes an interpretation that the work's vitality lies in Ch'unhyang's chastity and argues that the true power of the story—the source of its wide audience—instead resides in the poem that Yi Mong-nyong writes before revealing himself as a secret royal emissary at Pyŏn Hak-do's feast: "The fine wine in gold goblets is the blood of the people / the flavorsome food on jade plates is their fat."

Considering Brother's books, it must have been a work that analyzed class struggle. I never saw the name Kim Tong-sŏk once he was blacklisted after the war. With the recent thaw between North and South, however, most banned writers have been reinstated and their books are available once more. I've looked carefully for Kim's name but still haven't found it. Maybe he wasn't the great critic I'd thought.

Before the war, we moved three times within Tonam-dong itself. I assume that Brother's deepest plunge into leftist activity occurred when we lived near Samsŏn'gyo, but that's only a guess on my part. The South Korean Workers' Party was then at its most dynamic in directing an underground movement. Brother was a man possessed. He had changed so completely that he no longer seemed part of our family. He even prepared an escape route in case he was caught by surprise at night.

The kitchen of our house near Samsŏn'gyo had a back door that led to a narrow passageway between our fence and our neighbors'. The passageway was just wide enough for a person to squeeze through and ended in one direction at a high brick wall facing the street. If you went in the opposite direction, a labyrinth of an alley passed backyards all the way to another neighborhood. To reach that neighborhood by the usual route took much longer. If Brother ever had to flee quickly, he'd obviously use this shortcut, so sometimes Mother went out to look for obstacles in this dark maze. She patted herself on the back, saying, "We'd be in a real pickle without this escape route." But in spite of the advantages the house offered Brother, we suddenly up and left, less than a year after we'd moved in. Fortunately, I suppose, Brother wasn't the sole reason for our departure.

The house had four rooms. We each took our own bedroom, and Mother rented out the room closest to the gate since we needed the money. Her concern for Brother made her scrutinize prospective tenants closely. Nonetheless, despite her pains, the family that moved in turned out to be quite like Brother. Although they didn't seem badly off, the father didn't have a job. Soon enough, it dawned on us that suspicious people were gathering in their room. Mother immediately realized that we had a Red in our midst. Brother had stopped offering our house as a hide-out, so naturally Mother was dumbfounded when the tenants' room became a plotters' den. Brother had nothing to do with it. Mother blamed it on an evil spirit that was lurking about the house. She was inconsolable.

But Mother never thought of sending the family packing. She even worried about them, the way she might have sympathy for fellow sufferers of a disease. Not long after, the police surrounded our house and led the man away. Mother quickly abandoned the house in a state of shock and joined Uncle. She reacted like country folk who burn down a house in which everyone has died during an epidemic. Nonetheless, she was happy to allow the man's family—his wife, son, and daughter—to stay on until the house was sold.

11. The Eve Before the Storm

UNCLE'S PROPERTY LAY NEAR TONAM BRIDGE AND faced an avenue where streetcars ran. It had space for a shop and large inner quarters as well, so all five of us could live together without too much discomfort. I even got to have a room of my own. During our stay there, talk of a second marriage for Brother went into full swing. Our relatives often grumbled that Mother wasn't hurrying to arrange another wedding or, at the very least, make him stop his activity with the underground. I'm sure Mother would have liked nothing better than to do both, but she also wasn't prepared to take on projects doomed to failure. After all, she knew her son better than anyone.

Brother turned a deaf ear to arranged meetings with prospective marriage partners. But one day in a relative's house, he happened to set eyes on a young woman who was kin to a distant cousin. When someone asked in passing how she would do as a bride, Brother perked up. He asked me to look her over, but discreetly, so she wouldn't realize that she was being checked out. Although spying compromised my dignity, I was thrilled that Brother had come to me first. Fueled with a sense of mission, I hid near her house when I expected she'd be coming in and out and caught a glimpse of her. While she wasn't pretty as such, she projected intelligence, radiating strength and confidence rather than femininity. My impressions thoroughly satisfied Brother.

We were getting anxious because our Samsŏn'gyo house was slow in selling. After our tenant's arrest, his wife took the children to his family's home in the countryside and the room by the gate remained empty. Still, there was enough time between when our house was sold and when we moved to our own house again for Brother and his new bridal prospect to get to know each other. And so by the time we moved out of Uncle's, we'd welcomed a new family member into our household.

In my fifth year of secondary school, our class was divided into three streams: liberal arts, science, and home economics. We'd already been split into three homerooms when we were admitted, but now we were also divided evenly by major. I picked liberal arts without giving it serious thought. This track felt most congenial to me because I liked reading so much. It was hardly because I had literary ambitions at that point. Several girls in our class thought they had potential as writers and poets, and others agreed. Under the previous academic system, we'd have already graduated and gone to college, so now was the time for talent to bud. But I wasn't one of the talented ones. Girls with a conspicuously literary sensibility struck me as belonging to a world I'd never be part of.

The teacher in charge of the liberal arts stream was a novelist named Pak No-gap. He had just joined our school, and, as it happened, at that very moment his work was being serialized in the newspaper my family subscribed to. Although I'd read many novels, it was the first time I'd ever seen an author in the flesh. I was excited to have a genuine writer as a teacher. I searched Brother's bookcase and came upon a short story Mr. Pak had published in *Literature*. Discovering my teacher's work in this left-wing journal gave me a sense of affinity with, and sympathy for, him. I owed those feelings to the way Brother set himself apart from the mainstream.

Back then, special preparation for university entrance exams didn't exist. In the liberal arts stream, we spent several hours a week on literature and creative writing. Mr. Pak took charge of those classes, in addition to Korean. While he was my homeroom teacher, he published a novel called *Forty Years*. I made it a point to seek out and read his works, but they didn't influence me much. They were no fun, and I had to force myself through them. However, he was very strict in teaching writing style. What he hated most was passages overladen with emotion and strewn with exclamation marks—"Ahh!" "Ohh!" He abhorred them. You could almost sense gooseflesh rising on his skin as he tore into them. And, of course, he despised cliché. Until I met him, the only view I'd encountered was that literary flair meant knowing how to trot out flowery, sentimental language, and the girls who were deemed "literary types" had the knack for these turns of phrase. The usual attitude made Mr. Pak's tutoring stand out.

He gave me the wherewithal to conquer my inferiority complex toward "literary types" and to believe in myself as a writer. For the first time, I had a teacher I liked. Although his large, clear eyes conveyed the impression that he was strict, when he smiled this austerity vanished and his expression was like a child's. In winter, he usually wore a *turumagi*, a traditional long coat, but the fabric was inferior—stiff, coarse cotton, dyed black. Nonetheless, Mr. Pak taught Chinese characters as well, and when he got carried away by his own emotions as he recited classical poetry in his sonorous voice, that black *turumagi* suited him brilliantly.

Our liberal arts course turned out to be fun and free-wheeling. Some of my classmates hoped to major in literature or art at university, but the rest were more interested in having a good time than studying hard. Our desks were arranged so that two students sat together in the central rows, while a single desk lined the windows on either side. I was assigned a window desk that faced the school field. I sat alone but became friendly with the girls in front of and behind me. In front of me sat Han Mal-suk, who made her literary debut and became well known long before I did, and Yi Kyŏng-suk, who grew up to become a professor at Seoul National University College of Music. Behind me sat Kim Chong-suk, later a novelist and prolific translator. The four of us got to be good friends, and we'd fool around together during class.

When any of us brought an interesting novel, it would make the rounds among us. We'd hide it inside our textbooks and read it during class. If the teacher called on us, we'd wind up answering with some non sequitur that made the others laugh. From time to time, we passed notes among ourselves about fresh ideas we'd had. Days like that flew right by. Han Mal-suk brought in collections of stories by the Japanese writer Ryunosuke Akutagawa one by one, and we took turns reading them, entranced. At this point, though, I don't have the foggiest idea why we were so taken with them.

Kim Chong-suk's family ran Chongno Bookstore, the forerunner of Chongno Books. From her I borrowed *Literary Arts*, a serious journal, and, sometimes, new books. Back then, books weren't published anywhere near as frequently as they are today. I was filled with envy whenever I stopped by the store, for all those books seemed to be hers. Although it was Korea's biggest bookstore, it was family run, with all the members pitching in at the cash register, doing bookkeeping and minding the customers. Her grandfather always stood watch in the middle of the store during my visits. He made me nervous. Looking back, I can see I may well have been hoping for a chance to make off with a book or two.

I did have other talents besides being able to read a novel while pretending to pay attention in class. I was also good at sneaking into theaters and watching movies that were off-limits to students. Tongdo Cinema sat kitty-corner from Uncle's shop. They gave him free tickets in return for putting up posters on his shop windows and walls. He'd then hand them over to me or tempt me into accompanying him. I became a regular there and saw every new film.

I kept my patronage of Tongdo Cinema hidden from Mother and my classmates, but I visited other movie theaters with my friends often enough. Even in the dark, our white uniform collars stood out, so we'd tuck them inside our jackets and pretend that we weren't students. No one who bothered to look closely would have been fooled for a moment, but we still felt the thrill of thinking we'd gotten away with something.

Once Chong-suk and I went off during the day to the movie theater in the Hwashin Department Store. When a teacher was absent or had other business to attend to, class was canceled. That day, we had no class for two hours back to back, so we decided to skip out on school and go to a movie we'd been eager to see. My pulse raced every time I snuck, collar stealthily tucked away, into the mysterious darkness and its expectant murmurs. Skipping class made it all that much more exciting.

Immediately after Liberation, the power supply from the North had been cut off. Although the situation improved slightly afterward, electricity still went out frequently. That day was especially bad. Every time the film got interesting, the screen went blank and whistles of protest rang out. The management did its best to placate the audience, quickly bringing in a singer to perform an operetta of some sort on the candlelit stage. We patiently waited, leaving only after the movie had completed a cycle and reached the point when we'd entered. Neither of us had a watch, and so we were unaware how much time had passed. We certainly had no inkling that it would already be dusk.

We raced back to school. It was barely a stone's throw from the cinema, but by the time we arrived we were panting, our hearts pounding. The classroom had already been cleaned and was empty, of course, save for the two book bags atop our desks. The blackboard held a stern order for us from Mr. Pak: go immediately to the teachers' lounge. We rushed down, but all the teachers had left for the day. The nerve that led us to the theater had evaporated. If I didn't see Mr. Pak that very evening, I thought, I wouldn't be able to sleep. Chong-suk shared my naïve anxiety. There was always a teacher on night duty to keep an eye on the school property, so we went to see him. We were so desperate to find out where Mr. Pak lived that he took out a stack of faculty dossiers and showed them to us. The information included not only our teacher's address, but a hand-drawn map to his house.

I discovered that Mr. Pak lived in my old neighborhood of Hyŏnjŏ-dong. A lump rose in my throat, and my affection for him surged. The teacher on night duty seemed to know the area and said that it wasn't one where we'd find a house readily from a map. I thought, though, from studying it that I had a general idea where it was. I was confident I could find it, but I didn't explain to Chong-suk why. I just said, "Let's go." It wasn't entirely a sense of shame that kept me from admitting I knew Hyŏnjŏ-dong. I was also worried that locating the house might not prove as easy as I hoped.

The streetcars were still running, so we made it as far as Yŏngch'ŏn at the bottom of the hill. But finding the house did indeed take a long time. The neighborhood had changed a lot since I'd lived there, and at night the convoluted alleys seemed to twist more than ever. I pretended that the area was new to me, afraid that Chong-suk might make some disparaging remark about it.

Finally we found Mr. Pak's home. It had a tiny single-door gate, and from the outside, the impoverished household was in full view. His wife told us that he hadn't returned yet. As we explained why we were there, my respect for him became more intense. Mother scolded me for coming home late, but the next morning when we went to see Mr. Pak in the teachers' lounge, he didn't make an issue of what had happened. He graciously said that we shouldn't have troubled ourselves to come to his house over something so trivial. Afterward, I felt as though a special bond had been forged between the two of us, a solidarity based on Hyŏnjŏ-dong.

Around this time, Brother had a son. The arrival of my nephew was just about the most blessed event possible for a family like ours with few male offspring. My uncle could scarcely contain his joy. The baby might as well have been his own grandson. My family was full of praise for Brother's wife. Her arrival was now seen as a stroke of great fortune, and not simply because she'd given birth to a son to carry on the family name. The anxiety that had haunted our family eased once she joined us. Brother hadn't pulled out from the underground, but everyone could see that she coped sensibly, neither fussing nor reacting frantically like Mother.

She supported Brother fully but had no qualms about reminding him that as head of the household he had duties that he tended to neglect. Just as you could know how precious rice was only when you'd gone hungry, she'd say, you could struggle for the proletariat only if you'd eked out a living. My sister-in-law had a unique way with words; she made Mother and me feel as though she were speaking on our behalf, but in a compelling way that gave no sting to Brother's pride. I suspect that Brother felt immediately attracted to her because he'd sensed her intuitive skill in dealing with men. He badly needed advice and comfort in those days.

Brother kept his distance from the underground. What was more, he had apparently joined the National Guidance Alliance, a government-sponsored group for reformed Communist sympathizers. He then got a job as a Korean teacher at Koyang Middle School in Shindo in Koyang County, not far from Kup'abal. It's never been clear to me whether he joined the National Guidance Alliance to land a job or he became a member once he started working, but I believe there was a psychological and material relation between the two.

Almost a year had passed since the South-only election that established the Republic of Korea. The most fundamental policy of the fledgling state was not merely to crack down on leftists, but to eradicate them. Staunch Communists faced heading north across the thirty-eighth parallel or going to prison. At least the alliance had been set up as a way out for idealistic, innocent sympathizers. Brother made his decision to join, whether coaxed or coerced, without consulting the family. We learned about it only when he got himself into an inebriated stupor one day like some kind of ruffian.

Brother threw a ridiculous temper tantrum. He wasn't himself at all. Of course, in his defense, he was dead drunk. He bawled, blaming Mother, as if he'd deserted the leftists and joined the alliance all for her. After his tirade, he passed out. Mother just gazed at him sadly and muttered, "What's with you, getting all liquored up and maudlin? This isn't like you." This was the biggest insult she could fling at her son; she'd never even violated the superstition not to walk around his head as he lay sleeping. Nonetheless, she seemed to fear the consequences of Brother's ideological about-face more than he did himself.

Afterward, out of Brother's earshot, Mother let on how anxious she was. She'd made a nuisance of herself trying to get Brother out of the clutches of the left, but now she had tinges of regret. She even displayed a lingering attachment to the cause. I'm still not sure why. Was it one of her usual contradictions—fear of an outlawed ideology and concern for Brother's safety, but a desire to believe in the importance of a cause he'd risk himself for? Or was it an ominous premonition that sparked her loyalty?

Her attitude took me by surprise. I was quite cheeky and teased her as a "watermelon": hard-shelled right-winger on the outside, Red on the inside. Although she tried not to let on, it was clear that Brother's desertion made her miserable for a long time, and she grew more tiresome than when she'd been doing everything in her power to get him away from the leftists. Not even motherly love was immune from being sucked into the ideological struggles of the day and becoming nightmarish. I'd rather not dwell on this ugly period.

Today the school where Brother taught stands within Seoul itself and near a subway line. Given transportation in the late 1940s, though, commuting wasn't a real option. He stayed at a boarding house near the school and cycled home once a week, arriving on Saturday afternoon and leaving again early Monday morning.

Although the school wasn't an agricultural institution, its holdings included a considerable number of fields and paddies. On payday, along with his salary, he received enough rice to last for a month. Brother would ride home proudly, rice bag strapped to the back of his bike. Sometimes potatoes or sweet potatoes were thrown in as a bonus. Back then, staples accounted for a high portion of a family's expenses; this new contribution immediately stabilized our finances and gave Brother newfound confidence. He gradually shed the shadows that trailed him and became a typical head of household, with all the requisite qualifications.

The first thing Brother did when he came home on Saturdays was hurry to the public bath in front of our house. It wasn't just because it was next door. He'd wind up coated in dust as he cycled home through the city streets, and his devotion to his son made it impossible to cuddle him in that state. After bathing, he'd change into a loose, comfortable outfit and become completely engrossed in playing with his little boy. Meanwhile, my sister-in-law would send adoring looks at the pair as she cooked, delicious smells wafting from the vegetables and fish sizzling in the kitchen. I felt isolated from their circle of three, but not in a way that triggered jealousy.

I, too, relished the peace that had returned to my family after so long. I felt a languid sort of joy, as though I were soaking in a soothing hot pool. Only Mother seemed odd. One might have expected her to be the most relieved of all, but not so. Her attachment to the past that Brother had disavowed surfaced spasmodically. Pouring the grain he had brought from school into the rice chest, she'd sigh, "Our gullets are gang lords." She implied that Brother wouldn't have defected if he'd been free from concern about feeding his family. Maybe Brother's drunken outburst had turned into a thorn that pricked her now and then. Or maybe the peace and self-sufficiency we were enjoying for the first time in so long was so precious that she feared losing it. She herself seemed aware of this; every once in a while, she'd sound me out.

"Your brother is acting like a real Commie now, isn't he? What could be more Red than 'wokking' like a dog, day in, day out, to keep your family from starving?"

Her tone was enthusiastic, obsequious even, as though she were excusing him not to me, but to some evil eye that had witnessed Brother's desertion. Her deliberate mispronunciation of "working" as "wokking" was strange. She spoke impeccable standard Korean, but the way that word grated suggested that she did it intentionally. When she referred to the South Korean Workers Party, she always gave it an ugly ring, stressing "Wokkers."

But I think she meddled in Brother's ideological beliefs only because they were against the law, not because she had any real understanding of the Communist Party. In fact, her lack of sophistication led her to a generally favorable impression of Communism, which explains why Brother's decision to leave the cause troubled her more than Brother himself. Mother equated conversion with betrayal, and although she couldn't bear the thought of a fugitive son, she must have found a traitor more distasteful. She'd up and move houses in a spasm—a clever trick she'd hit upon to cut off Brother's contacts, without having him branded a turncoat. Her fear of breaking the law surpassed any aversion she ever had toward Communism.

This mention of betrayal calls to mind a more recent incident, some forty years after the one I'm describing. Before my mother passed away, a leg injury kept her virtually housebound. Although a devout Buddhist, she could no longer make temple visits. Her only hobbies were watching television and reading. She liked to look at the books I owned when she came and stayed with my family. After I embraced Catholicism, she came to enjoy Bible stories written for novices and books of meditation designed to nurture faith. She said they were very good and even kept some at her bedside to reread. I once asked whether she had any interest in converting. Not only me, but all her grandsons and their wives had become Catholics long ago, and she'd never objected when, one after another, we took on a new religion. My suggestion almost felt belated.

To my astonishment, serious displeasure appeared on Mother's face. She scolded me furiously. How could her own daughter say such a thing? No one had ever doubted that she'd serve but one husband when she was widowed at age thirty. No one had even pitied her. I immediately, albeit with some difficulty, stifled laughter at her absurd comparison. How could religious conversion possibly be like fidelity to a deceased spouse? But suddenly incidents from days gone by that I didn't want to remember came flooding back. It dawned on me that her proud, tenacious chastity had discomfited us at unexpected moments. It lurked viciously behind the cozy family harmony that Brother had labored to achieve.

After that encounter, I never again entertained the idea of urging Mother to convert. I never even saw her reading Christian books again. She obviously thought that she'd lose face in front of me if she, a Buddhist, showed interest in books espousing belief in Jesus. Mother was tiresome. But we most resemble our families in those aspects we most dislike about ourselves. Just as Mother feared losing face before Brother and me, I, too, struggled to maintain dignity before her. I had the most trouble when it came to the books I'd written.

The first thing I did to prepare for one of Mother's visits was put my own books on top of the bookcase, spines turned inward. When she entered my study to look for something to read, she could easily have asked, "Where are all your own books?" But she never did. I had the vague impression that she might have gotten hold of them through other channels, but I never gave her one. Irrational as it sounds, I felt reluctant to reveal potentially embarrassing aspects of myself to her, even if I exposed them to the rest of the world like an exhibitionist.

When I was serializing a novel in a newspaper, it wasn't easy to keep what I'd written from Mother's eye. The best method for both of us was to pretend that nothing was out of the ordinary; she and I were adept at reading each other's mind without a word. After one of my books came out in the *Dong-A Daily*, a magazine reporter pressured me for a joint interview with my mother. I turned her down. Our relationship was not such that I could dismiss her flatly, however. I tried to get out of it politely by saying that she'd need Mother's agreement. But soon I heard that she'd received Mother's permission, although it hadn't been easy.

My mother then lived in Hwagok-dong, so I accompanied the reporter to her home. Mother answered the questions put to her with aplomb, although it was her first interview. Inwardly, I couldn't have been prouder. As a wrap-up question, the reporter asked whether Mother had read my serialized novel.

"We subscribe to that paper, too."

Mother, assuming a haughty expression, began by stressing that it wasn't my work that made her read the newspaper. I smiled bitterly. The answer was vintage Mother. The reporter then prompted her for her impressions of the novel. My heart shriveled. I'm usually dauntless and critics' comments, good or bad, roll right off me, but Mother's next remark, pointed and cold-hearted, stung me for a long time to come.

"Well, I don't know if I'd really call it a novel."

My heart thumped, and my face burned. It was like standing in front of a bonfire. I nursed my resentment by pledging never to make such a hurtful remark to others.

Enough digression. Let me bring my meandering back to when we lived in Tonam-dong, behind the public bath.

In my eyes, the nervousness that occasionally percolated to the surface in Mother was unreasonable. There was nothing to be afraid of. As far as I was concerned, Brother had finally found his niche. Our years in Hyŏnjŏ-dong had left a deep impression on him, and he simply had to stay true to his roots, because he felt indebted to that neighborhood and its residents. An innocent sense of justice might have spawned his leftist sympathies, but he was too weak and fond of comfort to put his beliefs to the test. While the people of Hyŏnjŏ-dong were making gruel out of bean dregs, not having enough to eat their fill, he'd invited me out for a Western meal to celebrate getting into school, and he saw to it that his tubercular fiancée had a private hospital room.

Needless to say, Brother wanted to give his son, the apple of his eye, a secure upbringing. It made no difference that the organization he'd belonged to condemned this longing for security as petit-bourgeois. Brother and his change of heart were as transparent to me as Mother was. I may have had no worldly experience whatsoever, but I at least had the arrogance of my youth.

In 1950, I turned nineteen. I was part of the only graduating class for whom high school's golden final year lasted just nine months. Starting with Liberation in August 1945, and continuing until 1949, we followed the American academic calendar, with the school year beginning in September. Under the Japanese, the year had begun in April and ended in March. In 1950, however, in a transitional measure to bring the end of the school year back to March, the calendar was shortened by three months, and we finished in May. My high-school class was the only one to have had the good fortune of a May graduation. When I see university entrance examinations falling in the dead of winter or admission ceremonies and graduations held on chilly early spring days, I realize how lucky we were.

That May was particularly beautiful. Unlike nowadays, flowers didn't bloom seemingly at random. Leaves, like blossoms, came out only in May, the season of lilacs, peonies, roses, and wisteria. The school compound was redolent of flowers and buzzing with bees. For the first time in all my years of education, I made the honor roll and received an award at graduation. Mother, Brother, Sister-in-law, Uncle, and Auntie all came to the ceremony to celebrate. I was elated, although I acted blasé. I had aced the exam to enter the Korean Department of Seoul National University's College of Liberal Arts and Sciences. At the time, pure academics were stressed, perhaps a remnant of Japanese imperialism, and SNU's College of Liberal Arts stood at the top of the ladder, billing itself the "college of colleges." Only after the war did trends move in favor of more applied studies.

Having passed the entrance exam without putting any effort into it, my arrogance became irrepressible. I was floating. Few students went on to college back then, so there were no cram schools. After a couple of practice runs, we were left to our own devices in studying for the exam. All I did was borrow a book of potential questions, thanks to Chong-suk's generosity. The book, printed on pulp paper, was quite bulky and unwieldy. Another friend was waiting her turn, so I concentrated on the book for just three or four days. It seemed to neatly sum up what we'd learned. I don't know what happened to the book after we were done with it. It might have been sold at Chong-suk's family's bookstore, just as with the novels we shared. My family could have afforded a copy for me, but I think adolescent vanity about passing the exams while pretending not to study pushed me not to ask.

The entrance exams were held at the end of April when the College of Liberal Arts was at its most beautiful. This area has since become Marronnier Park, and College Stream has been covered over, but then it flowed all the way from the entrance of Tongsung-dong to Ihwa-dong. A row of dazzling forsythias lined one side of the stream. Cherry blossoms were strewn giddily about campus, and chestnut trees were in bloom. Since streetcars were the only public transportation, I'd exit the main college gate, cross the street, pass the School of Medicine, and head for Wonnam-dong via the University Hospital front gate.

I adored the path connecting the School of Medicine and the University Hospital. Maybe it was the enchanting daydreams the scenery encouraged in a late teenager, or maybe it was the way the trees, flowers, grass, and warm breeze of the path quickened my pulse, but its attraction couldn't be explained away simply as natural beauty.

What most captivated me in preparing for college was a sense of impending freedom. Leaving high school meant that escape from all types of restrictions was in the offing, but above all, liberation from my mother. Without marriage, I otherwise couldn't even dream of escaping her control, and to say I hadn't fantasized about it would be a lie. It was my dream of dreams, my most cherished desire. And now the reality of personal liberation lay just around the corner. How to use such tremendous freedom? Every option had its attractions. I could put it to good use or bad, treat it prudently or squander it. I would conspire with this freedom in everything I'd do. For me, this dream was more splendid than the May sunshine that brought the roses and lilacs and peonies into bloom.

The possibility of release from Mother's clutches burst upon me suddenly in the spring of 1950. One weekend, Brother made a rather exaggerated show of exhaustion upon cycling home from school. My sister-in-law was already pregnant with a second child and suffering from morning sickness. Despite the burning desire for offspring in our family, for her to carry a second child so soon, before the first had even turned one year old, put a strain on both mother and baby. Just yesterday, we'd been thrilled with Brother's position as a teacher at a countryside school, but now we were showing signs of listlessness with our staid life, in which the only change to be expected was the addition of new family members. Brother spoke up nonchalantly as the dinner tray was brought in.

"Looks like a house at the school will be available soon. It's bigger than ours and comes with a vegetable patch. Might be nice to spend time there . . ."

Mother immediately picked up where he had trailed off.

"Are you saying it's ours for the asking? The school's official residence?"

I couldn't help but smile at Mother, who wanted to turn this house at the school into an official residence, but I hardly thought moving there could become reality.

"Sure. It'll be vacant soon, but no one is applying for it. I just mentioned it because the principal asked today if I'd be interested. It's nothing. Forget about it."

"Let's do it."

"What?"

At this resolute, all-too-simple decision, everyone stopped eating and stared at Mother.

"After three years of boarding house meals, your bones go hollow. You're getting run-down already, and it's only been six months or so. It makes me nervous." She then turned to my sister-in-law: "That goes for you too. It's not easy for a young couple to live like this."

"But Mother, what about Wan-suh?" Brother tilted his chin toward me.

"If she gets into university, she can go from Uncle's. They'll all like that."

Mother could speak confidently because of how Uncle and Auntie doted on me. I felt just as close to them. Elder Uncle now had a son and three daughters, and at one point, Younger Uncle, still childless, tried to bring one of the girls from the countryside to raise. For over a year, Uncle and Auntie lavished enormous affection on my cousin, but she missed her mother and the countryside so much that she had to be sent home. I'd seen their heartbreak from close quarters and tried to be nicer to them. They showered their devotion on me, as though I were the only one they could lavish love on. And although I was overjoyed at the prospect of boarding with them, our special relationship had nothing to do with it. My focus was on breaking away from Mother. That was enough.

Uncle's house had a room for me. When we lived with them, I had a room to myself, but at home I still shared with Mother. Although we had a spare room, we left it empty to save on firewood. I wanted to use it in the summertime, but I was afraid of hurting Mother's feelings and couldn't bring myself to broach the subject. For the same reason, I took extra care not to let on how thrilled I was about moving out. No matter how good Uncle and Auntie were to me, they still weren't immediate family. I held a rice cake in each hand, admission to university and freedom, and it wasn't the case that I could choose only one, as the saying goes. The thought that it'd be all or nothing had kept me in a high state of tension until exam day.

As soon as the house at Brother's school had been brought up, Mother wanted to see it. I went with her. We took a streetcar to the Yŏngch'ŏn terminus and then had to wait a long, long time for a country bus to Kup'abal. Walking from Kup'abal to Koyang Middle School was no picnic either. There had been a long drought that spring, and the clay path sent up clouds of dust. In a flash, my black shoes looked as though they belonged to a peasant. Gazing down at them gave me real empathy for what Brother went through.

The house was already basically vacant, containing just some furniture abandoned by its previous tenant, a teacher who'd resigned due to illness. It wasn't much to look at, but Mother made a half-hearted tour, first going over to the vegetable patch.

She squatted there, holding the position for a long time. I thought she was peeing and faced the other way. Eventually I turned around again and discovered that she was playing with the dirt, like a child. When her eyes met mine, the humble, bashful smile she flashed made me think of a potato flower.

"I want to move here right away. The soil is as fertile as can be. Imagine, letting such good earth go to waste!"

The warm spring sunshine was the sort to make you drowsy. Vegetables were sprouting in nearby gardens, but this patch lay fallow. My pulse quickened as I imagined coming home on weekends and dashing toward Mother, arms raised high, while she weeded. I pictured her amid waving leaves of peppers, lettuce, cucumbers, squash, sesame, and all sorts of greens. The vegetable patch meant that I wouldn't just be going home, but home to the countryside. The image stirred me as much as my vision of impending freedom. The two would fit together perfectly.

As it happened, we were also on the verge of losing our house in Pakchŏk Hamlet. Elder Uncle had lost his taste for the village after Liberation. He'd wandered from place to place at first, but now he shut himself up at his concubine's in Kaesŏng, and our family's fortune was dwindling fast. What's more, the issue of my cousins' education had arisen. Brother and Younger Uncle agreed that it was time to bid farewell to Pakchŏk Hamlet. They'd bring my cousins to Seoul and start fresh. The plan was taking concrete shape.

As soon as I passed my entrance exams, Mother commissioned a real-estate agent to rent our house in Tonamdong. Then she busied herself with preparations for the move. Brother wanted to shift house during his school vacation, but Mother made haste, as though catastrophe awaited if we didn't have freshly picked lettuce to wrap our rice in when summer rolled around. She became a woman possessed. As usual, her spasmodic energy came back to her with the move.

"Looks like moving is your hobby, Mom," I teased, seeing her eagerness to pack up again after just over a year. Mother was so caught up in the move that she seemed indifferent about leaving me behind at Uncle's. I was slightly put out.

But Mother sighed. "There's an old proverb that says you move when your days are numbered." She seemed in a far-off world.

Mother was still haunted by her own demons. Just as she'd run away in vain from the leftists, she was trying to flee the consequences of Brother's defection from their cause. To me, her fears were neurotic and irrational. I thought that moving would be the best treatment for her.

That May held a special beauty for Mother and me, filled as we both were with dreams for the future. But of all years and all Mays, it was May 1950. Mother was a woman endowed with an unusual wisdom of her own, but she didn't realize as yet how silly it was to inflate expectations without bracing for them to burst. June was fast approaching.

12. Epiphany

SCHOOL ENDED IN MAY, AND SO THE NEW ACADEMIC year followed on, naturally, in early June, but our admissions ceremony wasn't held until the middle of the month. A tenant was found to rent our house, a contract signed, and a second installment of contract money accepted. My room at Uncle's was papered. Likewise, the house at Brother's school was papered and fixed up. Mother picked an auspicious moving day according to the traditional method of divination, and we were waiting for it to arrive. When Brother returned for the weekend, we divided up the books we'd each take to our new homes. But then, only several days into the term, June 25 rolled around.

A report came that the Korean People's Army had attempted to push south across the thirty-eighth parallel. Border clashes were common enough, but the ROK Army had always driven the North back, so we didn't take the latest news too seriously. Even if it escalated into all-out war this time, we never dreamed that anything major would occur before our move. This rather selfish way of thinking was based on our still fresh memories of World War II. We assumed that we'd have no reason to regret our move and that instead we'd wind up patting ourselves on the back over how clever we'd been to relocate to the countryside near Brother's school. The Syngman Rhee government tried to convey the impression that if war broke out we'd sweep northward, eat lunch in Pyongyang, and have dinner at the Yalu River. And although we certainly didn't take this propaganda at face value, their brainwashing wasn't to be dismissed so lightly. We took it for granted that the worst-case scenario would be a protracted conflict, with the two sides pushing to and fro somewhere north of the thirty-eighth parallel.

That Monday morning, Brother left for his school at dawn, and I went to college in Tongsung-dong. Military trucks were moving toward Miari Hill, carrying ROK soldiers in camouflage, their helmets covered in leaves taken from the trees lining the streets. When I caught sight of them, I had the shocking realization that war was indeed upon us, but I clapped enthusiastically and shouted my hurrahs along with the other pedestrians. After morning classes were over, someone suggested that we sneak in and listen to a lecture by the colorful literary critic Yang Chu-dong on the sly. The thought of sneaking in for lectures gave me the agreeable feeling that I'd become a university student. Even more exciting was the opportunity to see a famous scholar in the flesh. Although it wasn't "listening on the sly," soon after school started, I attended a lecture by renowned academic and poet Karam Yi Pyŏng-gi, my heart racing with excitement. I simply felt proud to glimpse a celebrity; I knew nothing about his scholarship or his accomplishments.

Unlike today, well-known scholars and other celebrities did not have much chance to appear in public, and neither their images nor their voices were widely recognized. They were more or less literally confined to the ivory tower. To set eyes on them was an intoxicating privilege of university students. Yang Chu-dong was immensely popular even then, and the class was standing room only. Crammed on my feet into the very back row, I was enthralled. My eyes were riveted on him as he roamed the podium, wit and knowledge cascading from him. The roar of artillery approached from time to time and shook the windowpanes in the lecture theater. Yang, small in stature but solidly built, continued unfazed. I found him thoroughly dashing.

By the time I headed home from school, things were rather different from what they'd been in the morning. Troops were still moving toward Miari Hill, but they now looked tragic, not valiant, and the citizens sending them off appeared nervous and half-hearted. Mother kept complaining throughout the night that at times like these families should be together. I was worried about Brother, too, and that made Mother's remarks all the more irritating. I resented not having a room of my own.

The next morning, gunshots boomed closer, as though coming from the other side of Miari Hill. According to breaking news, the ROK Army had crushed the Korean People's Army. The general public was urged to go about its daily activities. Assuming all had turned out as expected, I set out for school, but a stream of frightened refugees was making its way down along the streetcar tracks that stretched to Miari Hill. People tried to ask them questions as they passed by, wheeling their household goods on wagons, but were being held back by the police. From word of mouth we were able to establish that the refugees were coming from Ŭijŏngbu. Seeing them with my own eyes made me more frightened, but I took comfort in telling myself that they couldn't be innocent. Maybe they were evil landowners, or from the families of police who had led the crackdown on leftists, and had been terrified even before anything actually happened. Even though I didn't want the Korean People's Army to invade, not even as an idle fantasy, my thinking had been quite affected by leftist ideology.

Our lectures were canceled. Female students were sent home, while the boys were required to attend a rally in which they pledged northward reunification in the name of the Student National Defense Corps. I stood on the sidelines and briefly watched this rabble-rousing session. The cadres read out a resolution at the top of their lungs and led others in shouting slogans, but they weren't terribly reassuring.

I could sense the clouds of war thickening by the minute. To the accompaniment of incessant gunfire, pedestrians seemed to be rushing about randomly. I ran home, gripped by sudden fear for Brother. I prayed that he'd arrived while I was away, but no news had come. Mother was pacing outside our gate. When she spotted me, she mumbled, "Best to get out of here fast." Her blank gaze unnerved me. The situation had passed beyond simple urgency. Sister-in-law was in the kitchen frying rice on a pot lid flipped upside down. By that point, she was already seven months pregnant. She breathed heavily, her shoulders rising and falling. My infant nephew whimpered, gaunt and malnourished with his mother expecting again so soon, but she ignored him. I lost my temper, watching her brown the rice with a big wooden spatula like a zombie.

"Sister, what do you think you're doing?"

"What does it look like I'm doing? I'm getting rice flour ready," she snapped. Her tone was even more irritated than mine.

A stuffed canvas sack had been carelessly pitched out on the edge of the veranda. A quick glance made it clear that it was Mother who'd sewn the sack and that she'd then stuffed it hastily. My sister-in-law was obviously following her directions and cooking under duress, but I snatched the spatula from her.

"Don't tell me you're planning to flee in that state of yours."

"Do I have a choice? If your mother pushes us out, she pushes us out. I can't argue with her. But your brother has to come before she makes us go."

Suddenly, an earsplitting boom. Aftershocks, deafening as a mountain top caving in, rattled the glass of our doors. They resonated for a long time. Mother flew in and held open a sack of cloth. "Hurry up and pour the rice in."

"But we haven't ground it yet."

"Who has time to grind it? If you have to eat it a handful at a time, you're better off leaving it as it is."

She was in such a rush to put the half-burned rice in the bag that she didn't even scold us for our shoddy work. I assumed she'd streaked in because she'd glimpsed Brother in the distance. Sister-in-law was on the verge of tears, thinking that she was about to be driven out of the house. I pleaded with Mother: "Brother can go take refuge by himself. Sister-in-law doesn't have to go too."

"What are we in such a hurry for? He hasn't even come back yet."

She smiled ruefully, realizing how absurd her behavior had been in the confusion of the moment. She headed out once more.

Brother didn't return that evening. No phone call came to Uncle's store. Uncle, of course, had tried to reach Brother's school all day long, but in vain. Late that night, Uncle and Auntie came over to shelter with us. Not only did our snug residential neighborhood feel safer than the major avenue they lived on, but they thought it would be less frightening to have others around for support.

Brother's absence loomed larger when we were all together. As cannonballs whizzed past in the Seoul sky, we huddled in the room without budging. We buried ourselves sweatily under cotton-padded quilts, because dubious rumors floating around at the end of Japanese rule said that they gave protection from shrapnel. Beneath the quilt, Uncle listened closely to the radio. He would pipe up immediately whenever there was any comforting news.

Mother and Uncle could hardly have passed that night more differently from each other. No matter what we said, Mother refused to cover herself with a quilt or even to come into the room. She spent the entire night pacing our front yard and the alleyway outside our gate. But rather than wait idly for Brother, she observed what was going on, trying to glean information from passersby or from watching the movement of neighbors. She passed on to us that the line of refugees had slowed and that some, with nowhere to go, were even coming back. Once people stopped moving about, she sat frozen on the edge of the veranda, trying to pinpoint the location of the battlefront. She projected an expert's confidence, as she listened to bombs screech past and their explosions when they hit their targets.

Like Uncle, Mother wanted us to agree with her conjectures, but the two of them were at odds on every point and neither version was credible. They offered little comfort. I found it thoroughly baffling. It was as though we were watching a struggle between reality and propaganda. To see Mother so calm and dauntless after she'd been scared out of her wits during the day spooked me somehow. Finally, the battle noise quieted toward early morning, and Uncle urged us to go to sleep. He sounded relieved.

Yawning widely, he added, "Just like I thought. The president pledged he'd defend Seoul to the death."

Mother shot him a pitying look: "Are you saying you really believe that old fart?"

Uncle and Auntie left for their shop when day broke, assuming that they could open as usual. We didn't stop them. The silence outside made us think that things had calmed down. But Uncle soon returned, out of breath. The world, he informed us, had changed overnight. His voice was remote, stupefied.

Mother blanched: "Oh my lord, what should we do?"

She sounded delirious. I took her hand and found it trembling slightly. Uncle seemed puzzled by mother's change of heart. He joked, "What are you so worried about? You were bad-mouthing Syngman Rhee fearlessly before. Not such a bad turn of events, is it?"

He told us that crowds had gathered along the streets to welcome the Korean People's Army and urged us to go out fast and have a look. Mother sternly forbade us. Although Uncle, who'd accepted the president's words at face value, was ready to blow with the wind, the change in regime terrified Mother, despite her loathing for Syngman Rhee. Concern for Brother clearly was what made her so timid, but I still thought she was being excessive, since I already had calculating thoughts of my own: Brother's desertion of the cause might be a blot in his revolutionary résumé, but surely his circumstances would be taken into account.

Back then, I was truly cunning and shameless, but I wasn't like Uncle, who was essentially an opportunist. I was more resolute and hopeful. These hopes of mine became more concrete as I recalled Brother's days as an activist and my own fleeting sympathy with the movement, although I'd largely forgotten about it by then. While I focused on his leftist credentials, Mother's thoughts were on his desertion. Her fear was not so much that he'd be a target for revenge, but that shifting political currents might push my brother into another change of heart, leaving him a spineless good-for-nothing.

Mother headed out alone to confirm that things had indeed changed. She returned to touch base with us and then went all the way to the avenue along Anam Stream to wait for Brother. From the stream's edge, the backyard of Songbuk Police Station had been fully visible. Shuddering, Mother said that the Korean People's Army had occupied it and was rounding up reactionaries. Mother came back after watching for Brother's return so intensely that she'd strained her eyes. They were glazed over, drained of vitality. I tried to comfort her: "Don't worry. Brother's not going to be arrested. Now he can live the way he really believes." So I wished at least.

"Is that any way for a human being to behave?"

Mother's tone conveyed open contempt for me. That damn concept of loyalty again. She was impossible and, to me, laughable, with nothing to cling to except two sharply distinct ideologies, like the sun and the moon in the sky. But she wasn't as ludicrous as Brother, who soon made his appearance. Mother must have been waiting for him precisely so she could hide him. She may even have entertained the idea of shipping him straight off to Uncle or to her relatives.

As it happened, Brother returned just as Mother stepped into the house. The timing was utterly natural. Imagine a child keeping close watch over a morning glory and shifting her attention briefly. At that very moment, the flower blossoms.

But natural as the timing may have been, Brother looked more unnatural than he ever had in his entire life, and it wouldn't have been any different if Mother had met him at the corner where she'd stood watch: he entered with a truck full of prisoners in tow. I call them prisoners because their heads were shaved and they were in prison uniform, but they beamed with all the dignity of triumphant, medal-studded generals and more. In contrast, Brother wore everyday clothes and a blank expression. He looked as though he didn't have the slightest idea what he was doing. On Mother's face was a look of equally dull perplexity. One of the prisoners gently lifted her as she stood on the terrace stones and set her down on the veranda. When he prostrated himself in a bow to her, the others followed suit. Only then did she recognize that it was the man who had been taken away from our Samsŏn'gyo house. She grasped his hand and expressed sympathy about his hardships, but no color returned to her face.

Because Brother had been active in the movement at that point, he and the man had seen through each other's identity, although no direct connection existed between them in the leftist hierarchy. The man said that in prison he'd always been grateful to us, for keeping his family as tenants. His wife had told him of our concern for their plight.

The first thing the Korean People's Army did after entering Seoul on the morning of June 28 was to release those who'd been jailed for ideological reasons. The prisoners must have then just boarded trucks in their uniforms—they couldn't have had anything to change into, and even if they did, they wouldn't have, for prison garb itself became a proud revolutionary marker. They crisscrossed the city, responding to the crowds' applause and fanning their excitement in return.

In the countryside where Brother's school was located, upheaval had come quietly. He said that he hadn't taken matters seriously because the roar of artillery wasn't especially loud. But someone reported that the flag of the Communists had been raised that morning at the township office and the police station, and that a major battle had taken place in Seoul. Brother was hurrying home when he encountered the truck.

The man who relayed the news gave Brother a straw hat with a red ribbon and tied a red strip of fabric to his bicycle for him, but this made Brother uncomfortable, so he kept taking them off and putting them back on again while bicycling home, which goes to show how indecisive he was. Unsure which side he really supported, he would have gazed at those in the truck with ambivalence, since he couldn't shun them but couldn't cheer them on enthusiastically either. As Brother told it, when the truck approached, he edged back but someone held out a hand. Although Brother witnessed passionate handshakes and embraces between those on board and pedestrians that day, I picture him extending his own hand shyly. An emotional cry rang out, "Unbelievable! Meeting a comrade like this!" and Brother was then immediately hoisted up to join those in the truck. He didn't even have time to call out for his bicycle, the possession he held so dear. He was stuck for half a day amid the excitement, as out of place as an unhusked grain amid polished rice. And so Brother returned, reluctantly trailing an entourage.

Our cramped veranda soon replicated the festivity on the truck. Mother, Sister-in-law, and I cooked rice, boiled stew, and fried vegetable pancakes in the kitchen. We had an entire crate of tofu and a case of liquor delivered from the neighborhood grocery. The visitors ate and drank, and tirelessly sang revolutionary songs until our roof tiles hummed. Our small house seemed as though it would take off with their racket. Neighbors gathered outside our gate to peer in at the spectacle. Mother was in a daze, half out of her wits. Her legs trembled as she made one blunder after another, breaking dishes and confusing sugar with salt. More than once, she put her hand to her forehead and muttered, "What kind of omen is this?" To her, the arrivals were neither prisoners nor revolutionaries; they were simply an omen.

Yet even throughout it all, she served the men herself, rather than letting my sister-in-law or me do it. As she brought dishes around, she'd put on an anxious expression and say, "I bet your family is dying to see you!" Evidently taking her hint, all the men finally dispersed late that night.

The next day, our prospective tenant came to retrieve the money from the first two installments of the contract. We also felt that the contract had become invalid overnight and returned the money readily. Mother went up to the loft and rummaged about for quite a while before coming back down with it. She gave an embarrassed smile: "There were so many things I wanted to do with this money. I'd have been so ashamed if I'd spent any!"

Suddenly I remembered how her smile had reminded me of a potato flower as she stood in the vegetable patch at Brother's school. My heart ached. We had been about to move, but with the sudden interruption, our plan now seemed something out of the distant past. I was struck by an antirevolutionary thought: even if an earthly paradise were to be ushered in on this land, I didn't want it if it meant robbing Mother of her dream of a cozy hundred-*p'yŏng* vegetable patch. Mother had dreamed of becoming wealthier;

she intended to take the lump sum she collected after the final payment of the tenant's key money, invest it in Uncle's business, and then receive interest from him. And she wouldn't have to buy vegetables—she'd just grow them in her own garden.

After the festivities we'd hosted with the released revolutionaries, our neighbors treated us differently. They bowed deeply and repeatedly, afraid of us, as though apologetic for prior failure to recognize they had someone important in their midst. Although the situation seemed to be running directly opposite to what Mother had pictured, she was more anxious than she would have been if her worries had come to pass. But what was really happening, of course, was not what it appeared. One after another, Brother's old comrades came to see him. When they saw his indecision, they implied that he was losing an opportunity to make amends to the Workers' Party. Their tone alternated between cajolery and criticism. He kept excusing himself, saying that returning to school and instilling revolutionary spirit in farmers' sons was how he could best serve the party.

The truckload of omens prevented Mother from realizing the future plans she had so carefully laid. She plunged into despair, passing each day as though treading on thin ice. The neighbors who treated us like VIPs filled her with trepidation. Our gates opened into the same alley, and everyone went back and forth regularly, especially older women with grandchildren to look after. They visited one another so often that they could distinguish how the bean paste and soy sauce tasted in each house. Babies tend to adore getting out of the house, and every day grandmothers carried them about on their backs and visited their neighbors. To be excluded from sharing our concerns about food with such intimate acquaintances was very difficult. They didn't believe that we had to eat gruel or scrape rice from the bottom of the jar, just as they did. When they made a mass excursion to Ttuksŏm to buy fresh summer greens, only we were left out.

The sense of calamity extended beyond our own immediate family. This time, Uncle's conviction that chaos was superior to stability for traders proved wrong. His shop soon closed. He'd rented out half the building, as the side facing the avenue and its streetcars had enough space for two shops, but the other store closed too. Now vacant, the building must have looked like an empty storage facility, and so officers from the Korean People's Army requisitioned it as a stable for the horses that pulled their equipment wagons. Who could dare refuse?

According to what Auntie told us, these officers ranked high in the security apparatus and wanted not only to quarter their horses, but also to sleep and eat there. Auntie became their cook. At first, Auntie and Uncle hardly believed the disaster that had befallen them, but as food shortages grew worse, they thought it fortunate that at least they didn't have to worry about rice. They didn't even have to worry about side dishes. Once a steer was slaughtered and carved up, and although the soldiers shared the meat with another military unit, they feasted on it for two days straight until they got sick of it. They didn't have any option, really, since this occurred before refrigeration.

The smell of beef filled the neighborhood. Although Auntie had no choice but to cook it, she said she felt like she was committing a terrible crime. Uncle's main line of business was liquor wholesale, but the alcohol he'd hoarded as capital for future trading was discovered when the cattle were slaughtered. It disappeared that very day. Compensation for the confiscated booze or Auntie's labor was a pipe dream, but it remained an incredible stroke of luck that they could fill their bellies three times a day.

Auntie was ridden with guilt over this luxury she couldn't share, and said that she couldn't hold her head high in front of her neighbors. She wanted, at the very least, to distribute the scorched rice from the bottom of the pot, but the strict surveillance over food made it impossible. Although we heard that the soldiers said nothing about visits from relatives, we stopped going to Uncle's, for Auntie would obviously try to feed us behind their backs, even if just a bowl of rice. We'd had it drilled into us as we were growing up that appearing greedy at the table should be avoided at all costs; the mere thought that people would suspect us of visiting to be fed made my skin crawl. Auntie told us what was going on during her rare visits. And although she positively reeked of food, confined to the kitchen all day, not a grain of scorched rice made the journey with her. We expected no such thing, of course, but she'd excuse herself upon setting foot into our house.

"I was afraid they'd suspect me of sneaking food away, so I shook out my skirt in front of them before they even asked. Look, like this."

She fluttered her skirt so vigorously that her slip came into view. When our hunger grew more extreme, she cut off those infrequent night visits completely.

Brother was apparently biding his time and watching the situation develop. It didn't hurt that those in the local government office, which had turned into the People's Committee, and the head of our neighborhood People's Unit were observing to see if he was indeed a major figure. But the world was not about to allow him to steer a middle course indefinitely; men, young and middle-aged alike, were being hauled off the street to be sent to the Korean People's Army, and Brother was losing the opportunity to either go underground or make up to the party for his mistakes.

Exclusion from our neighbors and a sense of impending crisis left Mother's eyes vacant, and she didn't express her opinion. The derailment of her plans had robbed her of her powers of discernment. She grew fearful and taciturn. I don't know where her strength of character went, but she behaved as though she no longer had views of her own.

Brother finally returned to school in early August. One of his fellow teachers visited as part of a campaign to encourage others back to work, and that may have swayed him. Even if they couldn't expect a salary, this teacher said, rice rations might be in the picture. My sister-in-law was due in September, and Mother was desperate to save some rice, if only a few handfuls, so she could cook her a proper meal or two after the baby was born. Mother resorted to taking out the hulled millet used to stuff my nephew's pillow and making gruel from it along with some leathery vegetable leaves.

On his next visit, Brother's colleague brought an official letter confirming Brother's credentials and granting him right of safe passage. And so Brother reported to work, only to be conscripted for the "people's volunteer army" three days later. We didn't even know he'd been taken away. In the middle of the night, a rap came on Uncle's window. Uncle and Auntie went out and found Brother standing there, with two Korean People's Army soldiers holding guns behind him.

Uncle's house faced the avenue leading to Miari Hill, and they could always hear troop and civilian movements at night. Brother had asked for the understanding of his soldier escorts and stopped by briefly to give word of what was going on. With nothing in mind but the thought that they couldn't just let him leave a message like that and disappear, Auntie and Uncle followed him all the way to Miari Hill in their pajamas. They were at a loss about what to do and finally lost sight of him when one of the soldiers pushed them away with the barrel of his gun. They stood at the side of the road and took cold comfort from the parade of young men being dragged away under cover of darkness. After watching the procession until it disappeared, Auntie raced over to relay the news. We were stunned and refused to believe it. When day broke, I was all the more certain that Auntie had simply been imagining things and talking nonsense in the middle of the night. Mother immediately made preparations to leave for Kup'abal to find out what had really happened and told me to come along.

The ferocious bombing along the national highway compelled everyone to move by night. We were confronted with numerous air raids and would leap into fields or rice paddies, lying flat for a long while before picking ourselves up and continuing.

The news was true. Brother had indeed been conscripted. An order from on high had instigated the intense campaign to encourage teachers back to work. Every school was obligated to send several teachers for "reeducation," and in the midst of their reeducation, they were forced to "volunteer" for the army then and there. We had no one in particular to blame. The teacher who'd talked Brother into reporting to work had been dragged away as well. He hadn't deliberately fooled us; he'd been fooled too. If anything was to blame, it was rural innocence. What deceived us all was a much larger, organized force.

Red dragonflies flitted about in the fields, amid the ceaseless chirr of cicadas in the poplars. Our garden patch, without an owner to look after it, was now covered with purslanes. Maybe it was the effect of extreme hunger, but as we looked out at all this from the faculty lounge, where a sole aged and weary teacher remained, the terror of war seemed so far away as to be surreal. The teacher went out to the storage shed with an even more ancient-looking janitor and scooped some rice from a sack. We accepted it with deep gratitude. Mother carried a bundle on her head, and I carried one on my back. That evening, we ate our fill of rice for dinner. When Brother brought his first salary from school, Mother had lamented that our gullets were gang lords. She'd spoken too soon. She didn't say anything that evening, but the meal proved that hunger came before all other worries.

I'd returned to school long before this incident. Unlike Brother, I readily sympathized with the political changes that had occurred, the criticism of the Syngman Rhee government, the pledges made on behalf of workers and farmers. I applauded how the Communists pressed hard on the enemy's heels and felt a vivid revival of the excitement and fascination I'd experienced when I first came into contact with revolutionary pamphlets, a sensation I'd forgotten. I even wanted to brag about my brief involvement with the Democratic Youth League, as though I had great personal knowledge of leftist struggle. Besides, I had a sense of attachment to the university I had just entered. I wanted to participate in the revolution, and the university was the one institution where I fit.

I think I reported to school in mid-July. I was eager to attend, but the turmoil at home delayed me. Mother showed no interest in my attending. Her acute, uncontrollable anxiety caused even the jokes she used to crack in any situation to fall by the wayside. I felt that it took courage on my part to return to school. I discovered that the Liberal Arts building had been occupied by the Korean People's Army and that we were supposed to register at the College of Veterinary Medicine several blocks away. Besides Democratic Youth League cadres, there were just one or two students in each department. Our major task was to encourage others to come back to school. Each of us received several of our fellow students' dossiers, including the hand-drawn maps to their homes within them. Track down the absentees, we were told. Urge them to return. I learned later that students were frequently rounded up with this tactic and sent to the army, just as Brother had been. But even before I found out the real purpose of the campaign, I ignored the instructions. For one thing, I wasn't good at locating houses, and for another, it didn't make sense to me to try to talk anybody into returning to school. The issue wasn't regard for those who'd been targeted; it was my own self-respect.

Beyond that, every day we were kept occupied with nothing but stupid assignments. We had to copy down a list of reactionary students in the College of Liberal Arts again and again. I couldn't for the life of me understand why we had to keep copying the same list. We weren't even told who authored it.

We did have something that was supposed to pass for study hours at school, but I never saw a professor. I never saw so much as a professor's shadow throughout that period, for that matter. The Democratic Youth League ruled the school. Their "democratic" study method was to take turns reading Soviet Communist Party history or a full newspaper page of Leader Kim Il Sung's teaching, and then treat it with fawning adulation. Nothing is more exhausting than having to offer glowing praise when it doesn't flow naturally. I had the marked sensation of my vital energy evaporating. Despite reading the same text over and over, we had to maintain the peak of enthusiasm we'd shown the first time. The new lessons sounded no different, but we were expected to add a fresh spark to our fervor. Absurd.

Even if that had been possible, it would have been a fraud. I couldn't carry it off unless I muttered to myself what an idiot this leader was if he was so taken with charade.

I had a congenital hatred of school preparation. In high school, I had little choice but to review before tests, but I never bothered to look at lessons ahead of time. I was easily distracted too. During subjects I didn't care about, I'd let the lesson go in one ear and out the other and had the bad habit of reading novels in class. Even in subjects I liked, I preferred to listen to the teacher, letting my thoughts wander once in a while, without going over the material in advance. Only then did fresh knowledge jump out at me in its full glory. I didn't want to turn the class into a review session by preparing and robbing the subject matter of its freshness, so that it became like a spoiled fish. It may actually be that what I hated was review rather than looking at material ahead of time.

The Democratic Youth League lessons consisted of endless study of the obvious, things that elementary-school kids would have understood the first time around. I was so drained that I felt that I myself had become a spoiled fish, a specimen, stuffed and mounted. The sensation was so intense that even though there were surely handsome young men among those Democratic Youth League cadres I called Comrade, I didn't experience the slightest stir of emotion as I sat with them, shaking hands at every opportunity, our shoulders brushing.

I'm not talking about romance, but the spark preceding romance that exists only between men and women. The pull is there even if you are talking about brothers and sisters, fathers and daughters, or mothers and sons. Contact between men and women offers a subtle attraction—or whatever you want to call it—that isn't present in same-sex interaction. Somehow this feeling had simply dried up for me. It wasn't just in my head; it was a fact.

During the war, my menstrual cycle stopped. Later I learned that this was true of many women. Most attributed it to a lack of nutrition, and although that may have been the main reason, I suspect that some sort of psychological neutering took place as well. In fact, pondering how men and women increased North Korea's population became much more amusing for me than contemplating whether it was a true workers' paradise. The circumstances didn't change my desire to have fun. I stopped going to classes after Brother was conscripted. I won't say that it was because of him, but I was exhausted. I withered and fell away, like fruit with unpollinated seed. Even now, with the perspective of distance, that three-month period under the Korean People's Army seems far longer than it actually was.

Every evening, Mother set a bowl of pure well water on the condiment-jar platform in the yard and offered her devotion to the spirits. On nights when the moon sent forth beams of silver, or when she spent a particularly long time in prayer, she seemed just like a shaman.

I should have wanted the victory of the Korean People's Army, knowing that Brother had become part of it. But when I heard mortars from the south, ceaseless and continually intensifying, my heart raced with the opposite hope. The artillery roar, it turned out, came from ship cannons, as we learned from the wife of the revolutionary who'd been arrested at our house.

We'd heard nothing from the man himself once he left after the celebration at our house. Brother didn't tell us about him, but Mother wondered whether he was a big fish or simply a minnow. During his wife's visit, we learned that he had in fact been the vice chairman of the Inch'ŏn Municipal People's Committee. A heavyweight, all right. His wife, however, looked wretched. Worn and haggard, accompanied by a frightened son and daughter, she told us that the bombardment had reduced Inch'ŏn almost to ashes. The city itself would fall before long. An order had come for high-level party cadres to send their families north but to stand their ground to the bitter end.

The woman had stopped by on her way north. How bizarre that our fate was so intertwined with theirs. But my dominant emotion was irritation. I asked myself heartlessly why she was dropping by, instead of hurrying onward. What were we to them, anyway? Mother, however, took special care over their food and bedding. Early the next morning, she sent them on with a lengthy prayer that they encounter helping hands throughout their journey and arrive in Pyongyang with a minimum of hardship. I was furious. Cuttingly, I said, "Do you think her husband is going to rise to power again? You're wrong."

I thought that she'd be angry, but her expression immediately registered dread and disgust. It was as though I'd defiled her very thoughts.

"Stop it with that senseless mouth of yours! How can I hope for your brother to find help if I don't give it myself?"

I felt very ashamed.

One day, flames leapt into the sky from downtown, making us wonder if the whole world except our neighborhood had become a sea of fire. Bombs and cannonballs rained on the city without letting up. And of all days, my sister-in-law looked as though she would give birth that very morning. The difficulty of her first delivery made Mother afraid to care for her on her own; she told me to rush and fetch Auntie. I dashed out but had to be so cautious that it took me over an hour to make my way toward her house, on what would ordinarily have been less than a ten-minute journey.

The streets were deserted. Fierce artillery roared in all directions, descending murderously from above as if intent on reducing mountains to rubble. Machine-gun fire from airplanes strafed anything that moved below, swooping for the attack like hawks spotting chicks. I inched my way forward, taking cover beneath roof eaves and under trees. In the end, though, I had to turn back. I never made it to Auntie's. Crossing the avenue over the streetcar tracks proved an impossible obstacle.

Meanwhile, Sister-in-law had had an easy birth. She was crying quietly, her newborn second son at her side, while Mother prepared soup and rice for her. Wrinkles were prominent on the malnourished infant's face, no bigger than a sweet potato. He was so tiny that he had slipped out from her womb without causing any labor pains.

A few days later, the political situation flipped upside down again. The ROK Army and United Nations forces gained control of Seoul. For three months, young men seemed to have vanished, but now they spilled out onto the street from wherever it was that they'd hidden themselves so resourcefully. They hugged each other, their hair long and their faces as white as a sheet of paper. Embracing the triumphantly returning ROK Army, they cheered madly and danced. These young men could hardly have survived in hiding so long merely through sheer endurance and the protection of their families. We alone had been the fools.

That said, the full revelation of how many had been taken away or killed defied our wildest imagination. The scale was too immense, too cruel. Every conscript still alive had had a narrow escape; all owed their survival to fate. Anyone who has had a close scrape with death becomes bolder and overflows with desire to live a meaningful life. Those who'd managed to avoid conscription were filled with bloodthirsty passion for revenge, and we remained at war.

Nothing is more horrifying than a civil war in which it is kill or be killed. The enemy had neither a different skin color nor a different language; they simply belonged to the Communist Party. We felt deep gratitude to the UN forces, who, along with the ROK Army, had rescued us, but above all we felt thanks for the very existence of our nation, which made it possible for the UN forces to help us in the first place. Everyone, no matter who, was choking on surging patriotism.

But for us, patriotism and anti-Communism were identical. Neither could exist without the other; they were the palm and the back of the hand. Impatience with mere patriotism led to the creation of groups—youth associations and self-defense corps—whose very existence was predicated on smashing the Reds. Institutions for maintaining public security—government, police, soldiers, MPs— returned, but their main concern was ferreting out Communist elements. We were placed under martial law. Jails were clogged with Reds who'd been arrested for serving the enemy while it was in power. Summary convictions were rampant. The life of a Communist was not equal to a human being's. A pointed finger and an accusation of being a Red could see a man shot to death on the spot.

What the Communists had done was so outrageous that a barrage of complaints came forth. Anonymous accusations were frequent. Some denounced others to stave off the same fate befalling themselves. In a sense, the very act of surviving Communist rule could have been seen as an offense. After all, even those who held out in an attic crawl space had to have someone sneak in food for them. Their wives or mothers could have gone out to the Women's Federation and sung songs of the masses and praised the Leader more passionately than others.

At some level, everyone who had remained in Seoul could be accused of siding with the enemy, even innocent citizens whose only sin was to accept at face value the government's pledge to defend Seoul to the death. Individual circumstances weren't taken into account. If anyone wanted to claim to be completely innocent, it was best to have fled across the Han. Among proud anti-Communists, a privileged class emerged: those who had crossed the river. In their arrogance, they seemed to have forgotten that when they evacuated the government was urging the populace to go calmly about its daily business. Maybe a guilty conscience was prompting them to display their power preemptively. Otherwise, it wouldn't have been possible for the government, which had shown royal magnanimity in considering the situations of Japanese collaborators, to become so stern now.

A period of excruciating hardship descended on my family, but I bore the brunt of it. Our neighbors still saw us as a high-level Red household. The people living next door nearly fainted when Mother stepped out of our house after Seoul was recovered. That we stayed instead of fleeing north seemed not just a source of amazement to them, but annoyance. No, not just annoyance, but anxiety—fear, as though a time bomb were ticking away next door. We'd done nothing, but our very existence posed a threat to society. We had to be removed.

Our house was searched after our neighbors reported us. They alleged that Brother, Communist big shot that he was assumed to be, must have been in hiding, considering that we hadn't fled. Joining the people's volunteer army itself wasn't considered a great offense because almost no one had willingly taken part. Many soldiers and policemen had brothers who'd been dragged away as well.

We pleaded, crying and begging, trying to convince them that Brother had been forcibly conscripted. His wife had just given birth and Mother was too old, so I was led off as representative of the family. I was subjected to all sorts of humiliation, but at least they didn't arrest me. Even though jails were overflowing with supposed Reds, I was evidently not much of a catch in the eyes of the expert who dealt with Communists. I was lucky to have the interrogator I did. Amateurs are always more frighteningly zealous than professionals, and that much more so when they're playing vigilante.

The affair didn't end there. I was summoned constantly from then on. I never learned if charges were filed against us repeatedly or if I was being dragged around simply to be humiliated. I didn't even have the energy to be curious about it. All sorts of youth organizations wanted to see me. They called me a Red bitch. Red bastard, Red bitch, it didn't matter—anyone stained by red was no longer human. And since our humanity had been forfeited, we couldn't demand our human rights. Presentation of a warrant? Forget it. Institutions were scrambling to smoke out Reds, and as long as our neighbors suspected us, I was prey. They ridiculed me, cursed me, and threatened me. In comparison with the thoughts reflected in their eyes, what they actually did hardly felt like a violation.

They gazed at me as though I were a beast. Vermin. I became their plaything. Their worm. I crawled for them. They were like children, amusing themselves with a disgusting insect. Thankfully, at least, the body of a Red bitch was too loathsome, too foul to sexually abuse.

I came to resent my genteel upbringing. By genteel, I don't mean that I ate well, dressed well, and was treated with utmost respect, but simply that I'd grown up without the opportunity to get used to contempt.

Every night, I shook my head fiercely and thrashed about, trying to erase the memory of having had to act as a worm in front of them. Then I'd come to my senses and realize that I had to fight off my impulse to forget, seized by fear that if they remembered how they treated me while I alone forgot, I really might turn into a worm.

Yet I have forgotten more than I recall. The individual humiliations have been reduced to a single lump, and particular incidents come to me only in a vague, abstract way. This strikes me as evidence that I not only literally wriggled on the ground like a worm in front of them, but had mentally submitted to the violence. What could I do? Such are an ordinary person's limits, the limits that prevent us from going mad and make it possible to endure.

But what I went through was nothing compared with what happened to Uncle. My interrogator had been relatively benign. Essentially I had encountered the helping hand that Mother continually prayed for, a bowl of pure well water set before her.

Uncle and Auntie remained unscathed until mid-October. They were busily scrubbing away the smell of horse manure and preparing to open a new business. Their only worry was about us. They said that they couldn't focus on work whenever we came to mind. They regretted terribly not striking a deal to rescue Brother from being drafted. They had assumed that bribes wouldn't work with the Korean People's Army, but after hearing that someone had made the impossible happen, Uncle kept kicking himself over it. Why didn't they pull a gold ring off Auntie's finger and bribe the soldiers who'd come to take him away? Uncle bickered with Auntie, criticizing her for not having thought of the idea first—after all, she was a woman.

Uncle and Auntie's neighbors passed on a fatal tip to the authorities that the two had been tools of the Political Security Bureau and lived comfortably. They were arrested separately. One of Auntie's neighborhood friends came and told us that Auntie had received a summary conviction and been dragged off in a group to the hill behind Sŏngshin Girls' Middle School. A series of gunshots had followed. "Hurry and get her body," she urged.

Many went to rummage through the corpses, desperately hoping to find family members who'd been taken away. Some did find the bodies of loved ones.

We didn't go, horrible as it sounds. All the chaos—the constant house searches and summonses—held us back. More importantly, we were terrified of what might happen if it came out that we were close relatives of a Red who deserved to be put to death. In those confused, horrible moments, we sent word to Auntie's mother. She rushed over, absolutely frenzied, and examined one corpse after another, but Auntie's body was nowhere to be found.

We eventually learned from Auntie that the officer in charge had lined up the women separately from the men, apparently assuming that no crime of theirs could have merited execution, and handed them over to the police. Auntie was put on trial and released on probation before the January 4 retreat. Her mother thoroughly devoted herself to Auntie while she was in prison. We were powerless to help.

Uncle was taken to the police from the outset and sentenced to death. We learned this only through a letter delivered to us by a man who'd shared Uncle's prison cell. Uncle didn't understand why he had to be executed. "Please save me," he wrote. "Do whatever is necessary. Hire a lawyer if you have to." In that period, my family hit rock bottom, and we felt at our most isolated and worthless. With no influential relatives to lean on for support, we tottered like a radish whose roots had been cut.

So many had served the enemy that waiting in line to send in warm clothes to imprisoned family members took a whole day. As it happened, one of our kinsmen had long been a correctional officer. Mother asked for his help, but he turned a deaf ear. We shuddered at his heartlessness, but we understood perfectly well why a low-ranking civil servant would be reluctant to take up Uncle's cause. In order to line up at the prison as early as possible, Mother stayed overnight with a family she'd been close to in Hyŏnjŏ-dong. They treated her with warm sympathy. The poor were much more compassionate, Mother said.

Uncle was put to death. We were unable to offer even the most trifling assistance toward saving him. We never even found out when he was executed. No news arrived after his letter, no death notice, no summons to come and claim his body. Nothing. No evidence of his execution exists, but the January 4 retreat soon followed, and that was that. No trace of Uncle was ever found again. We'd always assumed that he met with a group execution. A Red's life was no better than that of a fly, and we, his family, were insects.

Our powerlessness to help Uncle originated in the new system of citizen identification cards. After the recovery of Seoul, civilians had to carry cards certifying their upstanding status in order to move about freely. Later, every citizen of the Republic of Korea was entitled to receive a card, but in the early days, the underlying purpose of the system was to distinguish potential Reds. A person's record was closely scrutinized before the card was approved.

In our case, problems arose even before we got to that stage. The neighborhood head pointedly overlooked us when she handed out application forms. This shocked us even more than when we'd been anonymously denounced to the authorities as Reds. The cards were the precondition for a semblance of human life; to slight us was tantamount to telling us to go to hell—literally. Mother had passively accepted all sorts of affliction as if dull-witted, but now she pounded the ground in lament, "This is going too far! We shared rice cakes to ward off spirits. We held each other's grandkids and let them poo on us no matter what kind of clothes we were wearing. How can they do this?"

We swallowed our pride and went to see the neighborhood head, saying that if she could just give us a form, we'd see what we could do. She said that she'd skipped us because she'd been one form short and that we should ask for one at the district office. The very woman who'd been head of the local People's Unit under the Communists was now back as neighborhood head and discriminating against us! We got our preliminary hearing, but had to bow and scrape to an officer before we received an application form. An organization that didn't know us conducted the more serious examination, so Sister-in-law and Mother got their cards without incident. Since I was a student, though, they told me to go to my university and get my student registration card first.

I had scaled one mountain, but another loomed before me. It didn't look like I'd be able to attend university again. I hadn't even gone near it, because I was afraid of punishment—going to classes under the Communists was taken as a clear sign of support for their cause. I heard that the Student National Defense Corps screened the students at every university, sometimes cruelly. Investigations were the rage, and in the process all sorts of awful things happened. I was petrified, but in the end I went, pledging to put up with any humiliation or harassment, for not having a citizen's card was equivalent to a death warrant.

At that stage the UN forces were using the College of Liberal Arts, so college business was being conducted in one of the houses that used to be furnished to professors in Tongsung-dong. I was already on a blacklist; the other students there whispered among themselves when they saw me fill out a registration form. My reputation was such that my card wasn't forthcoming right away. Several days later, though, the head of the investigation team interrogated me and, after a warning, issued me my card.

The student card took intense effort, but once I showed it, my citizen's card came without a hitch. I'm still grateful for the inspection I received at my university not just because it helped me get the card, but because for the first time in ages I was treated as a human being. I was also long thankful that I could be accused of having served the enemy and still be treated with decency, as it kept me from losing complete faith in people. The suspicion I was under made my gratitude all the keener, because the entire community was on edge. And nothing at the time was more frightening than our fellow citizens.

Did the victors have to be so ruthless as they pursued the enemy all the way to the Yalu? When ideology is at stake, it seems that conflict has room only for triumph and not for compassion.

Patriotic organizations sprouted. Every wall on every street was covered with slogans, all belligerent, all urging the denunciation of Communist atrocities, all urging the extermination of every last Red. But what hit me hardest was a shabby poster that simply read "Hurray for Freedom." I was physically and mentally exhausted, and when I saw it, my knees buckled. Was it freedom that would keep me from trading the humiliation and hardships I was going through for all the glory and riches of the North? What greater freedom existed here, that made me choose to stay, even if prison might be my ultimate reward for stoically enduring humiliation and hardships? Yes, I was free not to blindly follow the head of the state. I laughed bitterly at myself. But that dream of freedom offered a bulwark of hope as massive as a mountain.

Our forces pushed northward. Reunification lay just around the corner when the Chinese intervened and drove us back on the defensive. This time, instead of lying that we should calmly go about our daily business, the government hinted that strategic retreat might be necessary. Since the summer had proved so terrifying, the rich and the powerful busied themselves preparing to flee, while the poor packed their bundles, albeit not believing that the situation would come to that. Mother prayed constantly before her bowl of water. She and Sister-in-law were inconsolable. Every passing day was a waking nightmare, but they persevered, cherishing a ray of hope that Brother would return.

As the ROK forces advanced briskly northward, conscripts who had managed to desert the people's volunteer army or deliberately straggled behind returned home. When Mother came across young men in tattered clothes, she asked whether they were on their way back from the people's volunteer army. If so, she brought them home and fed them, asking one question after another. She rejoiced over their stories, exclaiming at them in the faith that such a joy might one day be ours as well. At every meal, she first scooped up rice into Brother's bowl. When wind rattled the gate, she rushed out. What would happen to her son if the ROK Army retreated before he had a chance to escape? Mother couldn't bring herself to even allow Brother's death into her imaginings, so she had no choice but to keep him as a Korean People's Army soldier in her mind.

It became a virtual certainty that the ROK would retreat much farther south than Seoul. When the city's population dwindled by half during the first cold spell of that year, Mother made an important decision.

"You have to flee, even if it means going alone."

I'd actually been intending to do so, but hearing Mother say it made me choke with grief. My leaving would mean that everyone else—Mother, Sister-in-law, my nephews—had to stake their fate with Brother. I couldn't picture him in the Korean People's Army, but it was all too clear what would happen if they threw their lot in with Brother. Even if Seoul were recovered and I returned after this "strategic retreat," the house would be empty. I could flee alone, but making up my mind to say a permanent goodbye wrenched my guts. Mother had already decided the matter, though. From the depths of clothing chests she withdrew the fabrics one by one that she'd prepared over the years for my wedding. She packed them up, repeating, "Live a good life, even if we can't."

But before I left, Brother came home looking like a beggar. He was really back! He could not have looked worse, but a triumphant return was hardly something we envied—at least, he hadn't returned as a Korean People's Army soldier. We embraced him, crying and laughing. Were we dreaming?

But almost immediately, his return made matters worse. He had changed so completely that our hearts sank. First of all, he was a physical wreck. We couldn't believe that he'd pushed through the front line and walked so far to get home in the condition he was in. But this was nothing compared with his complete lack of affect. He showed no joy in his homecoming, no desire to hold the son born in his absence. His thoughts were a mystery, but it wasn't that he was expressionless. His eyes darted about with anxiety. He started at the tiniest sound. At night, the rustle of wind and the scampering of mice terrified him, and fear remained on his face no matter what we said. A hot meal and a bed failed to calm him down. He couldn't sleep. Where had he been? What had he gone through? He obviously had an extraordinary tale to tell of how he had risked his life, but he told us nothing and showed no trace of willingness to talk. He now suffered from extreme paranoia.

Mother was at a loss. She related what had happened to Uncle and all we'd gone through and pleaded with him to pull himself together. But her attempts to jolt open the closed doorway to his thoughts with the news only aggravated his condition. Agitated, he begged us to flee right away, burying his head into the corner of the room and quaking.

"Let's get out of here. I'll die if the People's Army comes. Let's get out of here."

The urgency of the mass evacuations made him hypersensitive. He couldn't remain still. And so we entered his nightmare with him.

My solo departure was automatically called off. It wasn't time to cut ties with the rest of my family. If it had been, how could things have gone wrong so coincidentally? Even if Brother hadn't begged us, we were all eager to flee as soon as possible. We no longer had to picture casting our lot with the North; the mere thought of what we would likely go through if Seoul were recovered made our hair stand on end. Given the vengeance wreaked on those who'd stayed behind when the government promised to defend Seoul to the death, how would it treat citizens who remained when advised to flee? And all the more so, now that it had built a temporary bridge over the Han. We wanted to leave. Our desperation was making us crazy.

But several problems loomed for Brother, including that damn citizen's card. The fear of spies amid the refugees had given rise to stringent inspections around the city. Those who'd escaped from the people's volunteer army weren't necessarily branded Reds, but they still faced a strict screening process before their cards were issued. We didn't believe that Brother was up to it, and although he didn't want to go through screening either, he badgered us to secure a card for him as soon as possible.

"Why the hell can't we find someone with the clout to get me a citizen's card without all the rigmarole?"

He said this without a trace of shame. How could Brother—my brother, so full of integrity—have become so craven? It must have been his paranoia talking, but his gutlessness was even more difficult to take. I couldn't bear to witness it. But there was no way I could undo the bonds that had drawn us together once more.

Brother's pestering prompted Sister-in-law to think of the country school. Maybe we could rely on his fellow teachers' artless honesty and the respect that teachers commanded among villagers. She went first to talk things over with them. They were happy to cooperate, so she persuaded Brother to come along. There Brother could receive a provincial resident's card, if not exactly a citizen's card. Almost everyone had fled the village. The genuine sympathy extended by the handful of remaining teachers and villagers and relief about obtaining an official card helped Brother improve slightly, so Sister-in-law left him there and came home to make preparations to evacuate.

We were so eager to flee and so envious of those who could that we never thought through the difficulties that awaited us on the road. We were simply happy to fulfill our dream of escaping at last, to cross the river, climb over hills, and pass through fields. The more tangible problems—how we'd care for two infants, only a year apart, so that they wouldn't freeze to death; what we could bring to keep ourselves from starving—didn't bother me at all. Actually, these burdens sat on me alone, but my heart was soaring, as though someone awaited me across the Han who would shoulder my troubles and let me rest. We could hardly pack a refugee bundle like we were going on a picnic, but the feeling remained with me. All of us—not just me— had buried in our hearts the fear that we might not be able to pull off our escape. And so it came to pass.

News of the worst sort arrived. At night, fields near the highway and large buildings had been turning into makeshift camps for retreating UN and ROK Army soldiers. Back then, there was also something called the Youth Defense Force. I don't know how it differed from the ROK Army, but its soldiers were also armed and engaged in battle. They were now on the retreat, and some set up camp in Brother's school. Brother had been staying in the watchman's room and shared it one evening with an officer who was looking for a warm floor to bed down on. The following morning, a private took apart the officer's gun for a routine check, but it misfired and a bullet penetrated Brother's leg.

We rushed over as soon as we received the news. Brother had been left behind in a small clinic. Its middle-aged doctor had yet to evacuate, but the military unit had moved on. More information would scarcely have helped us, but even so, Brother refused to tell us anything beyond what we'd already heard. He was pale and had lost a great deal of blood, but he looked calmer than before. Although the doctor was kindly, his family was preparing to flee.

Brother's life wasn't in danger, he said, but an infection could prove extremely troublesome, so he explained how to care for him. Treatment was straightforward. The doctor showed me how to extract the bloodied gauze from the bullet hole that passed through Brother's leg and insert a new piece. That hole seemed to me a dark, gaping chasm into hell. As I watched, a fear came over me that I was about to be sucked in forever.

Brother didn't cry out in pain; he even smiled faintly. This serenity that came to him with the loss of all hope struck me as ghastly. The doctor fled with his family after giving us everything he had for Brother's treatment—gauze, dressing, antiseptic, ointment. The village emptied out. Three or four days after we became the sole occupants of the clinic, the final signal for the so-called January 4 retreat was given. We assumed that almost everyone had already left, but those who'd been watching the situation and nursing a tiny hope now poured out as one. From a low-flying helicopter, a voice amplified by a megaphone was urging escape, and the small clinic shook with the thump of running feet on the highway. But our hearts quaked more violently than the building itself.

Mother spoke up: "Let's leave. If they're telling us to go, let's get as far as we can, even if it means dying. Better to die than have them treat us so horribly again."

We'd been keeping our eyes on a rickety wagon in the clinic's backyard. The very few privileged enough to have access to cars had fled long ago. Later, people carried children and bundles of valuables on hastily put-together wagons—basically just wheels attached to a board. We placed Brother on the wagon, which must have been abandoned because it was so broken down. Mother and Sister-in-law each carried a baby on her back and bundles on her head and in her hands. I was in charge of rolling the wagon. It seemed to weigh half a ton. We jumped into the ranks of the final retreat, but found ourselves lagging farther and farther behind. After traversing Muak Hill, I collapsed in exhaustion. Dusk was falling.

"A little farther, just a little farther." Mother pressed on mercilessly.

"How can the bridge over the Han possibly be just a little farther?" I thought I'd explode with rage.

"Getting away isn't in the cards for us. It must be fate. Let's just pretend that we're escaping. I know a house in that neighborhood over there. We can stay and go back home when things change and people come back. That's the only way left."

Mother must have been plotting it all along. Speaking reasonably and calmly, she motioned to a large group of houses visible from the hill: Hyŏnjŏ-dong, the refuge-to-be for our mock escape. Hyŏnjŏ-dong again! Oddly, though, my heart calmed and new strength returned to my limbs, which only moments before I'd found impossible to move. The upward path to the steep neighborhood meant a detour, but we took it rather than the steps because of the wagon. The last batch of refugees was dashing down like startled rabbits in flight. Moving in the opposite direction, we arrived in our new shelter, huffing and puffing.

The house that Mother pinpointed belonged to the family she'd relied on when she was supplying necessities to Uncle when he was in prison. The family had left, and the house was locked. But the humbler the house, the looser the lock. We joined forces and tore it away, door fastener and all. The family had evidently left just minutes before. One side of the room was still warm; on the other, a small table lay scattered with half-eaten dishes. Teeth marks stood out on a long piece of radish kimchi. The first thing we did was to ransack every spot we thought might hold something to eat.

The food we had with us was inadequate, and no matter what circumstances we human beings find ourselves in, our stomachs come first, so we had no compunctions about what we were doing. There was no rice to cook in the house. All that was left was a handful of grain and half a bag of wheat flour. We didn't make supper but managed to stave off hunger with cold rice that had been left behind and used twigs and branches to feed the furnace under the floor. Amid that peace obtained when a situation can't get any worse, we fell into a deep sleep.

A new day broke. Brother stretched, saying that he'd slept well for the first time in ages. I felt frustrated and weighed down by my family. They were thinking about when the government would come back after its retreat, but ignoring the pressing matter at hand. How would we survive all the upheaval? I may have put Brother down from the wagon, but I wasn't relieved of my burden. To see how the world looked after this latest reversal, I cautiously stepped out of the gate.

The entire neighborhood was visible from our position on the hill. Directly below lay the prison, home to liberated revolutionaries, home to Uncle's execution. There was no human sound. Goosebumps spread over my flesh. It was as though a cold, steely dagger were fluttering down my spine. I'd never before experienced the total absence of people, and it spawned panic within me. No one was to be seen, not on the avenue visible all the way to Independence Gate. No one in the alleys, no one in the houses. No smoke rising from any dwelling, not the barest wisp. It would have been less frightening if, at the very least, a Communist flag had been hoisted in the prison. We were the only ones left behind in all of this large city. I alone was watching this vast emptiness, and we alone would view the unfolding of the unknown in the coming days. It all seemed impossible. Had I known a magic trick to make us disappear, I'd have used it.

But an abrupt change in perspective hit me. I felt as though I'd been chased into a dead end but then suddenly turned around. Surely there was meaning in my being the sole witness to it all. How many bizarre events had conspired to make us the only ones left behind? If I were the sole witness, I had the responsibility to record it. That would compensate for this series of freak occurrences. I would testify not only to this vast emptiness, but to all the hours I'd suffered as a worm. Only then would I escape being a worm.

From all this came a vision that I would write someday, and this premonition dispelled my fear. I stopped worrying about our meager food supply. The clustered, vacant houses were now my prey. I was certain that each held at least a few handfuls of wheat flour, a small container or two of barley. I had accepted my gullet as my gang boss and no longer felt ashamed about it. I already planned to steal from those houses.